A Novel
STATE OF ESPERANZA

MICHAEL CHINTIS

Copyright © 2025 by Michael Chintis

All rights reserved. No part of this publication may be reproduced, distributed, or transmitted in any form or by any means, including photocopying, recording, or other electronic or mechanical methods, without the prior written permission of the copyright owner and the publisher, except in the case of brief quotations embodied in critical reviews and certain other noncommercial uses permitted by copyright law. For permission requests, write to the publisher, addressed "Attention: Permissions Coordinator," at the address below.

CITIOFBOOKS, INC.
3736 Eubank NE Suite A1
Albuquerque, NM 87111-3579
www.citiofbooks.com
Hotline: 1 (877) 389-2759
Fax: 1 (505) 930-7244

Ordering Information:

Quantity sales. Special discounts are available on quantity purchases by corporations, associations, and others. For details, contact the publisher at the address above.

Printed in the United States of America.

ISBN-13:	Softcover	979-8-89391-768-0
	eBook	979-8-89391-770-3
	Hardback	979-8-89391-769-7

Library of Congress Control Number: 2025913193

TABLE OF CONTENTS

Dedication i
Prologue iii
Chapter 1 : The Hamlet - April 1, 1945 1
Chapter 2 : The Adoption 7
Chapter 2 1/2 : The Plan 15
Chapter 3 : Vivian and Ben Wallace 22
Chapter 4 : Time to Relocate 33
Chapter 4 ½ : The Path Forward 42
Chapter 5 : Margaret Then and Now 46
Chapter 5 1/2 : The beat goes on 53
Chapter 6 : A New Era Begins 59
Chapter 7 : Independence for Sofie 72
Chapter 9 : College Days–Sophie 80
Chapter 10 : Biology 101 96
Chapter 10 1/2 : 'Obla Di, Obla Da,' Life Goes On 102
Chapter 11 : School Days—Redo 114
Chapter 12 : Summer of 1961 - Sophia Gets a Job 119
Chapter 13 : Hi-ho…Off to Work We Go 136
Chapter 14 : The times they are a'changin 145
Chapter 14 1/2 : HELP!…I need somebody! 154
Chapter 15 : Breaking Up is Hard to Do 165
Chapter 16 : All the King Horses 177
Chapter 16 1/2 : Que Sera, Sera 184
Chapter 17 : Six Days on the Road 191
Chapter 18 : It's a New Dawn and a New Day and I'm Feeling Good ... 204
Chapter 19 : Old Man River 213
The Nine Commandments 216
Authors Final Note 217

Appendix A 219
Appendix B : Carbon Cycle 226
Appendix C 228
Appendix D : Los Alamos National Lab 230
Appendix E : Four corners power plant circa 1970 232
Appendix F 233
Appendix G : Uranium mining in New Mexico on Navajo Land 235
About the Author 237

DEDICATION

This book is dedicated to all the sons and daughters of New Mexico who have fought in the historic battles preserving our nations freedoms.

What a delightful book. The characters are very engaging and they take you through some of the southwests most notable history and development since statehood. The book is well researched and the story lines are based on actual events. A fine addition to my library.

- Marylou Morrow, Flagstaff photographer and historian.

I was glad to see the author address some of the issues faced by minority workers in the state after WWII. Were they were heroes one day then a miss- treated labor force the next. The 'red scare' tactics used by many at that time to detract from labor issues was effectively documented. The authors description of the dynamics of small town New Mexico brought back many memories for me as well.

- John Arsola relations consultant

History, intrigue, adventure, romance, it's all here. This is a fast moving book with well developed characters and interesting scenery without going overboard on description. It's something a person with a slight amount of NYC impatience can read without going "c'mon, get to the point". Well researched historical information is a plus in any novel and with his author's notes within the chapters Mike gives you the info right there as you read. It's a combination of US and New Mexican history with a fascinating story of a German orphan's life in America after WW2. This is a book that holds your interest right to the end and keeps you wondering about the lives of these people.

- Janice Petty Literary Critic, Tucson

PROLOGUE

From the journal of Lieutenant Benjamin Wallace

We were a platoon out of the 104th Infantry Division in April of 1945, outside a little hamlet near the city of Paderborn, Germany, halfway between Bonn and Berlin. I am sure the little town had a name, but if I ever knew it, it is lost to me now. I am a newly minted second lieutenant as a replacement for a casualty suffered during our blitzing advance through Europe in the past months. Winter was brutal and the fighting fierce. The Battle of the Bulge is now making some serious progress against the German offensive initiated last December. Spring has brought hope that our recent advances might mean the end is near.

The goal is to take Paderborn in the next few days, and our troops are being positioned to do just that. One challenge is we seem to be in a competition with the Russians to see who can hold the most territory when the fighting stops. In fact, they just left the hamlet the previous day, leaving behind their signature destruction and body count. We found no German soldier corpses, only civilians composed of old men, women and children; all young men were conscripted long before to fight the Fuhrer's battles. My orders are to plant the American flag here and secure this little village from Soviet occupation as well as cut off a retreat route for the Germans exiting Paderborn–simple enough that fifty men should do it. The Fighting Timberwolves are we.

My uncle said the sights I will see in battle will haunt me for my remaining days if I even make it out alive or in one piece. He always was a cheery bastard. He swears this is just another chapter in man's brutality against his fellow beings and it will continue until all of mankind has been erased.... "Don't just take my word for it... read your history, son! Seems this is our evolutionary punishment for having a brain. Surely no God would have gifted us with an organ that has the capacity for the brutality that war brings to his fellow men"(see what I mean about the cheery part).

Now, however, I don't give a shit if he's right. I just want to make it out with ALL my men. This additional responsibility has hit me harder than I anticipated, and I am finding I'm not very good at it!!! So, I hope this ends soon for all our sakes. If one of my men was to be the last to die in this war, well, that really would make my uncle's prophecy come true. Plus, I suspect my family back home would not like it much if it happened to me.

Author's note

In late 1944, during the wake of the Allied forces' successful D-Day invasion of Normandy, France, it seemed as if the Second World War was all but over. On Dec. 16, with the onset of winter, the German army launched a counteroffensive that was intended to cut through the Allied forces in a manner that would turn the tide of the war in Hitler's favor. The battle that ensued is known historically as the Battle of the Bulge. The courage and fortitude of the American Soldier was tested against great adversity. Nevertheless, the quality of his response ultimately meant the victory of freedom over tyranny.

PART ONE
WAR IS HELL

Chapter 1

The Hamlet - April 1, 1945

Ben

Cpl. Polanco. Pick some men and do a recon of the town to see what we might be up against in the next 24 hours. The siege of Paderborn begins tomorrow, and we need to be prepared for all situations. Command doesn't think it will take the Boche long to throw in the towel. There is not much fight left in them these days. Polanco tells me, "I know just the five needed," and he's off.

Ernie and I have been together since we hit Europe in the summer of last year and have been through some intense fighting over the winter. By some strange coincidence that can only happen during the calamity caused by a world war, we come from the same small county in New Mexico. Grant County can't even have a total population of 15,000 people. We were both too young for the draft when the war started. When war was imminent many young men from our part of New Mexico were sent to defend the Philippines and ended up as war prisoners after enduring the brutal Bataan Death March at the hands of the Japanese. So patriotism was at an all-time high. All available men were joining up as soon as they possibly could. In another oddity, Ernest, as he insists on being called, and I had never met before our bus ride to take our enlistment physical in El Paso, Texas.

Ernesto Polanco is small in stature, but like many with that trait, has learned not to back down from bigger men and big challenges. That, coupled with some innate intelligence, makes him a natural leader of men. I, on the other hand, am well over six feet tall and somewhat of a plodder. Our comrades have labeled us Mutt and Jeff. We work well together and have developed the trust needed to survive in the real-time situations war presents, so we let the label roll off our backs.

I know it won't take long for Cpl. Polanco to evaluate the present conditions and get the information necessary to defend our position. He returns soon afterward and reports that the real problem will be the Russians. They are not far away and will probably want to return soon to claim the town as a wartime conquest. He lays the dilemma at my feet with a shit-eatin' grin and says, "Time to earn your rank, gringo."

As much as I would like to open fire on this particular group of Russkies for the brutality they have inflicted in this particular hamlet, I inform the corporal I am going to do what every lieutenant does in this situation. I call the captain, hoping he will make the decision for me.

However, when faced with the predicament of firing on your allies to accomplish the mission directive of planting the American flag in this deserted town, his parting words to me were, "Use your own judgment until I get back to you." "CaCa," as they say in New Mexico, but I guess I should have seen that one coming. Nobody wants to be on the record for that decision.

I walk back to the re-con team. Ernie can see my body language and knows immediately what's up. I tell him to get five more men and make sure Hanlan is with them.

Hanlan is the only German speaker in our platoon and my hope is the Russians will have one as well. The corporal leads us to the town entrance that he is sure the Russians will use when they return. We set up a quasi-defensible position that won't be so threatening as to draw immediate fire.

We no sooner get established than here they come with a platoon about our size, *but with a tank*. The negotiation strategy I planned to use now seems a little feeble, but what the hell, I am not that quick a thinker to change now. Cpl. Hanlan and I advance to meet the Russians. Cpl. Polanco positions the remaining men and sends someone back for the rest of the platoon. The Russian soldiers advance toward us as if they expect Hanlan and me to step aside. They stop a few feet away and Hanlan asks if anyone in their platoon speaks German. To my great relief, the person he is talking with answers in German. I have already told Hanlan what to say and how to deliver our message, and he boldly does so. A lengthy conversation ensues between the obvious officer in charge and the soldier. The longer it goes, the less sanguine I am of avoiding some type of last-minute disaster. Finally, the Russians just turn and leave with their tank leading the way.

Ernie asks what I told Hanlan to say. I look at Ernie with sweat still beaded up on my forehead and tell him here is what Hanlan said, "We're here, you're not. We are both a long way from home. Let's not die on the last day of the war over a meaningless town." Ernie says, "Wow! Man, that's good! You earned that rank today!"

We watch the Russians retreat until we are sure they will not return. I tell the men to finish clearing the town and to look in every hidey-hole they can find. I don't want any snipers or saboteurs in our midst. This might be our new home for the next few days.

Ernie and I are walking on one side of the main street, and I can still hear him chuckling. What's so funny I ask? Ernie says, "Man, that was good back there. Took some real huevos, hombre. Wait till I tell that story back home. You will be a genuine hero!!"

I tell Ernie to cut the crap. You would have done much the same.

"Shit, Benji," he always calls me that when I call him Ernie. "I would have opened fire immediately for what they did to the innocents here. The last few days, I've begun to hate the Russians as much as the Germans for what they're doing in these small towns. You know these communities can't defend themselves and that's why they're getting targeted."

Yeah-yeah. War is hell, I tell Ernie. You got to remember the Germans were worse.

"I guess." And he continues saying, "Makes the differences between us Chicanos and gringos in Grant County seem pretty small. Plus, all these people fighting over here all look alike, not like back home, ¿que no?" Ernie can make my head hurt with his life philosophical views. But he brings up things I seldom considered.

We enter the next building on our side of the street. It appears to have been a clothing shop of some kind in the past. Ernie checks the downstairs basement while I finish upstairs.

A couple of minutes go by, and I hear Ernie call, "Hey Ben, come down and look at this!" As soon as I get halfway down the stairs, the smell hits me. What the hell is that? Ernie says immediately, "Spoken like a man who has always had indoor plumbing. That's shit, man… human shit. There's a box in the corner, maybe two days' worth". On heightened alert, we continue our search of the basement. I approach some shelving with a large box on top. I suspect I will find the source of the odor, but I am not sure I want to look. I call out, Ernesto, venga aqui, pronto, one of my few Spanish phrases.

Sofie

At first, I heard speaking and thought, *'Oh, good, they are Americans…'* Then I remember how awful the Russians are. I move to my hiding box quickly. All the mean men I have known in my seven years have worn some kind of uniform, so why should these be different?

I think there are two of them talking upstairs, but I know they will eventually look down here, hopefully not too closely. I see the torch light bouncing off the wall as one of them descends the stairs. He doesn't even reach the bottom before he calls out, and at that moment, I know they will find me. Both soldiers are in the dimly lit basement now and have probably discovered my toilet. I am doomed! As the torch light focuses closer to my hiding place, I freeze, motionless, and hope for the best. I would pray, but that hasn't worked in years. One soldier moves the box from the wall and his torch light blinds me, so he directs it from my face. His first kind gesture. The other soldier is also there, now speaking an unfamiliar language. Their voices are calm and without anger, so I remain calm as well. He gently pulls me from the box and gathers me in his arms. He is a giant, this man. But there is a kindness to his manner. If only he did not smell so foul. The other man is of normal size and joins us, looking at me with the kindest eyes I have seen in a long time. I begin to think I will be safe, and they mean me no harm.

Ben

Ernie, go get Hanlan, and I'll stay with the girl. Maybe we can get some communication going here. As Ernesto runs out to find Hanlan, I look down at this child in my arms as I walk up the stairs. We sit at the table and chairs we passed when we came in. She is surprisingly calm as her eyes continually move about and search my face–for what I am not sure. I place her in a chair and sit next to her, I then notice she is eyeing my canteen. Recognizing her dehydration and hunger, I remove the top of my canteen to offer her a drink. Surprisingly, she snatches it from my hands, drinks half of it in one go, and then hands it back, saying, "Danke." '*Composed*' is the word I think best describes her. She apparently has analyzed the situation and senses we mean her no harm. I get the feeling not much will surprise this kid after what she has witnessed.

Sofie

I don't say a thing as I walk between these two soldiers, the giant and the other, who speaks two languages at once. I think they are the only two friendly people left in the world and I don't want to leave their side. The third soldier who speaks the bad German walks behind us for a while, then leaves. The giant and the other soldier talk as we are walking. We walk down the main street. It is sad to see what's left of my little home town I now fear is ruined forever. What is my future? There are no people left to repair my town. I look around and find no familiar faces to reassure me. We approach the building where my uncle once worked. It is the biggest building in town besides the church. In front of the church, there is a tarpaulin covering dead people. Their heads and bodies are covered, but I recognize the shoes worn by my uncle, father, and mother. I pull the tarpaulin back to reveal the grotesque bodies of my family. I look at the giant and say, "Papa, Mutter, Onkel."

The giant quickly replaces the tarpaulin, and we move away from the church. Suddenly, several big trucks drive up with big red swastikas painted on the side. I am instantly terrified and grab the giant's hand. He kneels down and speaks softly to me. I point at the truck and say, "Bosch!!" It takes a minute before the smaller soldier walks to the truck, points at the Red Cross sign on the truck, shaking his head. "No! No! No!" he says. I am so used to seeing the Bosch symbol that I have failed to see it is a red cross. I now relax, but the giant picks me up anyway. He is so big I can see all the way to the end of the street. I feel safe when he holds me. He carries me into the church and the small soldier leaves, as if searching for something. Soon he returns with a giant woman who is beautiful, and all three talk at once.

Chapter 2

The Adoption

Maggie

For God's sake, Ben, what the fuck is Ernie talking about? We're fighting a war here, not running an orphanage. You just can't dump this shit on me while you two run off and create more bodies for us to fix or bury. Ben says, "Calm down, Maggie, and watch the mouth. There is a child present,"

Who cares? She can't speak English, anyway. I take a deep breath to even my voice out.

OK! OK! So, officer, what can I do to help you? Your corporal is making no sense, babbling on about some orphan we can't leave behind. God, Ben, this better be good. We're awfully busy here trying to set up this field hospital before the big push tomorrow against whatever city I don't give a shit about and occupied by who-cares-anymore.

"Well, Captain," Ben says, "you are the first person we thought of for this humanitarian mission. Let me explain."

Stop right there, I command in my best officer's voice. I really need to get back to my corpsmen and doctors. This hospital must be set up correctly, and I mean NOW! They have said we're going to be here for a while, so it needs to be done differently than the temp camps we have been using recently.

Calmly, Ben tells her, "Well, Captain, the short version is Ernest and I are heading toward the city you don't give a shit about and won't be around camp for a couple of days. AND we will not abandon this kid we found just after she identified the corpses of her family just outside this very church. We won't be a part of letting the Russians or Nazis get their hands on her. You know that! Just look at her. She's scared to death!"

She doesn't look that scared to me, as I watch Sofie's reaction to our conversation.

"Yeah! That's part of the problem," Ernie says. "I think she trusts us."

So, let me get this straight. I am supposed to put this little chica on ice while you two go off soldiering.

"Oh, no, Maggie," Ben says. "You have to feed her, find her a place to sleep, clothe her, and entertain her, too. And please give her a bath. She stinks! And that just ain't right."

Look who's talking, I say, as anger creeps back in my voice.

"One last thing before Ernest and I go to save the world: Be thinking about how we can get help for her. She has no one left in the village…family or friend. Ernie and I cannot see placing her in some wartime orphanage without exploring other options. Adios for now. We have to report back to our squadron for our orders. Tomorrow we are planting the American flag in Paderborn."

And what if you DON'T come back?

Ben replies with, "Well, Mom, you're just on your own, I guess!!"

FUCK YOU BOTH! I yell at their backs as they walk away.

Sofie tries to follow Ben and Ernie, but I hold her close. As Ben and Ernest look back, they put their friendliest waves and smiles on.

"That went well," Ernest says. "You think Sofie will be OK? And will Maggie still like us in the morning?"

"I think Sofie will be fine," Ben says, "BUT I am not sure about our friendship with Maggie. She never liked us that much anyway. What was left of our friendship just took a serious hit back there, if you know what I mean. That was a lot of disrespect for her and her rank. We put her in a bad spot alright."

As Ben and Ernie walk away, Ben says, "Desperate times require desperate measures!"

"Well, I just hope absence makes her heart grow fonder," Ernie replies.

Captain Margaret Beltran leads Sofie into the field hospital in search of Becky Baldwin, their designated German speaking corpsman. Like all good officers, she intends to pass the buck down rank and get back to the job at hand. Maggie is still furious as she walks up to Becky and tries not to take it out on this poor girl who is one of her best aides. I need your help here, corpsman. A snappy, "Yes, ma'am," is her standard reply.

This girl was just dropped at our doorstep, and I need you to gather some information from her so we can help her. Another, "Yes ma'am," follows and Maggie continues with guidance for Becky to get some meaningful information from this girl. Her name is Sophia or Sofie, something like that. Clean her up, and find her some clean clothes from somewhere. I need to go now, but I will be back in a couple of hours. Oh! Before I forget, tell her that her friends who brought her here have not forgotten about her and will return, but it may take them a few days. In the meantime, we will take care of her and make sure nothing bad happens. Impress on her she needs to do as we say. This is a war zone, not an orphanage. I am sure you can phrase that better than I just did.

Maggie returns later and finds Becky helping other corpsmen setting up surgical tables and the triage center. She pulls Becky aside, but before she can ask about Sofie, Becky starts in about what a good kid she is. "Come here, I will show you," she says. They walk to the WAC corpsmen quarters and Sophie looks up, dressed in some young boys' clothes and much cleaner than when I saw her last. She even smiles at me as I approach. Becky tells me she will provide details later, but that this poor girl is truly all alone in the world. The Russians tortured and murdered her entire family over the last few days, and she does not know where the remainder of the townspeople scattered.

Becky continues, "Look at this," and gestures to the barracks room around her. "She did almost all of this by herself. I just showed her once how to put the cots together. She is quite strong for her age, which is seven, by the way. I plan to have her unpack the bedding and distribute the blankets and pillows to each cot. Rather than dwelling on the events of the last few days, she appears keen to keep herself occupied. She wants to help and has said repeatedly how grateful she is that the Americans are here. She keeps talking about the giant that rescued her. I didn't know what to tell her. Do you know anything about that? Maybe she has had some hallucinations because of what she has been through recently."

I can't help but laugh as I tell Becky, It's Lieutenant Wallace, the big galoot-giant. He and Cpl. Polanco were the ones that found her hiding in a basement somewhere. When they dropped her off, under my protest, I might add, I practically had to pry her away from them.

"Well," Becky says, "she asks about them and wants to know when they will return. It is the only time she seems frightful that I have observed."

Becky, with surprise in her voice, says, "Mutt and Jeff! Who knew they could be endearing to anyone? Desperate times, I guess!" I then tell her that is exactly what 'they' said while trying to convince me to look after her.

Over the next few days, as the fighting for control of the area around the city continues, the battle becomes more chaotic, and the casualty load increases in the field hospital. Patients of all nationalities pass through. The lucky ones are transported further back for more long-term treatment.

All the Medical Staff has observed that Sofie can work as tirelessly as any of my corpsmen and nurses. She is continuously rotating clean linens for those ruined during medical procedures. Although Sofie is excluded from the triage and operating arenas, she gathers the dirty linens when they are thrown out the door, and stacks them for transport to the field laundry. She then stages clean ones for immediate use. Same goes for the barracks. Sofie takes the soiled sheets away and replaces them with clean ones whenever needed. Sofie has clearly had a positive effect on morale and has endeared herself to all the staff, including the medical doctors. She eats when the staff eats, sleeps when they do, and goes about her self-appointed duties with commitment. Everyone knows her story now and understands why she is more solemn than cheerful.

The doctor in charge of the field unit, Colonel Kelly, initially voiced his concern about her presence. But Sofie has silenced him and any other critics with a positive attitude and commitment to helping the Americans.

When Dr. Kelly asked why the girl was here and not in some German orphan center, Captain Beltran responded, "That girl deserves better. If we can help, why not? You know those places are just shit-holes. What are we fighting this war for anyway?" Well, word got out that Maggie and Colonel Kelly are firmly in the Sofie camp, and that was the last questioning comment heard.

Sofie has suddenly stopped going to the 'civilian patients' ward tent to pick up the dirty linens. Her demeanor has changed dramatically in the past two days and now she only reluctantly ventures outside of her barracks. It is all Becky and Margaret can do to even get her to eat in the mess hall.

Margaret says to Becky, "This scared kid is not the same helpful, pleasant child that we knew last week. What do you think…maybe a delayed trauma reaction?"

Becky says, "I don't think so. This behavior came on so suddenly, like normal one moment… paranoid the next. There was no gradual change. Something has happened and she won't talk to me about it. She keeps asking for '*the giant*'."

Maggie tells Becky, "Keep a close eye on her and if things don't change soon, we'll get some emotional counseling for her from the support staff that just arrived."

The next morning, Maggie and Colonel Kelly are walking to the mess tent when they see a man in civilian clothes grab Sofie by the arm and drag her between two tents. Maggie breaks into a full run after them, with Col. Kelly right behind. They both start yelling to let go of the girl. The man abandons Sofie and takes off, running for the camp perimeter gate. Maggie gathers Sofie up as Kelly continues after the civilian and yells for the guards to stop him.

The man desperately tries to escape but is tackled and subdued by two of the guards at the gate.

Colonel Kelly tells the guards, "Isolate this man in the stockade and don't let anyone near him until you hear from me. Is that clear?"

Kelly finds Maggie, Sofie, and Becky in his meeting room at the headquarters tent. The girl is sitting on Maggie's lap and Becky is quietly talking to her.

Suddenly, Becky turns to Colonel Kelly and says, "Sofie has recognized that man as a German officer from the village and apparently, he recognized her as well. She says he is a very bad man, and she has seen him execute people in the village."

Colonel Kelly immediately orders his aid to find the MP's and take him and Margaret to the stockade where the German is detained. At the stockade, Colonel Kelly finds the officer in charge, a young captain by the name of McGuirre. Kelly tells him what has happened in the camp with Sofie and the man they have in custody. Sofie saw him execute some civilians in the town. Captain McGuirre says, "Wait here, I'll be right back." After about ten minutes, the captain returns and tells Kelly, "That man you captured is a Waffen SS officer, complete with the Blood Tattoo under his arm. There are very few of them left. Since the war started going badly for the Germans and the writing was on the wall, they have either turned deserters, been executed by the Soviets when caught, or been executed by the local populations they had been abusing. Even some allied units, Americans included, have openly executed them even if they surrendered. Recently, though, command ordered us to send them to a prison dedicated to war crimes criminals for the trials that are surely coming. So, my standing orders are to transport the thugs to that prison for interrogation immediately upon capture. He will be placed in a prison van, under heavy guard, within the hour. Good work, Colonel. You and the Captain have bagged a real bogeyman."

On the way back to the hospital Margaret says, "No wonder this poor girl has been acting strange the past few days…she was scared to death! And who can blame her after what she has been through!"

When the meeting room clears and Becky had taken Sofie back to her barracks with orders not to leave her alone, Margaret turns to Kelly and says, "I am growing very fond of this kid and there is no way I'm leaving her here in some post war German orphanage. Surely there is a way to get her out of Germany and back to the states. Geez, Colonel, two smart people like us should be able to accomplish that mission."

Sofie

My face lights up as the giant and his smaller companion enter the hospital. I'm so happy and relieved at the same time.

This feeling seems very strange, especially after recently burying my Papa, Mama, and Uncle in the church yard less than a week ago. But I don't think anyone else besides these two soldiers, Becky, and Maggie cares whether I live or die. They alone stand between me and the bad people.

I think Maggie is telling them how I have been helping. Doing what I can to help the Americans defeat the Nazis and Russians. The two soldiers and Maggie talk and gesture towards me. She must be talking about how I have helped around the camp. Their faces get very concerned, and I know she is telling them about the SS Colonel that was taken away by the American soldiers. I have a sense of pride that I have not felt in a long while. I believe they are really starting to like me, and I am again a real part of something important.

Chapter 2 1/2

The Plan

Later that evening, after the three soldiers have washed the war from their bodies and are eating in the mess, Ben asks Maggie, "Well, Captain, have you given any thought on how we can get this girl back to the states?"

"Lieutenant," she says, "I have actually done more than think about it. I have put 'OUR' plan into action. After observing Sofie for the first few days while you two have been on your '*daddy vacation*,' I have come to the same conclusion: We cannot abandon her!"

Ernie asks, "So, what's up?"

"So, Corporal," Margaret says, "the plan is to have someone declared as guardian for Sofie to expedite her entry into the States. Apparently, Benjamin and Sofie both have a German cousin in common who has gone missing. Therefore, "he", as she gestures toward Ben with her fork, "is the logical choice."

"What the hell," says Ben. "I ain't got no cousin over here!!"

Maggie responds with "*Paperwork says you do,*" and plops a manila folder down in front of him. Ernesto breaks out laughing so hard he has tears and snot all over his face. As he gets up to gain some control, he says to Ben, "Payback is a bitch, que no, hombre," and he realizes Ben still doesn't get it. Maggie has exacted the perfect way to pay him back for putting her in the tight spot last week.

Maggie explains their plan. "Inside the folder, you will find your application for the legal guardianship of one Sophia Walder (Sofie) until your cousin Hans resurfaces...'*I don't hold much hope for that, do you?*' Colonel Kelly has approved your application at this level mainly because Sofie has some hearing problems resulting from the Russian artillery shell explosions. And, as it turns out, she can only get help from a specialist stateside."

Margaret continues, "We have already talked with Sofie. She agreed because she has no one left here, and she likes and trusts you–*go figure!*" She looks Ben straight in the eye and says, "You know what this means, don't you? '*It is either put up or shut up!*' This is a serious commitment, on your part especially. It's not like getting a puppy from the pound; this is seriously for better or worse stuff here. Considering her trauma, she may face a lifetime of challenges ahead that we can't anticipate. However, I think Ernest would add his support, as would I. But it is your name on the dotted line, as they say.... So, what will it be, Ben?"

Ben pauses for just a moment and responds with, "I could not live with myself if I didn't do this, not after what we have seen here and knowing what she has been through. To use one of your favorite phrases, '*What are we fighting this war for, anyway?*'"

Ben asks, "How in the world were you able to put all of this together so fast?"

"Well," Maggie explains, "you have not cornered the idea of helping orphaned German children. The phenomenon has caught on quickly as the tide of the war has revealed just how awful the Reich has treated its own citizens and just how many children need help. The concept itself is not a new one," she explains. "For instance, during WWI, the American Red Cross oversaw a program where each American Army unit operating in France adopted one French orphan. Once Colonel Kelly had this history, he contacted the Red Cross to facilitate this application for guardianship. It really helped that she is a family member and you are an officer in good standing. Ol' man Kelly has grown fond of Sofie as he has witnessed her working to better our cause here. Her courage in identifying the SS officer who terrorized her village put the Colonel on the path to expedite Sofie's adoption process. His weight behind this effort has pushed this over the finish line. A heartfelt thank-you on your part would be a gracious gesture he would appreciate."

The three friends sit and plot the strategy necessary to pull off mission 'Get Sofie Home.' They all agree that Sofie can continue to stay put until they have a clearer understanding of the future. If they're lucky, the guardianship paperwork will be finished soon, and they can arrange transportation to the States for Sofie.

The 144th continued its mission through the month of June, about two months after the German surrender on May 7, 1945. Subsequently, the 144th was transferred to the states for possible deployment in the Pacific theater.

However, after the Japanese surrender on August 15th, the ranks of the 144th returned to a pre-war scale, allowing Ernest and Ben to go back to New Mexico. Sofie continued to stay with Maggie in Germany, where the hospital unit continued to treat casualties and ready the patients for transfer back to the states. But now they have received orders to decommission the hospital unit, so Sofie will soon be air- transported to the Biggs Air Base in El Paso, Texas, along with other civilian personnel and patients exiting Germany.

The medical personnel from the decommissioned hospital unit are being shipped stateside, accompanying the wounded soldiers that need care during relocation to VA hospitals. Becky Baldwin is scheduled to be on a medical air transport destined for El Paso, Texas. She has agreed to take charge of Sofie and accompany her to the Biggs Air Base in El Paso along with other civilian personnel and wounded soldiers.

Margaret, Becky, and Colonel Kelly sit down with Sofie to describe what will be happening in the next few days. Sofie listens to them talk and seems to understand things are changing. When she learns of their intentions to transport her to America and reunite with the Giant and his friend, Sofie seems excited…but she is noticeably anxious about what the future holds for her.

Sofie

I listen to these nice people talk about me, and I can now understand some of their words. I try not to show how scared I am that they might abandon me here despite their promises to take me with them. If only the Giant was here!!!

Finally, Becky, the German speaker who likes me, explains what will happen next. I am so grateful that I grab Becky's hand and hold on as tight as I can. I don't want to let go. I will be on an airplane and will get to see the Giant and his friend again… AND…I will get to live in America in a place called New Mexico. Margaret and the Colonel assure me that flying is fun and a great adventure, but that I must always stay near Becky and do exactly what she says. Of course, I think to myself, *'my Mommy and Daddy taught me how to be a good girl and behave'*. Besides, I like Becky.

Becky and I board the big airplane and help make the wounded soldiers comfortable. I am getting good at knowing what is needed to make them more comfortable. Several of these men are so badly injured they are not even awake during the entire flight. Others are so excited about going home that they just talk and talk. Most find it funny that a 'German girl' is helping Americans. We make several stops where the badly injured, or maybe dead soldiers, are taken off and others are loaded on. Becky tells me that now we will be flying for a very long time. We use the toilet and get some food to take with us. Then the long flight to a new life begins. Next stop…America.

I have fallen asleep. I was so excited I didn't think that was possible. The jolt of the landing woke me, and people are moving throughout the plane, getting ready to depart. Becky says we will be here in a place called Maryland for at least one day before we leave for El Paso, Texas, where '*the giant*' will meet us.

The next day is much the same with injured soldiers being put on the plane along with other soldiers catching a ride west. They like talking with me, and Becky has taught me some words to use like "orphan" and "adoption" and "my American uncle." I like these Americans. They have such hope–something we had so little of in my small town after the German soldiers moved in and started rounding up those who were known to be Jews or those who helped the Jews. That was basically everyone in my town.

When we land and get off the plane, the Giant is waiting. He is with a woman who is clutching his arm with tears coming down her cheeks. Without his uniform, the Giant looks smaller, but his smile is just as big. I run to him, and he lifts me high in the air, then I grab him around the neck and hold tight. Now the woman is crying even more than before. I wonder what is wrong with her and hope it's not my fault.

When Becky comes over, they hug in a warm greeting that I have noticed Americans like to do. They talk for a while and then Becky kneels down, gives me a fierce hug, and says, "You are home now, little one. '*You are the bravest girl!!!*' I will never forget you and will tell stories about you to my children. I hope we will meet again someday. You are also the luckiest girl I know–to find wonderful people like these to care for you, although something tells me you can make your own luck, too."

I don't quite understand all that Becky is trying to tell me, but I tell her that I am so grateful for all her help and kindness when I needed it most. When Becky has said her goodbyes and walked away, the other woman kneels down to tell me in German that she is the giant's mom and that her name is Vivian. So starts my new life in America.

It took two days for the Red Cross to clear the paperwork and place Sofie in the official care of her Guardian. Ben's mom has never seen her son so excited. Vivian fretted for days over how Sofie would deal with all the changes and her new environment. Ben, of course, told her to relax, saying, "I have seen this kid deal with so much more. She has an unshakable composure for someone her age. You'll see what I mean. Sofie is a remarkable kid." From the moment Vivian saw Sofie and Ben together, she knew all their lives would change for the better. There is almost an aura about them when they are together. It's truly a miracle.

While they were driving from El Paso to Silver City, Sofie immediately noticed how far you can see. There are no trees until they make the turn north towards the mountains. This is such a strange land. She also had time to think about how dependent she was on Becky to help her talk with people. This will be difficult, she thinks, and feels a twinge of fear rise. She could only hope they would still like her now that Becky was gone. How were they going to talk???

Part Two

A Little History

How We Got Here

Chapter 3

Vivian and Ben Wallace

Vivian Wallace moved to Silver City, New Mexico from Gary, Indiana, in June 1931 when her sister said she could get her a job as a teacher at the 6th Street Elementary School. Her sister, Joyce, had moved there several years back. She followed her husband Mac, who took a job as a mechanic for a mining equipment company. Viv had in-tow a 6-year-old boy, Ben. Her husband had abandoned her when he got laid off from the steel plant and could not find work in Chicago. The depression had been most brutal in that part of the country. Vivian had a high school diploma and one year of college, which Joyce says makes her *'over-qualified'* for the teaching job in Silver City.

Southwestern New Mexico was isolated from the severe effects of the depression and year by year, Viv and Ben got by with the help of her sister and her husband Mac. 'Mac the Mechanic' was a self-proclaimed cynic and part time rounder. But overall, as a WWI vet, he was a responsible man. He treated his family well, including Viv and Ben. Ben called him Uncle Mac with some affection, and he eventually displaced Ben's still M.I.A. father.

Life in New Mexico is so different from Gary, Indiana, that Ben has turned inward and is reluctant to talk much around other kids. He is one of the bigger kids in his class which immediately causes him two serious problems. One, he is among the first chosen when teams are picked at recess despite not being the best coordinated athlete. This leads to number two, kids are always trying to pick a fight with him. The Mexican kids in particular are always wanting to fight because he is new to the school and he is as big as they are. The fact that his mom and aunt both work in the same school presents other problems for his social acceptance.

Mac has told him, "Don't worry too much about this newcomer crap. It will go away in a little while. But my advice to you is don't back-down when they challenge you. Fight as hard as you can. When you win a few of those fights, things will start getting better and you will even become friends with most of those classmates. It's just the way things are for newbies, but especially here in New Mexico."

School started getting better for Ben. He made decent grades and played on several Little League baseball teams over the years. Mac was right…some of those Mexican classmates he fought with became friends as the years went by. When high school rolled around, 'The Colts' had some good teams when he and his friends played. A solid comradery was established among all team members.

However, off the field there was still some undercurrents of tension and something else he could not put his finger on. Ben noticed that the Anglo parents and the Mexican parents don't socialize much and, with only a few exceptions, don't live in the same neighborhoods. Mac told him that's just the way it is in Grant County with the mines and all here. Ben doesn't know what that means, but what the hell. I'm only 16 so everything was fine by me. High School was going great, and I got a good steady girl…life is grand as they say.

Ben turned 18 in the middle of a World War. A mother's nightmare if there ever was one. Viv would not grant him permission to *'join-up'* when he graduated from high school at 17. This was a major rift between mother and child.

Recent headlines in all the New Mexico newspapers had chronicled the events of the 1,816 soldiers from the New Mexico

National Guard who had deployed to bolster the defense of the Philippines.

Bataan had fallen in April of 1942 forcing the Grant County men to become prisoners of war and endure the brutal 'Death March.' (Of the 1,816 men, only 829 would return home). To say patriotism was high would prove to be a significant understatement. Ben and all his friends were eager to serve their country and rescue their neighbors…saving them from further brutalities at the hands of the Japanese.

Vivian held her ground, though, and would not give in to her son's demand to join the army and serve!!

Now 19, Ben leaves for boot camp and training, whatever that means. At least Viv kept him home another year until the draft appeal expired. She is proud of the fact that he got at least one year of college in at the local school. He did well in math and science classes and has visions of a job in one of the local mines when the war is over.

Since he left for boot camp, he has only written his mother a couple of times. He doesn't quite know what tell her. He doesn't want her to worry, and he doesn't want to lie…so he just doesn't write. When he gets to Europe his unit is constantly on the move. If there is any down time, he just sleeps. Writing in the middle of a war is impossible.

Finally, a cease fire has been declared and the war is over. The fighting has all but stopped. Front line units like his, though, are still on high alert. There are deserters and Russian troops trying to grab all they can before they're forced back to their own country according to the cease fire provisions. He has a little time now, and some very good news, so he sits down to write "THE LETTER" as his mom now calls it.

May 7, 1945. It is VE day, victory in Europe. Germany has surrendered, and her son is still alive and well. This is a day she will mark on her calendar and celebrate along with all the other special days. Every year on that day, Viv gets the letter from Ben out of her bureau drawer and relives that moment after both Germany and Japan have surrendered and WWII is finally coming to an end.

Dear Mom,

Sorry about the lack of communication over the past year but I hope you understand the distractions we have had with these pesky Germans. Now the Russians are becoming frustrating as well. Well, the war has finally ended, and I should be back stateside within a month if the scuttlebutt we are hearing in true. I am safe now so don't worry about me any more plus I have met some terrific fellow New Mexicans over here. We have bonded with a pact to all get home safely. I will tell you more about that when I arrive home.

However, Mom, that is not the really good news. You won't believe it, but I have found your niece Sophia and she will come back home with me. The bad news though is that Uncle Hans is missing and presumed dead. So, for now, I am her official guardian! She will be coming to live with us in Silver as soon as the final paperwork clears and transportation can be arranged. Until then, one of those New Mexicans I referred to has agreed to watch out for her. Margaret Beltran is a nurse and captain in a medical unit here. She and Sofie have bonded, and I am sure Sofie will be well cared for until she gets to her new home.

Don't fret too much over this new development. You will immediately fall in love with her the way we have over here. I will explain the 'WE" thing in a later correspondence. Sofie doesn't speak much English yet, but she is trying very hard to be prepared for America. So, brush up on your German…haha. Except for the demise of poor Hans, this is great news for our family, and I cannot wait till you see for yourself just what a wonderful kid she really is. Don't worry now. I have not suffered any trauma to the head.

I must close this letter now and get back to what little soldering is left to be done over here.

Your Loving Son
Ben

P.S. I also can't wait for you to meet Ernest Polanco, a fellow Grant Countian. We have become best friends and have had each other's back from the time we landed in Europe.

Vivian recalls reading the letter several more times, and it still made no sense to her. Her sister also read the letter and says, "*What the hell is he talking about*". They were both worried that he had incurred some injury affecting his mental capabilities. Although, the last sentence in the letter assured them this was not the case and there would be more details to follow. Every year she reflects on how that letter forecast the changes her small family would experience and the joy of all the new people she would meet over the next few years.

Ben takes more classes from the local college on the GI bill, concentrating on geology and chemistry, hoping to hire on with the copper mining operations in Hurley, the biggest mine in the southwest. In little over a year later, he's hired and now works in the assay lab thanks to a contact that Mac knew. He and Sofie can now move out of Mom's house into one of their own in Hurley, NM, about 15 miles away. Most of the company's offices are there, as well as the mill, smelter, and lab. They are also closer to Ernie's homestead (two acres) in North Hurley. Ben hoped to reacquaint with a former sweetheart from before the war, but found most women shy away from the immediate responsibility of raising a young 'foreign' girl.

Sofie now calls Ben Dad, and he likes that. Although she occasionally has some flashback episodes such as nightmares, Sofie is now 10 years old and seems to have adjusted well to her new life. Ben also feels very content in 1949 New Mexico. Ben and Sofie go into Silver City a couple of times a month to visit his mom because she has a new boyfriend and can't quite seem to make it out to Hurley regularly. Besides, the smoke from the big smelter stack causes an adverse reaction in his mom and she can never stay too long when the smelter is feeding concentrates into the furnace. Ben has gotten a promotion within the lab and is now in a management position. With his monthly salary, he can easily support them both, especially with the company's housing benefit.

Ben has seen Sofie grow up before his very eyes, not only physically, but emotionally as well. True to her nature, she is a loving helpful kid and does not shy away from work or responsibility. The fact that she still does not talk much or display emotions sometimes worries him. But when he thinks about what she went through during the war he can't help but think she is doing just fine. He loves her more than he thought possible.

Sophie is good at school but still speaks with a German accent. This has posed some challenges in the friendship department. Nobody speaks German in this community…just Spanish and English. Ben helps her with the English and Ernest helps with the Spanish.

Her teachers say she is a very bright student and should be promoted to the next grade ahead of schedule, but they all seem to agree that can wait until her English is better. Ben is proud of her grades in math and science and Ernest says she is becoming very proficient in Spanish. The schools and the mines sponsor activities and sports programs for the kids in the communities. Sofie has sadly voiced the observation that ALL the activities are for the boys…no girls allowed. Recently a few softball teams have been formed but Sofie didn't want much to do with them. She would rather go the Ernie's place after school and help Lupe and play with his kids. Plus, she likes learning Spanish and is getting better and better.

Author's Note

The following is part of my research for writing this book. My Dad was part of the 200th Coastal Artillery was subsequently captured and then a war prisoner in Japan until the war ended. This episode has been chronicled in many history books over the decades. I thought my readers would be interested in this perspective.

Deployment in New Mexico

Nine and a half hours after the assault on Pearl Harbor, the Japanese began bombing Clark Field and Manila in the Philippines. About 1,800 New Mexicans and West Texans were deployed to the Philippines as personnel of the 200th Coastal Artillery. Around 500 men from the 200th were sent to Manila and assembled alongside Filipino soldiers into a makeshift anti-aircraft unit, subsequently known as the 515th Coast Artillery.

The following is an article from a U.S. Army Pacific theaters publication.

1942 - 1943, The Bataan Death March

The Battle of Bataan ended, April 9, 1942, when U.S. Gen. Edward P. King surrendered to Japanese Gen. Masaharu Homma. At that point, 75,000 Soldiers became prisoners of war: about 12,000 Americans and 63,000 Filipinos. What followed was one of the worst atrocities in modern wartime history—the Bataan Death March.

U.S. Gen. Edward P. King discusses surrender, 1942. Photo by U.S. Army.

During the Battle of Bataan, the American soldiers and Filipino soldiers of U.S. Army Gen. Douglas MacArthur's U.S. Army Forces in the Far East, or USAFFE, had held out for four months against the Imperial Japanese Army, while every other island and nation in the Pacific and Southeast Asia fell to the Japanese. By March 1942, Japan controlled all of the Western Pacific except the Philippines.

MacArthur's plan was to hold his ground on the Bataan Peninsula and Corregidor Island in the Philippines until the U.S. Navy could bring reinforcements and supplies from the United States. Once the reinforcements arrived, he planned to attack north from Bataan, defeat the Japanese army, and push onward to the Japanese islands to victory. But with the U.S. Navy in shambles after the attack on Pearl Harbor, there were no ships capable of bringing the needed reinforcements to Bataan.

The Japanese navy blockaded Bataan and nearby Corregidor, preventing food, ammunition and medicine from reaching the U.S. troops. For months, the Soldiers on Bataan lived on half rations in the hot tropical jungle. Nevertheless, they fought back against Japanese attacks and defeated the Japanese army at battles along the Bataan defense line and along the rugged coastline of the peninsula.

But without supplies, they could barely hold out. By the first of April 1942, most of the starving men had lost as much as 30 percent of their body weight. They became so weak that they could barely lift their weapons. As medical supplies ran out, malaria, dysentery and other tropical diseases ravaged their ranks. Approximately 10,000 men were confined to the two open-air jungle hospitals for wounds and illnesses, and less than half of the remainder could be considered "combat effective" defined as a man, who could walk 100 yards without staggering and still have enough strength left to fire his weapon.

U.S. Army National Guard and Filipino soldiers shown at the outset of the Bataan Death March. Allied forces were forced to surrender to the Japanese on April 9, 1942, the largest surrender in U.S. history. Photo by U.S. Army.

The Japanese army launched its final assault on Bataan, April 3, 1942. Although the starving American and Filipino soldiers fought as best they could, they were no match for the fresh troops the Japanese brought in for the attack. As Gen. Homma's army rolled back the front line on Bataan, Gen. Edward King, the American field commander, made a fateful decision, April 9, as he surrendered rather than see any more of his starving, diseased men slaughtered by the advancing Japanese army.

Once the surrender went into effect, the Japanese rounded up the American and Filipino soldiers and gathered them into groups of 100 on the only paved road that ran down the Bataan peninsula. The Japanese assigned four guards to each group. They lined the men up four abreast, and they began marching them north toward Camp O'Donnell in Tarlac province, 65 miles away.

As the emaciated men proceeded north up the highway in the blistering heat, the Japanese guards summarily shot or bayoneted any man who fell, attempted to escape, or stopped to quench his thirst at a roadside spigot or puddle. The men were given little water or food for the entire length of the Bataan Death March, which took about five days for each group to complete. The guards chased off, bayoneted or shot any Filipino civilian, who tried to give water or bits of food to the passing lines of prisoners. At various points along the route of the March, they singled out prisoners, sometimes in groups, tied them to trees or fences, and shot them to death as examples to the other soldiers.

The Japanese guards killed between 7,000 - 10,000 men during the death march but they kept no records and no one knows the exact number. If a man fell, it was a certain death, unless another could pick him up and support him.

When they got to their prison camp, Camp O'Donnell, conditions were even worse. Camp O'Donnell was a former Philippine army camp designed to accommodate about 10,000 men. The Japanese crammed 60,000 survivors of the death march into the camp. There was little running water, sparse food, no medical care, and only slit trenches along the sides of the camp for sanitation. The heat was intolerable, flies rose out of the latrines and covered the prisoner's food. Malaria, dysentery, beriberi and a host of other diseases swept through the crowds of men. They began to die at the rate of 400 per day. It got so bad that by July 1942, the Japanese replaced the camp commander, moved the American prisoners to another camp, Cabanatuan, and decided to parole the Filipino prisoners.

From September through December 1942, the Japanese gradually paroled the Filipino soldiers to their families and to the mayors of their hometowns, who would be held personally responsible for each man's conduct. To be paroled, a soldier had to sign an oath that he would not participate in guerrilla activity, and he had to be well enough to walk. Anyone who was too sick to walk was simply held in camp until he either got well or died. By the time Camp O'Donnell closed in January 1943, after eight months of operation, 26,000 of the 50,000 Filipino prisoners of war there had died.

The American prisoners fared no better. Conditions in Cabanatuan were marginally better than Camp O'Donnell, and the prisoner doctors were able to somewhat stem the disease and death rate. However, as U.S. forces pulled closer to the Philippines in 1944, the Japanese decided to evacuate the American prisoners to Japan and Manchuria, to use them as slave laborers in Japanese factories and coal mines. Thousands of men were crammed into the dark holds of cargo ships so tightly that the men could not sit or lay down. Again, food and water were scarce, sanitary facilities were virtually non-existent, and the heat in the closed holds of the ships was unbearable. Men suffocated to death standing up. In some cases, the guards would not even let the dead bodies be removed from the holds. The Japanese ships were unmarked and some of them were attacked by American planes and torpedoed by American submarines. Once they arrived at the slave labor camps, more of the men died of malnutrition and exposure. By the time Japan surrendered and the U.S. Army liberated the Bataan prisoners of war, two-thirds of the American prisoners had died in Japanese custody.

Chapter 4

Time to Relocate

Isidro, Yoli, and Margaret Beltran

Margaret has heard her father tell his border crossing story so many times now, but she is always impressed with the courage her parents showed when they relocated to the U.S. from Frontera Chihuahua during the Mexican Revolution. In the period between 1910 and 1920, Carrancistas and Villistas were nothing more than bandits plundering the towns in Northern Mexico (Frontera) for food, horses, and guns.

They would also conscript the men to fight and force women to do all sorts of things, including in some documented instances fighting alongside the "soldiers."

When Margaret was in high school, her class was given an assignment to write something about their family history. She went home and asked her dad if he would tell her the story of coming to this country again so she could write it down in order to complete her assignment.

She remembers looking her dad in the eye and asking, "Please try not to exaggerate like you always do, and don't use so much profanity."

Her dad said, "This may take a while, so let me get your mom to sit with us...she was there after all."

Once they were seated at the dining room table with some snacks and drinks (cerveza for dad), Isidro drew a deep breath and began the story.

Isidro

I foresaw nothing but chaos in our future when the *'Punitive Expedition'* was launched against Mexico for the attack on Fort Furlong and the town of Columbus, New Mexico, in 1916. You were just three months old at the time. Your mother and I feared the worst for our family if we remained in Mexico. So, we abandoned our home and headed for the U.S. We figured it would take us about two weeks to cover the 200 miles to El Paso, Texas. Since we would have to travel at night, the departure time was critical. It would have to coincide with the two-week period on both the waxing and waning sides of the full moon. Also, to maximize our chances of getting some kind of job, we wanted to start in the spring for the planting season in the Rio Grande Valley. April 23 was the day we chose to begin our new life.

Fortunately, we had only a couple of close encounters with fast moving Villista mounted patrols, who were in too much of a hurry to bother with a poor peasant family that had nothing they needed. In 14 days' travel, we made it to the outskirts of Juarez, Mexico, across the Rio Grande River from El Paso. I remember resting the remainder of the night while discussing with your mom the best strategy to enter the U.S. East of El Paso was downriver and into Texas, while Northwest was upriver and into New Mexico.

When the sun came up, we noticed a small cluster of houses and buildings about a half mile from our camp. We hoped someone in the village might have some useful information about crossing the river. We worked our courage up and all went together, hoping the villagers would welcome a family better than a single male traveler.

A short, stout man named Jesus Montoya came out to meet us with a hospitable greeting. He offered us some food and water. Jesus said he was only familiar with the area north of El Paso. He was working there just last fall to help with the melons and the cotton. He never went in the spring or summer because he was too busy with his own small rancho.

He told us he had worked for a man named Gorman and that Mr. Gorman is a good man that treats his workers fairly. Jesus said, "I am sure if you mention my name, it will go favorably. Senior Gorman and I have known each other for a while now".

He continued, "It is only two miles to the best crossing place from here. Make sure you're there before sunup because the spring is more unpredictable than the fall. The troubles between the U.S. and Mexico have made the crossing more dangerous than in the past."

"Cuidado, hombre!" were his last remarks.

The next morning I was up early after a night of fitful sleep I could not help wondering what the next day would hold for our futures. I distinctly remember getting to the river's edge before it was light. This was the first cloudy night we had encountered the entire trip, and the valley held a strange darkness, like looking through a dense black veil. Your mom and I were afraid of entering the river without being able to see, so we waited for a little more light. This decision would change our lives forever.

We were hiding in the thicket beside the river in the dark. We were very tense and unsure of what to expect. The coming light and the strangeness of the whole experience was unsettling. Then you began to fuss. Finally, I said, '*We must go now.*' But as we stepped into the shallow water, a figure emerged from nearby.

"Stop right there," the man commanded in a gravelly voice. "This is MY crossing, and you must pay to use it".

Yolonda interrupts at this point in the story saying, "We were so tense and afraid at that moment, When the bandit appeared seemingly out of nowhere It scared me so much I almost fainted and dropped you into the water."

Scared me plenty too confessed Isidro. I told him we have no money, so we will move to another crossing to the north. The man replied, "Ah, senior, I own that one as well. So, you MUST pay to cross."

I told him again that I still had no money. The man was of a stocky build and wore his pistola dangling from the front in true bandito style. His eyes glared from a face full of neglected whiskers. I could tell he was very confident that the outcome of this encounter would be the same as all the others against the poor peons that were unable to resist.

"Then maybe you have something to trade," he said to me.

Again, I indicated we had nothing of value in our possession. The bandit quickly responded, "Ah, but you do, senior. Perhaps 30 minutes with your pretty wife will be the payment…if she is any good. I will even let you watch."

The words were not even out of his mouth yet when I lunged at the man while pulling my knife from its sheath beneath my shirt. The bandit drew his gun expertly and was leveling the barrel. I had reacted so quickly out of fear for my family that I hit him with full force. However, the bandit managed to get a shot off, but I was on him by then and with adrenalin in my veins, I drove him down into the shallow water. The next few moments were a blur. I just kept driving the knife into him over and over again. I didn't even know what vital place my knife was finding. There was nothing but desperation driving me, and I could not control myself. I continued thrusting the knife over and over again until he quit struggling.

When I finally stood up, I was covered in a mixture of blood and muddy water. I immediately looked for you and your mom. I saw my Yoli crouched at the river's edge holding you. But she was not moving. *'Then I saw it!'* The bullet had struck her arm, and it was just dangling by her side. She remained so calm, holding you. Quite brave is my wife.

Yolonda interrupts the story here again and says, "I remember I could not figure out what was happening. Your dad and this man fighting in the water, and I could not even move my arm to hold you close. I began to cry uncontrollably…I did not feel so brave as your dad says now."

Isidro continues, then I cut off the lower part of my shirt sleeve, rolled it up, and twisted it around her upper arm just above the wound. She made not a sound.

"Probably passed out by then," Yolonda says.

As the bleeding slowed, I looked around and saw some people had gathered at the river's edge on the Mexican side. They were gesturing and yelling at us to cross to the American side quickly. The gunshot will bring unwanted attention to this area. In fact, several bystanders were now in the water, pushing the bandit's body into the deeper center of the river. One man then turned and helped us cross to the other side. Before I could even thank him, the man said, "Thank you and may God go with you. Morales was a bad hombre."

I knew I need to act quickly, so I gathered you under one arm and supported your mom with the other. Then we moved as fast as possible away from the river. We had to abandon all our belongings, and I remember wondering how I was going to explain this to Yoli. It was so exhausting, and our strength was diminishing with each passing moment. A panic surrounded me as the reality of the situation became clear. I realized I had no choice but to stop at the next house.

It was like all the others in this part of the world: a small adobe home with no yard and a narrow latilla covered porch. As we approached, a man came out to block my path. Then he saw Yoli was seriously injured. He had not even noticed there was a baby mixed up in all this mess until he set your mom and me on a porch bench. "Por Dios, what has happened here?" the man said.

I recall crying in a desperate voice, *'Please, she needs a doctor now'*. The man tells me there is a small clinic where a doctor sometimes comes about one-half mile straight up this road. I tried to stand but could barely support myself when that kind man said, "I will help senior, un momento," In a matter of minutes he returned with a homemade cart to help us move faster. I have never been so grateful.

The 'clinic' is nothing more than another small adobe building. Locked. No one was there. At this point, it becomes too much for me and I all but passed out from fatigue and desperation. The man says, "I will see if I can find the nurse who lives nearby. She sometimes helps the doctor."

I woke to find myself sitting on the steps of the building with my dying wife and infant daughter. In almost total despair, I wonder if this is all there is to this life? Can there be no justice? Exploited by leaders denying people the right to make a simple living for their families, or plundered by bandits posing as revolutionaries? Yoli and I, we have lived but 20 years. Our daughter brought us hope. *'Where is that hope now?'*

The next memory I have is of some strange man leaning over me, speaking to a woman next to him. I tried to sit upright but the woman gently pushed me back down.

"Mi esposa y mi hija!" I demand. The man tells me in very good Spanish that they are fine and are in the other room. He tells me they will take my wife to a local hospital where they will have to amputate her arm to save her life, but my baby daughter is nursing now and doing better. The man asks me what happened. But I am a stranger to this country, and I am afraid to respond. The man says he is a doctor and not the sheriff. But again, I still say nothing.

The doctor says he heard a report about an incident at a border crossing where a notorious bandit was killed. If you are the one that killed Muerte Morales, you are a hero and certainly not wanted for anything on this side of the border. Now he is talking about a killing, so I still say nothing.

The doctor tells me it will take many days before Yoli can travel. He then says, "I have a cousin who owns some farmland near here where you can probably stay until she can leave. If you are interested in looking for work, he hires 'Braceros' for temporary jobs. His name is Pete Gorman, and I know he would be very interested in the man that killed Muerte Morales."

The doctor saw my reaction to Gorman's name. He told me, "Go see your wife and daughter and tell them what will be happening." He adds, "She knows about her arm. She is very brave and is more concerned about you and little Margarit. Go to her now. The hospital transport will be here soon."

I will never forget that moment when I walked into the room where your mom was waiting. She looked so small, so frail. Yet, when she looked at me with a faint smile on her lovely face, I could see hope in her eyes.

Her next words to me have guided us to this wonderful life we now live. In a halting soft voice she said, "These Americans are so kind to help us when we have nothing. There is goodness at work here... *'God has delivered us to this place'*. Please let us stay. This is why we came, to find a place such as this. We could have a future here and raise our little Margarit. The doctor said I will be fine in a few days and has assured me you and Margarit will be fine until we can be together again. So, my brave husband…go fight for our future. I will join you soon."

I tell you, Margaret, if you could have witnessed your mother's bravery and determination at that moment, when we were at our most vulnerable, you would have cried just as I did. Your mom is the true strength of our family!

After they removed your mom's arm just above the elbow and she is recovering, the kind doctor takes me to his family's farm to meet Pete Gorman. When the doctor tells Pete the story of the demise of Muerte Morales, I can see in Mr. Gorman's expressive eyes that he is clearly impressed. Mr. Gorman looked me over, trying to judge my character, "Isidro, I need you to talk. You need to tell me what and why you are here."

I remember it like it was yesterday. I told Mr. Gorman what was happening to my beloved Mexico with the war between the different factions of revolutionaries. They are hardly more than bandits, raiding villages like mine for supplies and pleasures. Those *'cabrones'* are why I am here. They had stolen our future, and I could not subject my family to the conditions we were forced to endure at our home near Chihuahua. And, yes, I did kill one of those *'cabrones'* in the river by Juarez. He tried to rob me of my meager possessions and threatened to do unspeakable things to my wife. He got what he deserved.

Mr. Gorman looked directly at me and said, "Isidro, with a story like that, you know you can never go back to Mexico. So, what do YOU want now? You seem a man of determination to me and will get whatever it is you set your mind to. So what is it?"

Reality hit me in that instant. What Mr. Gorman said was true. We could never go back. I stood as tall and as proud as I could make my skinny body look and I told him, *'Well, I guess I am an American now.'* I can still see this comical look on Ole Pete's face when he said, "Well, let's work on that mañana. For now, gather up your daughter and follow me. I have a place you can stay until your wife can join you."

Mr. Gorman hesitated and turned to me abruptly, saying, "Isidro, this is a hard-working farm. What skills do you have that could be used around here?"

I told him I was used to hard work, long days, and had some blacksmithing experience. Mr. Gorman looked me over again and replied, "Those traits make good farmers, and we certainly need some help now. So let me show you where your family can stay for a while."

Right then, I said to myself, just look how hopeless my life seemed only a few hours past… Now my family's future is back in my own hands.

When her dad finished his story, Margaret looks down at her notebook and realizes she has not written even one word. She looks back and forth between her parents and thinks that this is not the same braggadocios story her father tells at dinner gatherings at the Gorman farm. This is my family's history, and it is so personal, I cannot possibly convey this emotion-packed saga in a short school assignment. Maybe a story about the time spent with her dad planting the pecan trees on their own farm they had just purchased would make a better assignment to turn in to her teacher.

Chapter 4 ½

The Path Forward

Thus, in 1916, just 4 years after New Mexico was granted statehood, Isidro Beltran started a lifetime friendship with the Gormans. After working at Gorman Farms for a year, Isidro has proven to be indispensable in both farm operations and the management of the migrant workers that have become essential to the farm operations.

One day, Mr. Gorman came to Isidro with some surprisingly good news (he thinks). The government has just initiated a program to naturalize foreign citizens that provide military service for at least one year. The small Beltran family is thriving in America. Isidro has come to love this country and the opportunity it provides. His love for America and his community makes him more than willing to do his part to gain his citizenship. Mr. Gorman tells Isidro his family can stay where they are and Yoli can continue helping around the main house until he returns.

Pete Gorman accompanied Isidro to Ft. Bliss, just outside El Paso, to be sure they did the enlistment into the Army and the paperwork correctly. Pete just knew that Isidro's courage and determination will see him through. After-all, the man who survived the Mexican Revolution and killed Muerte Morales ought to make it through a little skirmish in Europe.

Isidro stood before the enlistment officer and explained his immigration status and his desire to serve in the war against Germany. Although his English is halting, he conveys his commitment to the United States of America. Pete watches as

Isidro communicates his dream to become an American citizen. The officer looks at Pete and asks if he can vouch for this man. Pete gives a brief account of his relationship with Isidro and his family and what he has accomplished in their short time together.

The enlistment officer then accepts Isidro into the process of becoming a member of the American Expeditionary Force. The officer tells him, "Your final destination will undoubtedly be in Europe, probably France. As of now, the U.S. has only about 100,000 soldiers on active duty, so your training will be brief and intense. Although your English is passable, you will be sent to Georgia first for a three-month crash course in English. After that, you'll be assigned to the Texas 'Lone Star Division,' probably to 141st Infantry Regiment for immediate deployment to Europe. If all of this is still OK with you, I will expect you back here in three days to complete the enlistment and ship out to Fort Gordon, Georgia."

So Isidro goes to war after all. This time not to fight out of fear of retribution from some bandit, but to gain citizenship and freedom in his adopted home. Hope is an amazing tonic.

After his tour of duty, Isidro returned to 'his home' with a slight limp as a result of a GI can explosion during the Battle of St. Eteiene toward the end of the war. When pressed by Pete and Dr. Jim one afternoon, Isidro told them, "My experiences in Mexico with the Villistas and the basic training I got did not prepare me for the trench warfare I encountered in Europe. Every time the officers shouted, '*Over the Top*,' we would lose half our men before we drove the Germans from their trenches. Even though I was wounded in the leg, I had to keep soldiering. Finally, one day, we went over the top and the Germans just stood up and surrendered. We couldn't believe it! We thought it was a trick. They all just threw down their weapons and stood there… maybe a hundred or more where we were. Turns out, most of them had no ammo and hadn't eaten in days. Everyone in our unit got Badges of Military Merit. The fighting war ended for me right then. I swear if you yelled '*Over the Top*' now, I would be completely paralyzed with fear. The only negative effects I have now though is trouble sleeping now and then. But basically, I am the same man who enlisted. A small trade-off for becoming an American citizen."

Gorman Farms prepare to enter the 'Roaring Twenties' producing excellent crops, and their start-up dairy is well underway. Mr. Gorman welcomes Isidro home with a dinner at the main house, including Dr. Jim. Mr. Gorman can see a change in Isidro since his return from the war. For one thing, his English has improved dramatically. It is obvious Isidro has worked on that, plus he is bolder with his comments and conversation. He offers Isidro a supervisory position, which also means a better house for his family.

Mr. Gorman says, "I hope you can start tomorrow. There is a lot to do, my friend."

Isidro pulls Margarit onto his lap and declares, "Senior Gorman, what a journey you have put my family on, and we can never thank you enough." Dr. Jim says, "Don't be so fast there, Isidro. If I know my cousin, you'll earn every centavo he pays you."

Author's Note

"Over the Top": Experiences of Texan Mexicans in the Trenches

When President Woodrow Wilson declared war in 1917, the U.S. military force barely numbered 100,000 men, mostly concentrated in the state-level National Guard Units. Among the hundreds of thousands of men who registered for the first round of the draft that year were immigrants from all corners of the world, particularly Europe. Historian Nancy Ford recounts how the War Department was "shocked" to discover that approximately one-fourth of the draftees were either illiterate in their native language and/or functionally illiterate in English. War Department rules required volunteers or conscripts to read or write English in order to serve. In response, the War Department created the Foreign-speaking Soldier Subsection (FSS) in January of 1918 to quickly devise a means to teach recruits basic English and engage in Americanization programs. In Americans All!: Foreign-born Soldiers in World War I, Ford details how a successful English language curriculum developed at Fort Gordon, Georgia, was exported to several camps as "the Gordon Plan." Most soldiers only received three months of training, with mixed results at best.

The pertinent part of the naturalization act reads as follows:

If you are currently serving or previously served honorably in the U.S. armed forces during a designated period of hostilities, you may be eligible to apply for naturalization. While some general naturalization requirements apply under INA 329, other requirements may not apply or are reduced.

The designated periods of hostilities are listed below: Apr. 6, 1917 – Nov. 11, 1918

Sept 1, 1939 – Dec. 31, 1946

June 25, 1950 – July 1, 1955

Feb. 28, 1961 – Oct. 15, 1978

Aug. 2, 1990 – April 11, 1991

Sept. 11, 2001 – present

To establish eligibility under INA 329, you must:

Have served honorably in the U.S. armed forces during a designated period of hostility, and if separated, have been separated under honorable conditions from your qualifying period of service.

Chapter 5

Margaret Then and Now

Maturity

Margaret, as she demands to be called now, was one of the top students in the Gadsden High class of 1934. She thinks she could have been the best, except for the two 'B' grades she got in her Spanish classes because her parents refused to let her use Spanish around the house. Still, she is quite proud of herself, especially of the award for top math student. Her parents cheered as they announced her name when she received her diploma. Margaret had never seen her dad shed a tear until that moment. She still has never seen her mom cry.

A whole bunch of Gormans were there as well because two of her classmates were Gormans of some relation. But she thought Mr. Gorman and the doctor cheered loudest for her.

Doctor Jim, as she calls him, has offered her a job working in his office, as well as an assistant to his nurse. He also would like her to accompany him when he travels to the houses in the local farming community. It was an unexpected offer, and he told her to think about it and talk with her parents before giving an answer. Margaret told her parents at dinner that night what Dr. Jim had proposed. Her mother made the best argument to accept. "It is hard to say no to someone who saved you and your mom's life!"

Margaret joins Dr. Jim in his growing medical clinic. The Gorman clinic is housed in a nice modern building in Anthony,

NM. They see local patients on a regular basis for an office visit fee of $5.00. If they cannot pay at the time of the visit the fees are put on an accounts receivable ledger to be paid at a later date (or not at all in some cases). Dr. Jim or his head nurse also do home visits when necessary. Margaret almost always accompanies the person doing the home visit so both are not tied up and out of the office at the same time. They are trusting her more and more as the years go by and she is very proud of her accomplishments and her value to the community. As can be expected the clinic sees all forms of ailments typical of a rural farming community. Margaret has become very adept at treating the injuries common to physical demands of agricultural life; suturing cuts, setting broken bones and other trauma injuries. She has still not mastered any composure when dealing with infants and child birth. She just can't help but shy away from those patients and avoids them if possible. She just doesn't trust herself yet when there is so little room for error. Her boyfriend, a local deputy sheriff, tells her he has similar anxieties when dealing with young children. He tells her, "I can go into any of these local bars and break-up fights, but put a small child in front of me and I just seem to freeze up. They just seem so vulnerable and I am worthless to comfort them."

The Gorman clinic is starting to see wounded veterans coming back home from their service in both theaters of combat. Margaret has taken the lead in providing their care. Many are friends she has known since High School or are relatives of local community families. The war and the toll on the community are always topics of discussion at any local gatherings. Her boyfriend just volunteered and she has made up her mind to do the same.

She has discussed this urge to volunteer with her parents and Dr. Jim. Both have sensed her determination and have provided encouragement despite the fear for her safety. Dr Gorman has told her of a new program to train nurses and medical units to be positioned closer to the front lines. He tells her a medical colleague of his is part of the training staff at the hospital in El Paso.

Margaret looks Dr. Gorman in the eye and tells him, "Thank you Jim for all you have done for me and my family. More importantly to me personally, is your implied confidence in my ability to serve our country at this moment. Just give me that guy's name and I will do us proud…..I promise".

Jim gives her an emotion filled hug. He has known this remarkable young woman all of her life. He couldn't love her any more if she was his own daughter. "Just come back to us…..your community needs you..Comprende?" is all he can think to say.

Now, it is 1943 and as a 27-year-old, Margaret Beltran graduates from the Army Nurse Corp Cadet training center at William Beaumont hospital in El Paso, Texas. She then enters the Army Medical Corps with a rank of Captain, which was awarded to her due to her age and her work experience working for for Dr. James Gorman in the rural Rio Grande Valley of southern New Mexico.

Margaret excelled in the Medical Corp training program, and she even helped develop some of the curriculum and taught many of the classes. She has requested an assignment in the European Theater of military operations where field medical units were now placed closer to the front lines than ever before. Those units had reported a much higher recovery rate than prior operations. Previously, the first medical treatment a wounded soldier received was several miles removed from the front lines. She looked forward to being a part of this operation and, like all her friends, is eager to serve her country.

Author's Note

More than 59,000 American nurses served in the Army Nurse Corps during World War II. Nurses worked closer to the front lines than they ever had before. Within the "chain of evacuation" established by the Army Medical Department during the war, nurses served under fire in field hospitals and evacuation hospitals, on hospital trains and hospital ships, and as flight nurses on medical transport planes. The skill and dedication of these nurses contributed to the extremely low post-injury mortality rate among American military forces in every theater of the war. Overall, fewer than 4 percent of the American soldiers who received medical care in the field or underwent evacuation died from wounds or disease.

The tremendous workforce needs faced by the United States during World War II created numerous new social and economic opportunities for American women. Both society as a whole and the United States military found an increasing number of roles for women. As large numbers of women entered industry and many of the professions for the first time, the need for nurses clarified the status of the nursing profession. The Army reflected this changing attitude in June 1944 when it granted its nurses officers' commissions and full retirement privileges, dependents' allowances, and equal pay. Moreover, the government provided free education to nursing students between 1943 and 1948.

William Beaumont Army Medical Center–Cadet Nurse Corp training

Over there

When she departed the transport ship in France, she couldn't help but think that her father must have had the same anxiety and fears about entering the European war zone. When he returned home, he felt a great sense of pride as the government granted him his citizenship. Her pride of service was genuine as well. She literally felt her dad walking beside her as she disembarked the ship. Margaret and team were part of the 240th Medical Battalion headed for the town of St. Vith, about 100 miles from Frankfurt, Germany, near the Belgian border.

Since the German surprise counter offensive started in mid-December of 1944, the American forces had been routing the German Army in their own counter offensive called the Battle of the Bulge. The fighting had been very brutal, and the medical unit had scrambled to get in place to deal with the all the wounded soldiers in desperate need of medical attention. They all heard the reports that the 'Bulge' had become the largest and deadliest single battle fought by the allies in World War II so far. But it had proven to be the deciding battle in the war when reports showed the Germans were in disarray. The entire area they were heading for was reportedly in complete chaos at the moment, but the American Command assured all that stability was coming soon.

Margaret was assigned to the 42nd field hospital. Each of the field hospital centers are comprised of several special trauma surgical teams with hand-picked surgical units. Each team had two to three surgeons, one anesthesiologist or anesthetist, two to three nurses, and two to three surgical technicians. These teams were dispatched to the field hospitals to handle non- transportable casualties. She was the ranking officer in the support staff, with all the responsibilities inherent to that assignment.

Margaret knew that her previous experience with Dr. Gorman in treating snake bites, broken fingers, childbirth, and various minor surgeries hadn't prepared her for the grizzly wounds she encountered in the battlefield hospital. But she has more experience than all of those under her command and they looked to her for leadership and competence.

There was very little time to sleep when they finally got to the site where the hospital would be erected. It was truly a chaotic scene when they were simultaneously erecting the hospital and treating the wounded. Margaret couldn't believe how many young men died despite all their efforts. At times, she became completely dispirited, but she kept her feelings to herself, not wanting to affect those who depended on her.

When Colonel Kelly gathered the staff for an impromptu meeting Margaret could not really comprehend the meaning of the words, *'Hitler is dead and Germany has surrendered'*. There was not one peep of a victory cheer in the camp mess hall. Everyone in that room was thinking of all the desperately wounded soldiers that were needing their help at this very minute. The mood of the frontline troops that began coming through camp in just a matter of hours after the surrender declaration however was quite different. Smiles and laughter were every where and the atmosphere was becoming more boisterous by the minute. Soon the the whole camp was caught up in the joy of the moment. Margaret took real comfort in spreading the news to the wounded in the recovery ward. '**You won…It's time to go home**' she kept saying over and over again to every soldier she encountered, wounded or not.

America Saved the World

The war did not halt for the Medical Corps just because the guns stop firing. There were no magic words to make those wounded boys healthy again.

The aftermath of war became a heartbreaking experience because one realized the senselessness of war. Young men were wounded in ways that will render them 'dependent' for the rest of their lives. Too many died of their wounds, but for some, she thinks in some cases the survivors may envy the dead. They would never have to deal with all the pain, emotional scars and anguish that a disfigured, wounded man faces. Some would become the constant object of sympathy from friends and family back home. As if giving the most for his country wasn't enough? *Now that was a tragedy*. Most would never completely adjust to the aftermath of recovery.

When a war ends, everyone was eager to forget. But these men, the scarred reminders, kept dragging their community back to a time everyone wants to bury in the history books.

As soldiers returned to their hometowns, most were true local heroes and proudly wore their uniforms around the community for weeks after discharge.

It was almost a year before Margaret could return stateside, but she couldn't bring herself to go home home yet. She tried to explain this to her parents that she did not think her job was finished yet. There is a lot of unfinished business, is the way she tried to explain it.

So she extended her enlistment to assist the Veterans Administration staff in their regional hospitals, helping the returning soldiers. There was a small VA hospital in Grant County at Ft. Bayard, and she had been given a six-month TDY assignment there before reporting to the large VA center in Santa Fe. She simply couldn't wait to see Sofie. Even Ernesto and Benjamin would be a sight for sore eyes. These three are the only family she has outside of her parents and the Gormans. She thinks…They are enough for now!

Chapter 5 1/2

The beat goes on.

It's a Tuesday, and Maggie has picked up Sofie from Ernie's and is driving up to Ben's house with some good take-out from the Chavez Cafe. She looks forward to these Tuesday and Friday times at Ben's Hurley house.

They are sitting out under the big apricot tree in the backyard and sipping tequila while Sofie finishes her homework inside. Maggie suddenly asks Ben, "You ever pray?"

"Wow, Mags," he says, "Just jump right into it. Yeah, but not lately...not much since the war. What brought that on?"

Maggie replies, "I am just a little adrift now and looking for some direction. I can't do the nurse thing much longer. I know it's important and I am very good at it. BUT...I have seen too much, and I know more is coming."

"What do you mean by that?" Ben asks. "The war is over, and the wounded men will recover."

"Well, not all of them will...AND that is just part of the problem. Humans, they are the problem! World War I, then World War II. THEN what? I am working the wrong end of the equation here. I want to prevent, not fix...if that makes any sense."

She leans over and puts her hand on Ben's and says, "You saw firsthand those people coming out of those concentration camps. Could you, in your worst nightmares, imagine people treating other humans like that? Thank God we got Sofie out of there!! Ben, all those people in those camps prayed to some God for salvation, but, as I see it, it was the American Army that delivered. America was the savior of the world. We have proven our way of governing people is the best, not perfect mind you. I want to work to make it perfect, as impossible as that sounds."

She puts her other hand on Ben's and says, "AND you know what? New Mexico is the best of the best! Just look at us– Chicanos, Gringos, Native Americans, and even Texans can live together here."

Ben can feel the passion in her touch and voice and says, "You would get a different opinion from Ernie about that now. He just can't stomach that Mexican-Americans and Natives are still being treated as second-class citizens after the War. Hell, Maggie, your Hispanic roots are as deep as Ernie's. What do your parents say? You told me how your family entered this country and how your dad got his citizenship. How does your dad feel about this?"

Maggie says, "My Dad thinks things are getting better in his small slice of the country. Thanks to his hard work and the Gormans' help, he now has 10 acres of his own land planted with pecan trees, which he calls the wave of the future down here."

Maggie, all animated now, continues, "Yeah., but he makes my point. New Mexico is the oldest established colony in this country and should be in a leadership position to pave the way. I want to be one of those leaders! If *'All Men Are Created Equal,'* then why not re-start that effort here??? God, I love New Mexico. We have thrived with leaders of all stripes, good and bad–from Spanish royalty to Mexican, to mestizo, to Gringo, to religious zealots. And before them, the natives had a tenuous existence based on trade and good weather to grow their meager crops. Hell, the Navajos probably had the most sustainable civilization I have heard of."

Maggie looks up at Ben and says, "This is what I like most about my new and now dearest friend. We are holding each other's hands, and you are not even thinking about getting me in bed! From what little I know about men and women. This is quite rare and makes me cherish our relationship even more. Somehow, I know you feel the same. If we got all sexed up, this relationship would go to shit pretty fast. Look what we would lose, Ben. This thing we have going here with you, me, Sofie, and Ernesto, it would not survive our selfishness. Without imposing some limits and controlling our emotions, this journey we are on would get derailed. What a shame that would be. When Sofie entered our lives, we became woven into a fabric that binds us with a responsibility to improve life for all of us. I wake up every day grateful for the moment we became 'team Sofie.' I love you, Ben, more than I think I could love any husband. Plus, there is no cooking or cleaning… none of that domestic crap I know I could never put up with."

"Geez, Mags," Ben says, "thanks for bringing dinner. What's new with you, anyway?!" Maggie just laughs and says, "See what I mean?"

They move inside and call Sofie for dinner and as the tequila bottle loses some volume, Maggie tells Ben and Sofie she has enrolled in law school at UNM using the GI bill and will start with the fall semester. Dr. Jim knows a place for sale close to the school where she could live. Plus, even better, he knows a doctor friend looking for a part-time nurse to help with his practice. Maggie says, "See, it was meant to be."

Another Tuesday rolls around. Maggie and Ben are under the apricot tree again, and Ben says, "My turn now, Maggie. I talk…you listen."

"I can't shake the feeling I'm an interloper here in New Mexico, from Chicago. My Dad deserted Mom and me, and we basically came here because we had to. I didn't know shit about New Mexico–still don't, really. Back in Chicago, it was Italians here, Polish there, Jews over there, Greeks across Wayland Street, and so on. Wallace–what kind of name was that? Nobody knew what to do with a name like that! My Dad said stay in the neighborhood, stay in the neighborhood. It is one of my few memories of him. But, Mags, we were basically all white guys, and we still wanted nothing to do with each other. I come to Grant County and there are basically only two groups: Mexicans and gringos. Even back in Chicago, we were all Americans. When we moved to Silver City, we lived in a neighborhood where almost every family was white and my school classes were for the most part the same. But in sports and on the playground at recess, it is different. We were all thrown together. Bell rings to end recess and we go back to our respective corners. In little league baseball, MY team is mostly white guys and there are other teams like us. But there are also teams that were composed of mostly Mexican kids I knew from the school playground. 'Oh, well!' I say."

"Then came junior high school and high school, we are all placed in the same building, taking the same classes. What the hell?!…. Sports friends and class/neighborhood friends are now all together!! BUT It is clannish…..Mexicans hang with the Mexicans and us Gringos did the same, some exceptions for jocks and brainiacks. However, we still live in different sections of the community and our parents don't have dinner together so there was little opportunity for mixed close friendships. As we got older, some began wondering why. While for others, it is just another day in Grant County. *'So what,'* I think. It seems to work…but I can feel a kind of undercurrent, like an undeclared truce–thing about residential segregation that force the majority of Mexican kids to attend different schools or be in different classrooms. All this goes on with little or no discussion. There were some racial skirmishes in high school in the parking lot when things flared up…but these were uncommon. By and large, I left high school and entered the Army basically unaware of the racial tension around me was simmering on a hot stove."

Ben senses he unsure of where this is heading as he is talking about a subject he hasn't thought out in depth. He finally says to Maggie, "You can tell I don't know shit about this stuff and like talking about it even less. But, it sure makes my point. I love New Mexico but it is hard for me to explain how things work here."

Ben then holds up his hand to stop Maggie from intervening and says, "One last thing from me!….For me basic training changed everything. This was football times ten!!! We are all carrying guns, and we are told we MUST trust the person next to us. Life or death this time, not just winning some game. I look over at this guy next to me and he is a five-foot nothin' Mexican named Ernest, and I say to myself, GOD help me. Now, all these years later, I find out he is saying the same thing looking at me. God! Just listen to me go on about things I know nothing about. Maggie, your love of New Mexico is engrained in your very being. But me, I'm still trying to figure the place out. What I am coming to understand is that post WW II things are different and New Mexican history is a source of pride here. As much as I sensed the uneasy truce before, I now sense changes are coming…and fast. This strike talk in the mining district is gaining momentum, not only with labor, but with management as well."

Maggie finally stands up and says, "Are you done so I can say something?"

She takes the silence as a yes and declares, "Interloper, uh! Well, we are all interlopers. My "wetback" parents are the true definition of interloping, coming to this country illegally. What about Spanish missionaries enslaving native people who eventually revolted and ran them out? From Texan Confederates to Eastern industrialists buying up mineral rights, the list of interlopers goes on and on for New Mexico. The beauty of New Mexico is that the place has basically seen it all. People of different languages and different skin colors have succeeded here. Citizens here are not afraid of differences; some may not like it, but when change comes, almost all shrug their shoulders and say, "quién sabe" (who knows). For the most part, they don't let hate interfere with progress. For the majority, the desire to be respected rules the course of action, not the '*waste*' that hate and revenge bring."

She pauses for a moment then continues, "One last thing before you go get me some more tequila. Your two best friends have the names of Polanco and Beltran. I say you have graduated from the interloper class to…quién sabe!! Quit living in that science-chemistry brain of yours where only yes or no exists. Give hope some space to make the world bigger and better. You and me, Wallace–we will build on the New Mexico tradition, and changes will happen here first. You watch. We have seen the worst in Germany. That shit has no place here. We won't let it happen."

"Well, Margaret, you are going to make one hell of an attorney!! That is a fact!"

Chapter 6

A New Era Begins

Ernesto Polanco

Ernest was born in Grant County on the land he now lives with his wife, Lupe, and their two young children. Ernest and Lupe, along with his dad, built the small adobe building they now call home. It is nice but not fancy, which brings him security because it is paid for.

After the war, it did not take long for Ernie to get hired by the biggest smelter in the region. The proximity of the smelter location and his house lets Sofie come to his home several days a week after school until Ben gets off work. Sofie and Ernesto still have a special relationship, and Lupe is teaching her Spanish. Ernest is very proud of the fact that Sofie will soon speak three languages. He loves that girl!!

Shift work at the smelter means his schedule is continually changing, and his family must accommodate his variable eating and sleeping schedule. Ernie currently works as a tapperman. This job basically drains the molten copper away from the slag waste. The Pierce-Smith Converter Isle is a dangerous place to work, but the pay is better than at most of the smaller mines in the area. Smelter workers get from $10 to $13 a day, depending on the specific job and the price of copper.

There is labor unrest in the mining community, along with some racial issues that are causing a lot of strife among friends and family. The most prominent union organizer is Juan Chacon, who is the current president of the local chapter of the MMSW (Mine Mill and Smelter Workers). Ernesto's opinions align with other war veterans like Chacon and the newcomer, Clinton Jencks.

They believe it is time to change the way the labor force, especially the Mexican population, is treated. The MMSW is demanding an end to discriminatory working conditions and the dual wage system of two-tiered pay, different for Mexican-American workers compared to Anglo workers. There is talk in the community of a possible strike against one of the mines. It could happen as early as the fall and Ernest is preparing himself and his family for that event.

The local papers and even some national news centers are labeling the MMSW a communist organization in order to detract from the true reasons for the actions MMSW is taking. Those concerns were documented in an open letter to the state and local papers by MMSW, which reads, in part, as follows:

> *Grant County mining companies have segregated their workforces through control of entry into certain job categories. Higher-paying jobs considered "skilled," such as driving vehicles, operating machinery, working in the shops, and managing others, were off limits to workers of Mexican heritage. Housing segregation is also widespread. The larger companies and their predecessors maintained two types of company housing. Sturdy, multi- room "American" housing rented for between eight dollars and twenty-two dollars a month. For "Spanish-American" housing, however, workers paid a nominal fee for ground rent plus a monthly fee for electricity. These tenants also were required to construct their own cabins out of whatever materials were available. These living conditions can only be described as separate and unequal and are not acceptable to members of this community. For all we have sacrificed for this country and our community; post war America will not tolerate these conditions.*

This situation has caused some tense moments between Ernesto and Ben recently. Although the company Ernie and Ben work for has made its anti-union position clear, to date, it has taken a hands-off approach to the involvement of its workers in union activities. Sofie hears a lot more from Ernie's side of the issue than from Ben's. Recently, the Polanco house has become a meeting place for union sympathizers. Ernie sees no reason to shelter her from this topic. Ben is content for now and trusts Ernie to make the best decisions for Sofie. Ben is sympathetic to the union position, but his management position prevents him from being more vocal about the injustices in the mining community.

Ben and Ernie still have a special relationship that has continued since the war, and the shared commitment to Sofie continues to strengthen that bond. Every time Ernesto passes by Ben and Sofie's house on his way to the graveyard shift change at the Smelter, it reminds him how deeply he cares for these two members of '*his family.*'

Well, it has now happened. A strike has been called by the local 890 union of the MMSW against the Empire Zinc Mine in Hanover, New Mexico. It's set to start on October 17, 1950.

The tensions between the two friends increased sharply after Ernesto's place in North Hurley becomes a prominent gathering place for some of the striking workers. The miners from Empire Zinc drop by Ernie's house to get current information on how the community feels about the strike and to pick up food donated from area residents sympathetic to the striking miners.

The publishing of news articles that link the strike to communist activities has expanded from local coverage to regional, with even some national stories. "The Red Scare" has reached Grant County and with it comes outside influences from both sides. This comes at a particularly sensitive time in New Mexico because Julius and Ethel Rosenberg were recently arrested for espionage. The arrest warrants were issued just this past summer. Julius was arrested in July and Ethel in August. Julius initially fled to Mexico but was soon extradited back to the U.S. New Mexicans were extremely interested in the Rosenberg case as it involved secrets sold to the USSR about certain aspects of the Manhattan project conducted at Los Alamos during WWII and atomic research is still ongoing at the lab.

In addition to this event, Senator McCarthy from Wisconsin has just delivered a speech on February 9th of this year to the Republican Women's Club in Wheeling, West Virginia, claiming to have the names of 205 state department and federal employees that are card carrying members of the communist party. That speech and his accusations were carried on every major news agency in the country. Soon after, McCarthy and his advocates began persecuting suspected communists. The primary targets were entertainers, academics, left-leaning politicians, and labor activists. In almost all of these proceedings, *'suspicion ruled over evidence.'*

Several national union sympathizers have entered the picture, adding more drama and national interest. There is even talk of a documentary movie being made right in Grant County. The battle lines are being drawn, and Ben fears Sofie may be too close to any conflict that might erupt when she is at Ernie's place. People are increasingly committing acts of violence against strikers and their families, with even more violence is being promised.

Author's Note

The Empire strike took an unexpected twist when a district court ruled that the mine employees cannot man the picket lines at the entry gate to the mine. This ruling stated that the employees' employment contract specifies that if they picket the entrance of the company they work for, they will violate their contract. Thus, the company has the right to fire them and ultimately replace them.

In a hotly contested union meeting at the 890 Union Hall, the union designated the wives of the striking miners to replace the mine employees on the picket lines. Despite being jailed with their children in tow for several days, these brave women held the picket line until the strike ended after 15 months. Some women sustained injuries when 'scabs' (hired strike breakers) attempted to drive cars through the picket line that blocked the mine entrance. The union was ultimately successful in forcing the mine ownership to grant all of their significant demands.

This episode in the labor-management relationship and the treatment of hourly wage earners versus the management changed the dynamic of mining operations forever. It was also revealed that the underground work done by common laborers and muckers was done almost entirely by Hispanic workers in Arizona and New Mexico. They were paid far less than for the same jobs done by Anglos in places like Utah, Nevada, and Montana, even though some of those mines held common ownership. The discrimination of the Hispanic workforce and their families became apparent to the world.

The New Jersey Zinc Company, parent Company of Empire Zinc in Grant County, had records indicating that they employed 128 men at the Empire Zinc location in Hanover, NM. Of the 128 employees, 92 were Union Members with 80 Hispanic and 12 Anglos.

Grant County was being torn apart by all the labor and political unrest, but Ernesto Polanco cannot turn his back on his friends and neighbors. He continues to provide help to the striking miners and their brave wives, works on their behalf to collect food, clothing, and even monetary donations from the community.

One morning after his graveyard shift at the smelter, he drives into his property and sees two sheriff's vehicles parked in front of his house. As he pulls up next to them, two men get out of each car. Ernie gets out and asks, "What's up?" One of the deputies says, "We had a report of vandalism to your property and just came to investigate." Ernie looks around and now notices there has been some damage to his perimeter fencing facing the road and tells them it can be easily repaired and he will get to it this weekend.

He then says, "Thanks officers for coming out but I don't think any further action is needed." One of the officers informs him that it is not that simple. Since a complaint was filed, an investigation report must be completed.

Ernie then says "Look, I did not file a report, and I am not going to file any charges against anyone for these minor damages to my property. So, if you could just be on your way so I can get some sleep, that would be nice."

The Deputy then says, "Mr. Polanco, you don't seem to understand the situation here. We have a job to do here, and we are going to do it."

Ernie's next words started a series of events that had lasting effects for Ernie and his family, "Why don't you guys just get the hell off my property…is that plain enough for you? Hell, you probably did the damage yourselves just to harass me like you bully those striking miners and their wives. You guys are just a bunch of out-of-work cowboys the sheriff has deputized because he wants a show of force to intimidate the Mexican miners."

With that, the handcuffs come out and Ernie is thrown on the hood of the car and hit several times with a baton. Lupe comes running out of the house screaming at the deputies. When they turn to face her, Ernie yells to her, "Get back in the house and call Ben."

The deputies put Ernie in the back of the car with his hands cuffed from behind and take him to the county jail in Silver City. On the way to the jail, the deputies try to impress on Ernie that this is just the beginning if he doesn't change his ways with his communist buddies. He is thrown in jail, but he is not being beaten any more. The deputies heard him tell his wife to call some friend so they know that some visitor will be coming soon. Any more physical damage would look bad for the department. They have been getting enough bad press lately, thanks to those women on the picket line.

Ben gets the word at his office and heads out immediately for the jail. When he gets there, he finds Ernie is in a jovial mood despite being really pissed. The first words out of his mouth are, "I hope you called who I think you called." Ben then has his own laugh and says, "Yup, she will be here first thing in the morning, if you can hold out till then. If not, I can probably figure out a way to get you released this afternoon."

Ernie says, "Don't you dare! I wouldn't miss this show tomorrow for nothing. Just leave me right here in my front row seat."

At 9:00 o'clock on the dot, Margaret and a companion walk into the jail. The Sheriff is right behind them anticipating some trouble might be brewing.

Margaret recognizes the Sheriff and turns immediately to face him, "Sheriff, if you want any respect left for your department, you need to do exactly as I say. You have arrested a distinguished veteran of the U.S. Army that served with me and this other attorney to rid Europe of Hitler's Nazis. We are here to get this man released immediately and to file charges with the district attorney on behalf of Ernest Polanco for his false arrest and harassment at the hand of your deputies. There were also witnesses to the physical abuse my client received at the time of arrest. This charge will also be added when we file with the District Attorney. I might add a comment here of my own. You should be ashamed of yourself… treating a member of your community with such disdain for the freedoms he fought for. My guess is you never got near a front line if you even served, and you have never seen the abuse a Nazi regime can inflict, or you would not be trying to intimidate men like my client here. "*Now let this man out right now before I lose my temper!!!*"

As Ernie, Margaret and the other guy are walking to the car Ernie says, "Wow I can't wait till you're a full-fledged attorney. That was something back there".

"Yeah, I was plenty pissed at those pendejos. That's why I brought Jeff with me. He is a real attorney, just in case I ended up in there with you."

Ben

Ben is not looking forward to the upcoming conversation with Ernie. As he parks in front of Ernie's house, he's still not clear on how to approach the problem of Sofie spending so much time there.

"Hola, amigo," Ernie says as he greets Ben from the front porch and claps his shoulder as usual. "I know why you are here. So let's sit on this porch and get these words out." Ernie doesn't even wait for Ben to sit down before he blurts out, "I am worried about Sofie's safety at this house as much as you are. I don't think she should be here until the tension level drops a notch or two." With that said, he continues, "What is troubling me most *is you and me*. This issue of equality is fundamental to my beliefs and yours too, or so I thought. Ben, we cannot go back to the way it was before the war! Chicanos put their asses on the line for this country, just like you gringos. We won't be second-class citizens any longer. And, just for the record, fuck those communists for making this issue political! You know I could never support that side. My question to you, amigo, is why have you lost your courage now?"

Ernie looks directly at Ben and challenges, "Why doesn't our community see the inequality and show the same outrage as those miners at Empire Zinc? And where are you personally on this? I am sorry to say, I don't really know for sure."

Ernie continues with, "If you *'Corporate Cowboys'* running this mine we both work for had any Mexicans in management, I would bust their 'huevos' for some answers, too. But since there are zero Mexicans in our company management, I am asking YOU."

Ben thought the conversation would go in the Sofie direction and is caught off-guard by Ernie's direct guttural approach. However, he has obviously thought about this issue and needs just a moment to gather his thoughts before he responds to Ernie. The atmosphere on the porch is surprisingly calm even as the tension elevates between the two friends. After his emotional confrontation is delivered, Ernie seems relieved that it is finally out in the open.

'Now it is up to me,' thinks Ben. I need to find the language to convey my beliefs to my friend. He draws a deep breath and says "OK, here goes. BUT, Ernie, I want you to hear me through before you say anything."

About two weeks ago, James Woodall, the superintendent of the mine, requested I come to his office. This was out of the clear blue and I was nervous, to say the least. I walked into his office, and we greeted each other cordially and moved to a worktable in his office. He wasted no time in getting right to the point. This is what he told me.

I am summarizing but this is basically what he said; This unionization business is becoming very serious in Grant County and the company's executive management is asking for a forecast of where all this is going. They want to know what the impact of this union activity will have on our current operations. Plus, they want a long-term analysis of the situation as well.

I don't say a word to Mr. Woodall, but I can guess where this is going.

Woodall then spoke directly to me and said, "I know there are a lot of union sympathizers within our employee ranks. Your assay duties take you to all parts of the mine's operations, therefore, '*I want your opinion*'. You interact with personnel at all levels in our company structure where discussions of these union events are taking place. It is imperative that I know what the pulse of our workforce is."

After a brief pause, Mr. Woodall started up again and went right where I thought the conversation would be focused. He looked directly at me again and said, "Ben, you're friends with Ernesto Polanco, an employee in our smelter. Mr. Polanco has embraced some activities unfolding at the Empire Zinc Mine. Therefore, I believe you, more than most, can advise me and help develop a response to our executives."

I still don't say a word, but this time he waits me out.

Finally, I tell him, "Yes, Ernesto is my best friend. BUT, if you want info from Ernest, you need to ask him and not me."

Mr. Woodall then told me, "That will happen in due time, but not before I hear some other viewpoints and become better informed. However, you, Mr. Wallace, are in my office NOW, and I need some facts, as well as your opinions regarding this situation. I believe you are in a position to help, not only me and the company, but this community as well. So let me ask you this. Do you think this unionization movement in Grant County will spread outside of the Empire Mine to the larger operations, like Kennecott and Phelps Dodge?"

I don't hesitate with my response to Mr. Woodall. "Not tomorrow, but if we don't change our operations and make them more equitable towards our Mexican-American community, it is inevitable. But you don't need me to tell you that. You read that post in the local paper a while back and know a lot of that applies to our company. I would also add that there is not one Hispanic in our management ranks that I know of at the present time. This alone speaks volumes about the changes that must occur."

"Well," Mr. Woodall says, "those are comments I can appreciate. One final thing. Is the communist party involved in the Union Local 890 here in Grant County?"

I had to suppress a laugh at this point and here's what I told him, "Mr. Woodall, most of the union members and sympathizers here believe area mining management, meaning you, is spreading that rumor to divert a real discussion of the issues. They think it is a union busting strategy by the company."

I tell Ernest that I have had many subsequent thoughts about that meeting and always come away with the same conclusion: I have never belonged to a union, and since I am in management, probably never will. However, over the past several years, I have experienced firsthand that almost *'all industries exploit their labor force if they can'*. And labor unions are a just means to level the bargaining power for the workers. I also say I believe I am better positioned to serve the working community of Grant County from within the management ranks.

There is silence between the two friends, but their differences seemed resolved for now.

"OK," I tell Ernie. "Let me have a talk with Sofie and make some other arrangements for her after school. She won't like it, though, and I will be on her bad list for a while. She loves it out here and has said, 'I don't really have any friends my age…they are boring.' She really believes you and Lupe cannot do without her."

Author's Note

This is an excerpt from The University Of New Mexico Press about the documentary movie "Salt of the Earth." It is an extraordinary movie accurately depicting the tense situation that gripped Grant County at the time. The courage of the miner's wives is quite remarkable; there was little precedent for that type of suffrage fortitude.

~ UNM Press

This impassioned history tells a story of censorship and politics during the early Cold War. The author recounts the 1950 Empire Zinc Strike in Bayard, New Mexico, the making of the extraordinary motion picture Salt of the Earth by Local 890 of the International Union of Mine, Mill, and Smelter Workers, and the film's suppression by Hollywood, federal and state governments, and organized labor. This disturbing episode reflects the intense fear that gripped America during the Cold War and reveals the unsavory side of the rapprochement between organized labor and big business in the 1950s. In the face of intense political opposition, blackballed union activists, blacklisted Hollywood artists and writers, and Local 890 united to write a script, raise money, hire actors and crews, and make and distribute the film. Rediscovered in the 1970s, Salt of the Earth is a revealing celluloid document of socially conscious unionism that sought to break down racial barriers, bridge class divisions, and emphasize the role of women. Lorence has interviewed participants in the strike and film such as Clinton Jencks and Paul Jarrico and has consulted private and public archives to reconstruct the story of this extraordinary documentary and the coordinated efforts to suppress it.

Part Three

Ownership

It is my life now

Chapter 7

Independence for Sofie

Number 1–Teacher's Pet

I got my seductive powers when I was sixteen. And let me tell you what a power trip that was! I just knew I had received one of those superwoman powers you only see in those comic books sold in the drugstore downtown. Young people should not possess these capabilities. And I did my part to prove that adage was true.

My first victim came when I received an F in geometry. My Dad (I ceased using the term 'My Dad' during this rebellious phase, although deep down I still thought of him as that) was more upset with me than I have ever seen. Looking back on this time I am sure now that my many puberty antics precipitated his reaction. He was always, and still is, an even-tempered man who carefully weighs the words he chooses. He made the proclamation that if improvements weren't made by the next grade report, limitations on my freedom would be imposed. This demonstrated a total disregard for my new found social life.

Tutoring seemed to be the best method to remediate the situation, as it showed both effort and commitment on my part to get my grade off the floor.

My math teacher, Mr. Hargraves (every girl in school had a crush on him), said Tuesday after last period would work for him, but he could only spare 30 minutes because of other obligations. Fifteen minutes into the session, I was totally surprised that my physicality was making him behave differently than in the formal class. I was used to boys behaving in a primal fashion, but not a grown man. WOW!!! Suddenly, he wrapped up the session and assigned me a few practice problems to work on. We arranged to meet again on the following Tuesday.

When next Tuesday rolled around, I wasn't sure what was going to happen. BUT I had a good idea of what I wanted to happen, and I was prepared. I asked Marlene what it was like for her the first time.

She said, "Starts out bad and ends up good is my best recollection." She also told me, "It happened pretty fast and real time thinking was in short supply."

So, with Marlene's tutorial on first encounters as my only reference, I entered Mr. Hargrave's room at 3:30 hoping the 30-minute rule would be waved. First thing I noticed was that he had a different body language than at 10:00 am that morning. In less than five minutes, the space between us vanished, as if there was a gravity field around me he could not resist. My brain was now in a 'WOW' phase and geometric proofs was not the cause.

When he was standing over my shoulder with his leg against my side, I suddenly became lightheaded and air was hard to find.

The word stop was in neither of our thoughts then.

There wasn't any kissing or groping like my teenage boyfriends do. He was an experienced man whose caresses and touches found all the right places the first time. No wasted motion, as they say in the sports world. I was up out of my desk with my back to him and I felt his arousal immediately. Something inside me melted. Somehow his hand worked around my waist and down the front of my skirt, and his fingers were seeking my opening. I was wet with anticipation. Hurriedly, I was trying to get my skirt down while he was lowering his pants.

So bent over a schoolteacher's desk was my first time.

Moments later, we are putting ourselves back together, and there is now plenty of space between us. Other emotions have entered the room. Embarrassment, fear, uncertainty, and a real suspicion of each other. What happens now!! We were driven by something primal and now somehow, we must trust each other.

Well, I got my homework assignment and was out the door in much less than 30 minutes. Another 'WOW' moment!! I really did like the penetration, even though I did not get a good look at his cock because all the action was behind me. I vowed next time would be different. Now, I wanted more than a geometry lesson from Mr. Hargraves.

It turned out that next week's tutorial would be our last. Although the next encounter was physically more satisfying, it seems we both could not overcome the emotional deficits caused by our actions. So, without another word spoken, it was over in that instant. And we both knew it. But, at that moment, somehow, we also knew we could trust each other; both realizing we had a lot to lose if we were found out. Right then, my brain was telling me, men are soooo much better than boys when it comes to this sex business. So says a sixteen-year-old after the only sexual encounter in her life.

The law of unintended consequences really came into play as the next few weeks of geometry class unfolded. Mr. Hargraves and I developed a strange sort of friendship. We were afraid more tutoring would end in disaster, but he really wanted to help me improve my grade. He crafted a perfect plan. Whenever I got my homework back for each section of the chapter, there was always a problem at the bottom with these directions: *'Make sure you understand how to do this'*. So, in this way, he fed me the chapter test questions ahead of time, BUT it was still up to me to make sure I could do them.

'And that's how F's turn into A's and daddy is happy.'

There is an interesting postscript to this incident: The more I began to understand math, the more I learned to really like and appreciate math and science. Go figure!!!

Thank you, Mr. Hargraves, wherever you are today.

Number 2–The Fixer-Upper

Next up on the list is Dave Carbajal, a local mechanic in a one-person shop. The second person to encounter my seductive powers.

My uncle Ernesto gave me a car for my 17th birthday, a beautiful 1949 two-door Ford coupe. It just needed a few touch-up items. He said it would run well enough to make it to Dave's shop in Bayard and he would help me with what needed to be done.

As I pull up to this surprisingly nice, neat building and got out of MY car, a big rugged looking Mexican man greets me.

"Tu debes ser Sofie."

"Ernest dijo que podrías venir."

"Con mucho gusto chica."

"Para mi tambien," I reply.

As we banter back-in-forth in Spanish, I can see he is enjoying the talk with a nice-looking gringa who is almost as tall as he is. He looks me square in the eye and I try to hold his gaze, "Your Spanish is pretty good, your uncle's influence, I can tell."

"Poco a poco va mejorando," I reply.

He drives my Ford around the block and down the street and then pulls it into a service bay behind the shop. He gets out and says, "Algunos buenos, algunos malo. Vuelve la próxima semana, probablemente el Miércoles."

"So, if it will be ready by Wednesday of next week, then you already know what you are going to do and what it will probably cost, ¿que no?" I say. "Show me so I will know as well."

"Cuando"? he asks.

"Ahora," now I say.

"Ay! Your uncle warned me about you!!"

So, we start my 'car school,' as Dave calls it. In a couple of hours, we have found what needs to be done to fix the brakes, suspension, exhaust, and steering (something about linkage). He tells me these are the basics that will make it safe to drive locally. Eventually, all the belts and hoses will need replacement for any distance traveling.

"Quantos, how much?" I ask.

About $200 for the basics and about $150 for the rest, he says.

"What if I help?"

He laughs and says, "Then it will be much more!! What can you do??"

"Nada," I reply, and that is when car school really starts.

Dave's analysis proves correct, and it takes about twice as long with my 'help.' When we're done, I am beyond proud, and the car performs beautifully. Dave pronounces it safe to drive and has already told Tio Ernesto. My uncle came by for the inspection that morning and paid Dave for the work, as well as my schooling.

That wasn't our agreement, I tell Dave, and he says, "Tu tío es un hombre orgulloso y testarudo." Yes, I tell him, Uncle Ernesto is proud and stubborn, or I wouldn't even be here. But that wasn't our agreement, so I offer, "Let me help in the shop for a while. I know that several repairs have been delayed while you've been working on my car. It's summer, and I will be bored to death…….Come on, Dave," I beg with my best pouty voice.

With something akin to the Spanish version of *'no good deed goes unpunished'* along with some choice Mexican cuss words, I am now the newest and only employee ever at Dave's auto shop. Did I forget to mention Dave has a gym attached to the garage. Boxing stuff, mainly, with some weights and a bench. WOW! a complete entertainment facility.

After about a week in my new career, I have this thought in the back of my head that Dave isn't getting the full benefits of my talents that he deserves. So I up the charm and invade his space every chance I get. As we work closely together one day, I can feel him becoming affected by my superpowers.

Suddenly he slams his fist down on the workbench and says, "Chica, que estas hacienda?" "I'm not doin nothin," I say. Well, "Basta, ahora. Stop now," he says in both English and Spanish so the message is clear. "Cuántos años tiene?" he asks. Seventeen, I reply. "No bueno, chica, not for you or for me. Besides, either my conscience or your uncle would kill me. I actually enjoy having you around and you are finally becoming somewhat helpful– DON'T MESS IT UP……. Comprende?!

WOW!! So much for superpowers. Maybe they don't work on Mexicans or men over 30?? More research may be required.

I spent the rest of my 17th summer mostly in Dave's Garage/Gym, where I earned my elementary degrees in mechanics and boxing. Dave also taught me soooo much more.

Number 3–Grant County's Finest

Tom Siefert was a star athlete in Grant County. He was about three years older than me. Everyone was sure he would be just as successful in college, but all Tom wanted to do was work for the county sheriff's department.

I hadn't thought of him for a while until he stopped me in my Ford, speeding between Silver City and Mimbres, on my way to the UNM Campus in Albuquerque. He was still as handsome as I remembered when all the girls were awed by him in high school. As he gave me my citation, he asked me for a date.

A speeding ticket! My powers seemed to be fading with age!

He said, "How about going to Pete and Tillie's in Palomas, Mexico? Great food and dancing afterward. I really do not want any conflicts or trouble with the Sheriff's department."

Well, my superpowers returned, and Jim not only was an excellent dancer, but he was a good pistolero as well. He bought me a Ruger 38 Special revolver with a 2-inch barrel for my 19th birthday. So now I went to gun school. Tom and I went shooting almost every weekend at his parents' ranch on the Lordsburg highway. He had access to many calibers of weapons, from 22-caliber varmit guns to 12- gauge shotguns, and some higher-powered hunting rifles. I learned to load, shoot, and maintain all types of firearms. But he was insistent that if I was to carry my revolver or keep it nearby, I must be very proficient with all aspects of that gun in particular.

Well, we practiced and practiced, firing from all positions as well as rapid retrieval and re- holstering. He recreated his service training program at his ranch, where I got the complete benefit of his knowledge and attention to detail, as if I were a police officer. Another WOW!!

In the four years since being granted my superpowers, I have:

1. Raised my geometry grade from an F to A and gained an enhanced appreciation of math and science.

2. Learned basic auto mechanics and boxing skills. Both of which I still enjoy today.

3. Gained a good understanding of the firearm world and am very good with my little 38. Plus, I have not got another speeding ticket.

Some say in this era of women's lib and equal rights, men are holding them back from achieving their dreams and goals. I say, find the right man and use your powers!!!!

Chapter 9

College Days–Sophie

What a head rush college is for a small-town girl moving to the big city with no one looking over your shoulder being the monitor or moral police. But, on the other hand, my parents have basically handed that duty off to me. They are placing a lot of faith in my ability to make good, independent decisions, so I feel a responsibility to succeed here and make them proud.

Mom graduated from law school a few years back and she has been renting her Albuquerque house to students for the past couple of years, just waiting for me. It is now my turn to enter college, so I move into this nice furnished house close to the UNM campus. It even has a small garage for my beautiful 1949 Ford. What a set-up. I feel the responsibility to succeed mounting every day.

When people ask me about home and who mom and dad are, how am I supposed to answer that? Well, it is different every time. How do you tell people you really have three parents? Dad and Uncle Ernest pulled me from that box and Ben (Dad) adopted me. But Maggie taught me about Kotex and tampons and what all that bleeding crap was about. I also live in her house while I am in school. So, isn't that MOM? In my new Albuquerque world, Ben is Dad, Maggie is Mom and Ernie is Uncle. There is no need for any further explanations at this time.

I choose history as a major and chemistry as a minor and begin my formal education. Also, through some connections of Dave and uncle Ernie, I get a part-time job at a small but busy auto shop owned and operated by Chuy Mendoza. I run for parts, clean-up, keep customers happy, and basically try to stay out of the way. The money I earn is not much but keeps me from writing or calling home for spending money. The atmosphere around the shop is nice and most everyone is respectful to the gringa who can speak Spanish.

I like all my classes and especially look forward to learning about the history of the major civilizations that have risen and fallen. With very few exceptions, the take-away seems to be… humans are never satisfied and will always fuck it up. Another major challenge though-out history has been how to deal with religious 'cults.' We are talking about Islam, Judaism, Christian, Mormon, and the rest. They preach love and brotherhood with certain goals required to reach 'heaven.' Then the next thing you know, they are slaughtering their neighbors and proclaiming God wanted it. They never fail to attach some divine justification for the actions that, coincidentally, make them wealthy and powerful. I can't help but reflect on my circumstances and my personal salvation, at the hands of the Americans, from the Nazis and Russians. But you can see and feel that "trouble is brewing", as Ernie says, in 1957 America. I have heard Margaret tell Dad and Uncle Ernie that the Declaration of Independence and The Constitution are the two most beautifully crafted writings in the history of the human language. Still, so many will not embrace the tenets of *'equality for all'* and are willing to even sabotage those ideals for prejudice, religious fervor, and greed. Even in our own country, prejudice targets minority races, certain religions, and even women. To this day, despite wars being recently fought to eradicate those primitive notions, they persist.

It is the end of the week at the shop and Armando has brought one of his cars in to be 're- conditioned,' as he calls it. He occasionally brings cars in like this and uses our space and tools to do the work. He splits the profit with Chuy when he sells the car, so it kind of makes it worth it for Chuy. Armando is one of those light complected Chicanos with a barrel chest and just the way he handles the larger car parts you can tell he is very strong. Chuy has warned me once to steer clear of him, but that had the almost opposite effect on me. It is the end of a busy day, and we are enjoying a beer before we all head home. After we have had a couple of beers Armando and I start flirting with each other as we have in the past. He comes over and sits beside me and the heat index instantly rises. I see Chuy and his cousin Al glance our way and Chuy slowly shakes his head. This pisses me off because I know I can handle myself, so I lean in some to see what will happen. Well, now. Armando likes this. Soon his hand is on my knee and he is whispering nice things in my ear. Chuy stands up and storms out, saying he is going to pick up some parts for tomorrow and will be back in a while. He has not been gone long before Armando has pulled me to my feet and has his arms around me. His hands are finding the right places and he knows it.

There is a break room attached to the shop with a sofa and he pulls me in. I don't resist. He is a handsome, virile man and I admit I am aroused as well. He shuts the door and joins me on the couch and pure passion begins to take over. Next, I am being pushed down on my back and Armando is undoing the buttons on his jeans.

I tell him, "Slow down, slow down…we are both going to get what we want here." He looks at me with an odd grin on his face and immediately slaps me very hard on the side of my head and then back- hands me equally hard on the other side just to follow through. I am barely conscious of what is happening. As I start to come around, he is just thrusting and thrusting inside me until he is finished.

He says, "Is that what you meant by getting what we want? Cause I sure did."

I am still not quite coherent when he orders me to turn over for round two. When I don't move, he immediately slaps me again on the sides of my head and I disappear into another fog. As I regain some of my senses, I see him standing over me, buttoning his jeans. He says nothing and just walks out the door. I have no clothes. I am so shocked about what just happened I cannot even move. Dizzy and disoriented, I slowly try to put myself back together so I can leave.

I have just been raped! What do I do now?

It takes more than a few minutes for me to find my clothes so I can enter the shop. No one there. Chuy and Al are nowhere to be seen. I can't think straight. Do I call the cops? I feel so ashamed and damaged. I look in a mirror and can see very little evidence of the beating I took.

Remembering what I learned from my boxing lessons, I realized that the open-handed blows to the sides of my head were intended to render me dazed without leaving any marks. Some redness and a little swelling behind my ears is all that keeps me from looking normal. NO! The cops will not help me now.

My car is still out front with the keys in it, so I just drive home. It is not too far to my house and when I walk through door, it just seems so normal. Like a typical Friday getting home after work. But… holy shit!! I am a mess. And, I have no idea what to do now. Like a zombie, I move to the bathroom and start some water for a bath. I walk back into the living room and pick up the phone, but I can't think of who to call or what to say. I strip my clothes off and shove them in the trash and climb in the tub.

Somehow it is now Sunday afternoon and Chuy's voice is calling for me to open the door. I don't even remember getting into bed. He will not go away and now he is threatening to break the door down. I struggle to my feet, a little groggy and very thirsty. When I open the door, he comes in and we sit at the kitchen table. His voice is packed with an emotion he cannot contain; somewhere between anger and anguish.

He says, "I know what happened. I know what Armando did to you. Al heard it start and couldn't deal with it, so he ran to find me. By the time he found me and we got back, he was gone and you were too. I am so sorry, chica. I know he is a bad man, but I thought nothing would happen with Albert there. He is just so afraid of Armando he did nothing. I never should have left. Yesterday I came by but no one responded to my pounding on the door. I saw your car here…I didn't know what to do so I just left."

I look at him and he is really hurting from the guilt inside. But I don't know what to say either. Shame and confusion still have a grip on me. Chuy continues, "I couldn't deal with this on my own, so I called Dave. He said he would leave first thing in the morning and will be at my shop before noon. I didn't know what else to do, even though I knew it would make you mad."

There is so much anger welling up inside me, I can't even form words. Only spit comes from my mouth. Finally, when I manage to speak, my words carry such shame and anger that they almost knock Chuy from his chair.

Chuy looks at me and says, "Dave will know what to do. Dave always knows what to do. Even in prison camp, those Japs couldn't break him. He always knew what to do to save us and himself. He will know now, too. I am not leaving you again until he gets here."

There is nothing more I can say or do, so I just go back to bed, curl into a ball, and wait for someone to save me. But I cannot sleep anymore and the more I lay there, the angrier I get at what Armando did to me. *'He took something from me.'* Maybe Dave 'IS' the person to help me. Just the words *'help me'* pisses me off. I can't remember feeling so 'helpless' since Dad pulled me from that box in Germany.

When Dave arrives, he has Uncle Ernie with him. As soon as they enter the house, I burst into sobs and clutch Ernest around the neck and won't let go. We stand that way until I am sure I can stand by myself. I think, has it only been two days since…what do I call it besides what it was–a rape. Two days! Where is my composure? It is something I am known for and now it has deserted me. It was smart of Dave to bring Ernie. He has been with me longer than anyone, and I definitely need some help with this.

The four of us sit at the table. Immediately, Dave says, "Chuy, you had better get out of here right now. I am so pissed at you I can barely contain myself. I'll come to your shop mañana, and we will talk. Adios, for now."

When Chuy leaves, Uncle Ernie takes over, "Tell me how you are, and don't lie to me, Sofie. We have been through too much together and experienced many bad things. Together, we can be completely honest."

My composure starts creeping back as my uncle takes my hand. "Physically I am fine," I say, "but I tell you… I'm really shaken by this; worse than I thought possible after two days have gone by. I have this crazy thought that keeps flitting through my head. Is this what happened to my Mother in her dying minutes before some Russian choked the life out of her? Rape is not a thing that is talked about even among women. I can see why now. The shame and the guilt attached to it…well, I certainly haven't overcome it yet".

I tell Dave, "Don't be so tough on Chuy. He warned me about Armando's reputation. But you know me, I always think

I can take care of myself. Hell, I even flirted with him and gave encouragement. When Chuy left the shop, things just got very spontaneous. The next thing I know I was in the break-room with Armando alone. Even when I knew the sex was probably going to happen, I did not protest too much…just told him to slow it down. WHY?! Why did he hit me? Why did he beat me? Why did he fuck me so brutally?"

"Ernie, I know I can put terrible events in a place that won't be harmful to me or others. I have done so before. BUT, this will stay with me for a long, long time."

I turn and look at Dave and say;"I have thought about this and he's done this before. He knew how to do this and exactly what he wanted out of it. He also knew how he could get away with it and the police would never be called. Dave, I know this because of the way he hit me. He used an open hand, more of a hard slap to the ear area, very powerful but not as damaging as a fist. No cuts, no deep bruises, it just rattles your brains and makes you disoriented and helpless. His blows were no accident. He knew exactly what effect they would have and they would leave very little physical evidence for the police to question. He is one mean SOB and has some built-up hate for women from somewhere. There was no need to do what he did. I was willing to go along with the sex. But, he wanted something different, and he took it."

Ernie says, "Are you going to be alright by yourself for a while because we need to talk with Chuy now?"

"Yeah," I say, "but I have two questions before you leave. First, have you told Ben and Maggie yet? And second, what the hell do you two think you are going to do now?"

Ernie says, "The short answers to those questions are '*not yet and nothing*'."

He pauses and then says, "Pretty soon we need to call Ben and Maggie. You know they will be hysterical, so we better be ready to deal with that. But right now, let's hold off if you are OK with that. Dave and I need the rest of the day to assess the situation, so we have the bigger picture. Hopefully, waiting a little longer will not send them spinning off their axis."

Ernie continues, "What happened to you should never happen to anyone. But it has happened! I can see you are beginning to deal with this, so when I have regained some of 'MY OWN' senses, we'll call them. Get some rest, if you can. Dave and I will bring something to eat when we return."

When they leave, I am almost ready to pass out from exhaustion. I am so thankful I belong to this amazing family. I feel safe and somewhat peaceful for the first time since Friday. As I sit there gaining strength to make my way to the bedroom, I realize that during this conversation, my Uncle Ernest has lost his Grant County Mexican accent and sounds like an Army corporal again.

Ernie and Dave begin the conversation with Chuy by issuing a muted apology after hearing Sofie's story. Although Ernie was clearly still upset with him for leaving when he knew Armando had a shady reputation.

Ernie says, "You must not have any daughters."

Chuy shakes his head and issues his umpteenth apology, then says, "but I have some information where Armando might be. My cousin Albert asked around and found that he uses several other garages to refurbish cars up and down the Rio Grande Valley all the way from El Paso to Espanola. He gets most of his cars from the oil fields in eastern New Mexico and west Texas;

probably stolen. I should have figured this out when he first started bringing me cars a couple of years back, but he seemed like a nice enough guy then, so I just didn't bother to check. Plus, he always paid his bill and gave me some of his sales profit. Anyway, Albert says he moved his car that was in our garage to a shop in Belen, just about 50 miles south of here."

Ernie asks, "what kind of car was he working on?"

"Oh man," says Chuy, "It is a beautiful 1953 Bel Air sport coupe with a power glide tranny. It was primed and ready to be painted blue."

Dave asks Chuy some questions about the auto demolition salvage yard operating in Albuquerque down by the railroad tracks south of town. "Yeah," says Chuy, "I use them from time to time to make some extra on the junk cars left at my shop. A good friend of mine is a foreman there. Why're you asking?"

"Same as you, man. I have junk cars at my shop that need to be moved out." Dave looks around the shop yard and spots a parted-out 1946 Ford Coupe, then looks Chuy squarely in the eye and says, "Tell your foreman friend that you are bringing a rusted out 1946 Ford coupe in Tuesday morning for immediate disposal. If he needs some extra to make this a priority, I'll expect you to take care of that…just to square things, if you know what I mean."

Chuy swallows hard and nods his head, then says, "I'll arrange everything by Tuesday morning."

After talking with Chuy, Ernie and Dave have a better picture of the situation so Ernie decides to call Maggie. He makes the phone call immediately from the shop office before he loses his courage. He tells her he just got into town and says, "Look, something has just come up that needs your attention, so let's meet at Sofie's house in about an hour." There is a pause on Maggie's end and he hears the concern in her voice when she finally speaks. He quickly assures her, "things are fine, but this is important and has some urgency. I will fill you in when we get there."

Maggie says "Ernie, are you OK? You sound different somehow."

"Yeah," he says, "I'm fine and I am heading over to Sofie's now. See you soon." He hangs up before Maggie can ask another question.

Maggie gets out of car and sees Ernie and Dave sitting on the front step. As she rushes up, she barely acknowledges Dave and says, "Jeez Ernie, Dave's here, too? You got me really worried now. What's happening?"

"I am going to let Sofie tell you. Dave and I have something we need to take care of, and Sofie needs you right now. Mags, she is OK. She just needs her mom. Dave and I probably won't be back until Tuesday afternoon sometime. We left some food for you two on the kitchen table."

As they leave, Dave says, "Boy, is Ben going to be pissed when he finds out he is the last to know about this mess. I wouldn't want to be in your shoes, hombre." They get in Ernie's car and head south toward Belen just as the sun sets and providing a beautiful New Mexico sunset over the Rio Grande Valley.

Monday has been a really shitty day, with probably more to follow. Ernest and Dave are silent as they drive to Belen in search of The Grande Garage.

It's just past six pm when they pull up across the street from the garage located on a dirt road just off the main drag through Belen. Two of the three bay doors are still open with the work lights on and Mexican Music blaring from inside. They immediately spot the primed '53 sitting just outside one of the bays. The two men still say nothing as they watch and wait. Soon Armando emerges from the shop with a beer in hand and gets in the car. Ernie puts the car in gear and follows him as he heads back to the main paved road, then south. There is very little traffic, so Ernie lets him get a ways ahead.

Dave finally says, "I got two bits says he ain't going home. He'll head for the bar." Ernie still says nothing, his eyes are riveted on the Chevy tail lights. Ernie's jaw is clenched so tight that Dave thinks he can hear grinding teeth above the motor noise.

Sure enough, Armando pulls into the gravel parking lot of the Stage Bar and strolls inside. Dave says, "what now amigo?"

"Well, this looks like an army recon mission to me. I think I'll go in and do some scouting. What do you think, Sargent?"

Dave says, "Thanks for recognizing that you're out-ranked here, Corporal. I just have one concern about you taking the point. Can you follow the plan when you enter that bar room and keep your cool when you face Armando?"

"Well, obviously I am the only one to do it," says Ernie. "You walk into that bar with that punching bag you call a face plus those callouses all over your knuckles…that guy ain't leaving that bar with you, that's for sure! So, I'm the only one in this car that can get this guy out so we can deal with him. I'm going in there now, so you be ready when WE come out. Comprende, amigo?!"

Ernie walks in the bar and immediately says, "Hey who owns that '53 coupe out there?" Armando turns around but before he can say anything Ernie sees his reaction and says "man she's a beauty. My brother has one just like that. Since he left for California, I have been looking for one. You're fixin her up right,

I can see that! What color you thinking about for paint? What about the interior? Man, that's MY specialty, the interiors–seats, headliners, dashboards, floors. You got any ideas? Maybe I can help you. Hey my name is Beto, and I got a shop in Corrales. Maybe you heard of it, 'BB's'?"

Armando says nothing, but he is still listening so Ernie continues, "If maybe she is for sale as is…I might be interested. I have a buyer in mind for a quick profit, but he's ready to act now and won't wait much longer. So, what do you say?!"

"Maybe," Armando says.

Ernie pauses, then offers, "Hey, let me take a quick close-up look, and then maybe we can make a cash deal right now. Let me buy you another one of those Coors."

Ernie and Armando drink two more beers and talk cars. Finally, Ernie stands and says "Well what about it man, are you goin' to show me that car up close or not? I gotta get going."

Armando says, "Sure I'm interested, let's go."

The two walk out into a misting rain and walk toward the car when Dave steps in front of them. With the incredible speed only a trained boxer has, he delivers a powerful straight right to the middle of Armando's face. As he falls back, Ernie catches him and Dave begins slapping him with powerful forehands and backhands. Ernie shouts into his ear, "anything about this familiar to you, pendejo?" Ernie wraps a rubber hose around Armando's neck and throws him to the ground, placing his knee in the middle of Armando's back. He pulls back with all the vengeance he can deliver until there is no life left in his body.

Dave reaches into Armando's pocket for the keys and opens the trunk of the '53 Ford and they throw the body in. Ernie says, "Nice work sergeant, I'll follow you to Chuy's shop."

They spent the rest of the night trying to sleep in the break room on the couch and a cot. Chuy arrives about 7:00am and gets the trailer with the '46 coupe on it attached to the truck. He has already spotted Armando's car when Ernie walks out and asks, "is everything ready at the salvage yard?"

Chuy nods and says, "Yeah, but it cost me $100 to make it happen the way you and Dave wanted." Dave comes up and says, "I'm sure you can find a home for that '53 of Armando's, so get your $100 back from that. AND make sure Sofie gets her back pay… Comprende?"

Chuy says, "There are some ol' boys up in Espanola that will change the look so nobody will recognize it. The car you see there will just disappear with no trace possible. So don't worry."

Well, Ernie says, "Let's get this little project wrapped up. I'm eager to see how this compactor/crusher works. I have never seen one operate before. Where does the heap of junk go from here? I may want to follow-up just to understand the complete process."

Chuy says, "The guy at the yard said they have a shipment headed to the El Paso furnace tomorrow, and this car should be pig-steel by the end of the week. They don't let the junk stack-up."

Dave adds, "Chuy, forgiveness is at hand. Sofie says it wasn't your fault and what you are doing here will close the deal with me. What about you Ernie? She's your niece." Ernie gives him a side-ways glance and says, "I still want to see this crusher process, so let's get this hunk of junk down there and get back to Sofie and Maggie."

The crane sets the chunk of steel that used to be a 1946 Ford on the train flatcar before noon. Confident that their plan was a success, Ernie and Dave stop at a Lotaburger for some food to take back to Sophie's. Maggie and Sofie are sitting at the kitchen table. The green chile burgers smell wonderful. There is little conversation as they enjoy the food until Maggie says, "We called Ben while you boys were doing 'who knows what' and he should be here within the hour."

Ernie finally asks, "So how did he take being the last to know?"

"Not well," says Sofie. "He basically said I am leaving now and hung up the phone."

When Ben finally arrives, the four people stand up to greet him, but Sofie rushes up and throws her arms around him, not letting him move. Sofie, still holding him with her head against his big chest, says, "Dad, I am so glad you're here now. I'm just fine now, so don't be too upset, I couldn't deal with that now. Once you know the whole story, you will see why it could not have gone any differently. As I was telling Mom, ever since you three rescued me from that basement of that house in Germany, I continue to have a blessed and magical life. A girl couldn't have a better family than you, Maggie, Uncle Ernie, plus now Dave. I feel so loved."

"Come sit here and I will tell you everything that happened. I have my composure back. Maggie has helped me put this episode into some perspective that I can stash away in a hidden part of my brain. She says this event will resurface from time to time, but as time passes, it will ease. I will not let this change my plans and goals. I love you and will let nothing ever come between me and my family."

Ben has nothing to say after that greeting except, "Nothing and nobody can divide family Beltran-Polanco-Wallace."

"Dad, I think Uncle Dave has earned some place in this family as well."

After Sofie has patiently told her story, leaving out only a few details, Ben asks, "So where is this Armando asshole now, in case someone wants deliver a message or something?"

Dave speaks up for the first time and says, "Ernie and I tried to find that out ourselves, as we also had an important message to deliver. But, best we can tell, he is heading to El Paso. With a head start like that, he will be very difficult to find. He may even be in Mexico by now. I have a lot of connections in the car world around the southwest and if he ever surfaces, I'm sure I will hear about it."

Maggie says, "You tough guys get out of here now. Sofie and I were in the middle of an intelligent conversation. Something that is impossible with even one man in the room, much less three. Let's meet at Goode's for breakfast tomorrow at 8:00. OK?"

When they leave, Maggie turns to Sofie and says, "Now, where were we with this vagina theory of yours? It has me fascinated. I love these mother- daughter talks."

So Sofie continues, "Regina, referring to royalty, sounds a lot like vagina to me. Ever since I was a young girl and figured out what a vagina was, I couldn't help but associate it with royalty. I still have never heard a man outside of the medical field use the word vagina. They have no respect for the anatomical part and therefore lack respect for the woman. A woman's anatomical sexual part is something vulgar to them and carries demeaning sounding names like cunt or pussy or others equally debasing. I'm coming to think it's part of an agenda to keep women subservient to men."

She tells Maggie about the time she thought she had some special powers that could make men do what she wanted. Now, she says, "It seems like all I am doing is playing defense, trying to keep guys out of my privates. An image keeps appearing in my mind of the high school basketball games I used to watch where one team was trying to put the ball in the basket and the other was desperate to prevent that from happening."

"So, Mom, please tell me, how do I get back to playing offense? I hate this defense crap!!"

Maggie says, "Well, I think that is a conversation for another day. We have too much to do right now."

Chapter 10

Biology 101

Six weeks later, Sofie pays a visit to Maggie's office. Maggie looks up as Sofie enters. "Wow! What a pleasant surprise. Uh oh, what's wrong?"

"Yeah, you could certainly say something is wrong. I'm pregnant."

There is nothing but silence and concerned expressions in the room.

Maggie says, "Oh my! Where to begin?"

Sofie, with tears welling up in her eyes, finally says, "To think, just two months ago we were such a happy family, all of us heading in a positive direction. Mom, I have literally just fucked all that up; me and my precious royal vagina."

Maggie comes from behind the desk and holds Sofie in a tight embrace for the longest time. As their embrace separates, both women face each other with tears running down their faces. Maggie gives Sofie a steel stare and says, "*This is not your fault*!! So get that thought out of your head forever. Come over here. Let's sit on the couch and talk. I believe that there is nothing you and I, plus our family, cannot deal with. Just look at who we are and where we have been. *'This is serious'*. But, there are solutions. Women throughout history have been in this exact situation and have found the right remedy for them. Many of those women were quite notable, I might add…we will do the same."

"First, have you told anyone yet? Do you want me to call your dad?"

Sofie says, "I called him first thing when I was sure of my status. He said go talk to your mom immediately and he would be here on Saturday. I didn't want a repeat of the last crisis I caused by leaving him out of the information loop of my current crisis. What a mess I am. Just send me back to Germany."

"Oh, Sofie, Sofie, Sofie! Stop that nonsense talk and let's get to work on what our immediate future might look like. There are obvious solutions to this, so let's take a pause and consider what would be best for you. I know you have considered the obvious ones, but think of what will be best for YOU. Keep in mind your family has lots of resources. I'll bring something to eat to your house before six tonight, *and I promise you,* WE will come up with a plan for the future. So, what would you like me to bring to eat? Any cravings?"

Sofie says, "I can't get enough of those Blake's Lotaburgers with onion rings lately."

"OK," Maggie says, "I will see you at six tonight and we will begin the solution phase of this dilemma."

When Sofie leaves, Maggie dials Dr. Jim Gorman to get his opinion on possible options. The doctor tells Maggie, "With your medical background, there is nobody better to advise poor Sofie. Being pregnant from a rape seems heaping misery on misery. How is she holding up?"

Maggie says, "Well, she just left my office, and is doing as well as you would expect. She has a history of overcoming serious obstacles, as you know, and I have no doubt she will draw on that strength to get past this as well."

"Where is the father in all of this," Jim asks, "and will he resurface at some inappropriate time?"

Maggie responds, "No! He is not coming back from where he went. I can guarantee that."

"OK! There might be an option for Sofie that I would highly recommend. I have a patient friend of mine who has been trying to get pregnant for several years now. She and her husband have recently been investigating the adoption process. I'll tell them of Sofie's situation and emphasize how well I know her. Just tell me a little about the Dad and I will call them to see if they are interested. I'm sure they will want to meet Sofie. But even if Sofie balks at the idea of a meeting, that may not be a deal-breaker."

Maggie says, "That is a viable approach I didn't consider. It might just fit the bill. I'm going to meet with her tonight and present that option to her. It is just a guess on my part, but giving birth followed by an adoption, will have some appeal to her. Based on her background, I don't see her aborting. If this is a possibility for your friend, it may be a win-win. Thank you so much, Jim. Let me know, sooner better than later, obviously."

As soon as Dr. Jim hangs up, Maggie places a call to her parents. While the phone is ringing, she thinks how glad she is that Sofie feels she can come to her mom at times like this. Now I am going to call *"MY MOM"*. When Yoli answers, Maggie says, "Mom, just the person I needed to talk with."

She doesn't waste much time on small talk and gets right to the point in describing the dilemma she and Sofie are now dealing with. She tells her mom about the conversation with Dr. Jim, as Yoli still calls him. Yoli immediately says, "Of course, Sofie can stay with us as long as she needs to, if that's what you're asking. She can be as busy as she wants to be. We are always gardening now that we have a greenhouse, plus the cars and farm equipment are always in need of a good mechanic. I find it so fascinating where that girl's interests wander."

"Thanks, Mom," Maggie says. "I need to meet Sofie at her place for dinner. She has this craving for onion rings. Did you have any cravings when you were pregnant with me?"

Yoli tells her, "Figs! I drove your poor dad to his wit's end trying to find figs. There were a couple of growers in the area that started producing fig crops about the time we left."

Yoli then tells Maggie, "Let us know if we can be of any help with this situation. Ay Por Dios! That poor girl has sure had more than her share of hard times in her life. Yet, somehow she endures. Brave, brave girl, my granddaughter."

Maggie hangs up the phone and thinks, what an amazing family she has–caring, smart, and courageous, all of them.

She walks into Sofie's with burgers and sees Ben is already there. They eat quickly and there is a lull in the conversation as Sofie cleans up. When they gather around the table, Sofie says, "Let me talk first and get my thoughts out in the open before you two start doing the parenting thing, OK." Ben and Maggie look at each other, both shrug at the same time, and wait for her to begin.

Sofie starts, "OK, this is a *'my problem'* that has quickly become an *'our problem.'* I am lucky to have you two as parents and the rest of my family to rely on. I promise I will be there for you, IF you ever need me. Here's how I see the situation.

> One: I cannot live with the guilt of an abortion for the rest of my life.

> Two: I am not going back to Grant County and balloon up with family and friends doting all around me.

> Three: I don't want to waddle around the University with morning sickness and doctor visits while classmates give me the evil eye.

Four: Giving birth scares the shit out of me and, no offense here, but my parents have no experience in this either. Isn't that ironic.

Five: If I am reading this correctly…I take it *'the rapist-father'* will not be involved in his child's life. Ever!"

Sofie says, "I know I've eliminated a few solutions in that diatribe I just delivered, but I obviously have no clear direction other than, *I need help NOW!* While you two digest that a moment, I am going to go into the kitchen and burst into tears. I will be back momentarily!!"

"Wow," Ben says. "That's our daughter!!"

"Yeah! Ain't she something," Maggie agrees.

Ben then faces Maggie and asks, "So you got any ideas? I just drove five hours in a car by myself thinking about possible remedies, but I got nothing left after her list of conditions."

"Well," Maggie says, "I made a couple of phone calls, and one course of action she hasn't shot down yet may be a possibility. I think it at least provides us with a starting point. It involves my parents and the Gormans, but let's wait till Sofie returns and we can all go through it all together. My head is still spinning with the details. It will be good to lay it all out to see if it makes sense for everyone, including YOUR daughter."

When Sofie comes back to the living room Maggie presents the proposal given to her from Dr. Gorman. Maggie explains to Sofie how the next nine months might play out if Dr. Jim can convinced his friends this is their best course of action to parenthood. Of course, she will have to agree to involving the Gormans and Maggie's parents in this course of action.

She then delivers a stern caution for Sofie. "You think about this, mija, and be careful not to add a number six to your list of conditions. In your situation, you could run out of options quickly. We need to let Dr. Jim know what to tell his friends soon. Just so you know, your grandparents would love to help you, and they will sincerely welcome you into their home. Helping is right in my mom's wheelhouse and my dad says bring your tools!"

Sofie doesn't even hesitate. "Let the good doctor know am so grateful, and I am all in. Just tell me what I need to do."

Maggie says, "You tell him yourself. We are leaving for Las Cruces tomorrow so he can explain how this will unfold and answer all your questions. Your Dad and I also agree this initial information phase is critical, and he's coming with us. Also, Dr. Gorman wants to meet you and assess your physical condition. He is a critical part of this plan and he needs to be comfortable with you and how you're reacting. This is a serious situation. What we decide now affects the lives of others beyond our family. Futures are at stake here, but I am confident that, together, we can create a positive outcome for all involved."

Ben has just been watching and listening. Two amazing women just took a life-altering situation and developed a viable positive solution. But Ben also realizes just how fragile this plan is, as they are plotting the next few steps. The consequences for missteps are dire. However, there are so many competent people working for the best outcome here, he is confident they will control the circumstance, and not the other way around.

Chapter 10 1/2

'Obla Di, Obla Da,' Life Goes On

It is now becoming apparent that bending over and kneeling down will soon be serious issues. Sofie trades her gardening trowel in for a pair of pliers.

Isidro tells her, "There are several tractors on the farm and the Gorman farms that need some routine maintenance. It's just dirty work, but it still needs to be done. I can't spare anyone to do this work right now, so it would be a big help to me and Mr. Gorman, if you can manage."

"Maybe a full month's worth of work at pregnant woman pace," he laughs at his own joke.

Sofie says, "We'll see about that. Just you make sure the right parts are with the right tractor, and I will make sure the work gets done before this kid decides he needs a change of address. As long as there is no dragging this big belly under tractors, and I can do the work standing, I will be fine"

Sophie likes this kind of meaningful busywork. It keeps her mind from wandering to the time when the baby is born and she must turn it over to the strangers she has only met once, six months ago. Everyone has said these people are wonderful and will be terrific parents. She has given her word to never be involved, unless asked, or to interfere (in any way) with the raising of her child. What did they call it in the legal agreement they signed… 'stalking.'

Of course she will do as expected, but she likes it less and less as her belly grows. Everyone has worked so hard to make this happen in the best interest of all. She cannot selfishly deviate from the plan at this late date.

Yoli has been such a comfort, counseling her about controlling her emotions and assuring her this community is like a family that will nurture her child while providing him or her with every opportunity. As Yoli has said, "This is the best of an unfortunate situation, and everyone will come out of this with their futures intact."

Sofie can see where her mom gets her strength and determination. Much like Sofie's coming to America, the Beltran's arrival in this country was just as dramatic as her own. They were determined to make the most of it...and they have.

Ben and Ernie have come for visits frequently and they have been to the horse races at Sunland Park several times for a pleasant distraction. Both men get along well with the Gormans and Maggie's family. Maggie has also come down from Albuquerque several times, and they talk on the phone often. The last time her mom came down, a really extraordinary thing happened.

The Gormans invited us all to dinner for a special occasion. They wouldn't say what it was until we got there. When Mom and I arrived at the Gorman house, we noticed Ernie's car, along with several others, parked out front. Mom said that was odd as we walk up to the front door. Mr. Gorman meets us and we headed to the large formal dining room. As we enter, there is such an enthusiastic greeting that Mom and I are momentarily stunned. Some spontaneous applause also broke out. Mom looked at Mr. Gorman with a serious questioning look and said, "What's all this Pete? You old goat…What are you up to now?"

That is when the night took a real sharp turn for Ms Margaret Beltran

Mr. Gorman said, "Please Ms. Beltran, you and Sofie sit with your friends over there and I will explain." When Maggie sat down, Ernie took her hand and held it tightly. Now, Maggie was really starting to worry; she can't imagine what Mr. Gorman has planned.

Pete Gorman takes his place of power at the head table and looks at Maggie. "Margaret, don't fret. This is all good here, as you will soon see."

Gorman begins by saying, "Thank you all for coming tonight to help me make my sales pitch. I know you are all busy, but I believe what we are doing here tonight is quite important for all of us. Well, let me cut right to it. Ms. Beltran, we are all gathered here to ask you to run for the vacant congressional seat to the U.S. congress in the 1958 election."

Maggie looks around then says, "Pardon my language here, but, Pete, you have gone fucking senile." To her surprise, everyone just laughed.

Pete continues, "Look, I am going to let my son Josh take over, since it is his idea. He has put this all together, plus that will eliminate the senility issue, as Margaret has so eloquently phrased it."

Josh is a larger version of his dad but still has that quick Gorman mind. He had expanded the Gorman empire, both geographically and through diversity, gaining great respect in this part of the state. Josh had become the recognized leader of the business community.

Maggie took a quick peek at her parents at the end of the table, but they will not return her gaze. When Josh speaks, he gets her full attention. "As you all know, a congressional at-large seat is now vacant due to the untimely death of one of our representatives."

Maggie can't help herself as she interrupts. "I will now expand my *'crazy'* diagnosis to include everyone in this room. Who in the hell am I? To think anyone outside this room would even know me, much less vote for me to fill an important position like that. It is just lunacy."

Undeterred, Josh says, "Well, Margaret, let me tell you exactly who you are. Then I think you'll see that it is almost a certainty that… *'YOU will win that congressional seat.'*"

He continues, "It has been too long since we in this part of the state have had the representation we deserve. The oil interests in the eastern part of the state have had their say; now it is our turn! The farmers, ranchers, miners, colleges, and business owners in this part of the state are fed up with being ignored. They want to be heard…And you can be their voice if you so choose. Now let's get back to *'who is Margaret Beltran?'*"

"First, she is the first-generation daughter of an immigrant to this country who gained his citizenship serving in the military defending this country. Also, her parents had an immediate impact on their border community by eliminating the border scourge Muerte Morales from our midst.… My dad made me put that in. But he wouldn't explain why.…he just said the old-timers here would get it.

Second, she has worked with my uncle to serve her community's medical needs after graduating from the local high school.

Third, she served her country with distinction as a Captain in the Army Nursing Corp, where she put herself in harm's way, just minutes removed from front-line fighting, while saving the lives of wounded American soldiers.

Fourth, she continued her dedication to the soldiers of this country by being directly involved in staffing and modernizing the VA hospitals in New Mexico, thus helping our returning vets re-enter their communities.

Fifth, she has attained her law degree from the University of New Mexico and opened her own practice specializing in labor and contract issues.

And finally, she and her dear friends seated next to her have adopted and raised one of the most remarkable young women in our community."

Josh looks around the room, then back at Maggie saying, "Maggie, *THAT IS WHO YOU ARE*. And that is why you *WILL* win that seat and represent your state."

Then the entire room bursts into applause. Sofie was openly crying, trying to hand her mom a tissue because she can see tears welling up in her eyes too. Maggie leans over and whispers to her daughter, "Not yet, mija, I have something to say first."

Maggie stands up with all her famous composure. The room grows quiet as she speaks. "First of all, I have known and loved the Gormans like my own family for as long as I can remember. I had no idea that Señor Gorman could be so sneaky. He and apparently others in this room have executed the *'don't let Margaret know'* plan to perfection, even involving my parents and best friends with this deception. To them, I say, '*I will deal with you later*.'"

She then says, "Now, to the issue at hand….. It is extremely humbling to see how much time and effort all of you have spent to embarrass me in front of my daughter. Well, Pete, you and these wonderful people have laid the perfect trap. And although I am still somewhat miffed, I am also very, very honored that you think I can really do this. You also have hit the right nerve of my *'call to service'* nature. I love this state and this country."

So, still somewhat shell-shocked and more than a little overwhelmed, Maggie continued, "You all have put me in a position where the answer must be… YES!"

"And," she concludes, "I don't want to think about it any longer tonight. The task is too daunting and I might change my mind. But, with this support, *HOW CAN WE FAIL*? So let's move forward. And now, I think I better stop talking before I make a fool of myself."

Pete gets to his feet and almost shouts. "*I KNEW IT…* the moment Josh spoke her name, I knew she was the one to become only our second female representative in the state's history. Thank you, Margaret, for your continued service."

As Maggie sat down, Sofie looks at her mom and says, "I had no idea."

"Hush, hush and hand me that tissue now," Maggie said.

The dinner is boisterous, and conversations are loud but joyous. Many people come up to pledge their support. Most of them she knows quite well, but there are a few she does not. She assumes they are part of Josh's election team that he has personally chosen to help with the campaign. The immense power of this position flashes before her in an instant and she gives a brief prayer that she is worthy.

After most have left, she sits down with Ben, Ernie, and Sofie. She sees the pride in their faces. They are so genuinely happy for her that she cannot be upset any longer. She gave both of the guys an enormous hug at the same time and expressed how much she loves them. "OK, I forgive you. End of story. I'll need both of you if I'm going to make it through this. It's all so new and challenging."

Sofie can't contain herself any longer and said, "Mom, I'm just blown away, as they say today, of what you have accomplished and the number of people who admire you. I am so proud!"

"Oh, Sofie, I am just doing what I can like your Dad and Ernest here. It all counts!"

Now Maggie's mom comes up and gives one of her famous *'un abrazo uno mano'* and says, "We are so proud and love you mucho."

"Just so you know, that Muerte Morales thing was none of my doing. Ol' man Gorman has always got some kind of thrill from that," her dad said, laughing.

Maggie says, "I love you, Dad, but how could you keep this from me? It put me in an impossible position. It was impossible to say NO."

"You have answered your own question Mija" her father says with a chuckle, "You will be great and there is no one better than you to be in a leadership role for this state and our country."

Adam Shilito is Margaret's campaign manager. He is a longtime friend of the Gorman family and handles all of their real estate transactions. As such, he knows a lot of *'the right people'* throughout the state. He has arranged a campaign whistle stop trip to some of the important cities in the eastern part of the state. The journey starts with Las Cruces in Doña Ana County, Alamogordo in Otero County, and Ruidoso in Lincoln County. It also continues to Roswell in Chaves County, and ends in Carlsbad in Eddy County. A grueling one week if there ever was one. As Adam put it, "A lot of empty spaces and a lot of empty minds as well." Let's fill the minds of those good New Mexicans with the plans for a *'United future of New Mexico.'*

The Eastern part of New Mexico has experienced an economic boom since the war. The Permian Basin oil field extends into that part of New Mexico from the center of its structure in west Texas. Oil and natural gas dominate and drive the business in those critical eastern counties. One company in particular, El Paso Natural Gas (EPNG), just completed a pipeline all the way from Jal, New Mexico, to the California border to deliver energy to that fast-growing state. EPNG now employs thousands of New Mexicans across the southern part of the state and is expanding its operations in the San Juan Basin in Farmington, New Mexico, as well.

Adam tells her that these companies make healthy donations to political candidates and can sway many voters if they so chose. Since New Mexico's population is still well under a million people, the two House of Representative candidates are elected on an at-large basis by popular vote across the entire state. Needless to say, the votes in this part of the state are vital to our success.

Margaret and Adam are on the last leg of the trip, heading from Roswell to Carlsbad. They think the trip has gone well and the people seem receptive to Margaret and her platform of priorities for New Mexico. Adam tells her this next group will be similar to the one in Farmington last week where they addressed uranium miners and oil field workers. Adam pleads with her to not be so confrontational in dealing with some sensitive subjects like the unionizing of workers that some oil company executive brought up in the Farmington gathering.

Maggie looks sideways at Adam as he drives and says, "Look, I just pointed out that all workers in this country have the right to seek unionization according to the provisions of the National Labor Relations Board."

Adam says, "OK, OK, we all get that, but you didn't have to say the part about... maybe he should be equally concerned about treating his employees fairly to eliminate the need for union talk.'"

"Yeah," Maggie says, "maybe that was a little bit too much spice for that conversation. I will watch myself here. This is the last stop, right?!"

As the week-long campaign winds down, Margaret and Adam are exhausted and a little tired of each other's company, so they say little as they drive.

They arrive at the venue for the town hall gathering and dinner at The Riverside Golf Course and Adam reminds her again, "This crowd will test you similar to the one in Farmington. These ol' boys work in the oil fields and the potash mine and are a little full of themselves." As Margaret gets out of the car, she can't help noticing the beautiful setting. The stylish adobe building right on the Pecos River, with the sun low in the sky, it is *'Enchanting'*... just as the state motto says.

The dinner was fine, with yet another version of *'Campaign Ribs and Chicken,'* as Adam referred to them. There is a sizable gathering of about a hundred people that have come to meet the candidate. Again there are very few women or minority representation in the room. A clanging of a glass and a brief introduction precedes Margaret's walk to the podium. She gives a brief bio of herself and a few of the more important items that she has included on her platform. High on the list for this part of the state are interstate transport of products, regulatory oversight of operations, permitting, and, of course, labor.

She is nearing the end of her allotted time and opens the room for questions. After several questions related to her personal background, one gentleman stands and asks, "What makes you think you can represent this part of New Mexico?" His question has an abrasive tone, and Margaret ponders how to answer this blunted question.

She gathers herself up to her full five-feet-ten- inch height, then looks briefly at Adam, who has noticed her body language and has all but disappeared in his chair. So, Margaret says to herself, '*OK, here we go,*' and begins her response.

She looks directly at the man and begins. "I am pausing just a minute, trying to understand your meaning behind that question and the tone that went with it. Surely that can't be any reference to my Mexican and Latino heritage as we have already had two governors of Mexican decent in this state and you know that Senator Dennis Chaves is into his fourth term now. So, I'm thinking it is my gender and marital status that is giving you some heartburn here. Look... I love New Mexico and this country that has been so good to me and my family. But I know love is not enough. I have had my character and determination tested like many of you in this room did during WWII and its aftermath. When war was declared, I joined an elite nursing corps that trained right here in neighboring El Paso. Our training was intense because our medical units would be just yards from frontline fighting in order to give our wounded the best possible chance of recovery. So, after my training, I packed my Kotex and other feminine supplies and went where the fighting was. Snipers shot at our medical units, and we were a frequent target of artillery shells. Some in my unit didn't make it back home. Just like a lot of you Eddy County folk, who lost friends and comrades in the Pacific theater...I lost them in the Battle of the Bulge. I continued to serve when I returned, helping the VA hospitals prepare for what was coming when these men with mangled bodies and tormented minds returned home. I have subsequently earned my law degree from UNM. So, I am ready to serve my country again. With your support, I hope I can represent all the people of this great state and show America that New Mexico knows how to do things right."

She looks around the room and asks, "Any more questions?" She's not surprised when no one else has a question. As she gathers her things to depart the podium she looks one last time over the still silent room and says, "Thank you all for coming tonight." As she leaves the room there is only a scattering of applause.

Adam finally catches up to her and says, "Wow, where did that come from?"

Margaret just looks at him, saying, "Guess it has been a long week. Don't talk to me on the drive back home, OKAY."

There were excerpts from Margaret's *feminine supplies'* speech printed in every newspaper across the state. Two months later, those same papers had headlines that read "Beltran Wins in Landslide".

So, as the eventful year of 1958 comes to an end, Sofie has given birth to a baby boy and given him to his adoptive parents. And her mom is the newly elected congressional representative for the U.S. House of Representatives from New Mexico.

Author's Note

This is from the National Labor Relations Board Articles

Your Rights during Union Organizing

You have the right to form, join or assist a union. You have the right to organize a union to negotiate with your employer over your terms and conditions of employment. This includes your right to distribute union literature, wear union buttons t-shirts, or other insignia (except in unusual "special circumstances"), solicit coworkers to sign union authorization cards, and discuss the union with coworkers.

Supervisors and managers cannot spy on you (or make it appear that they are doing so), coercively question you, threaten you or bribe you regarding your union activity or the union activities of your co-workers. You can't be fired, disciplined, demoted, or penalized in any way for engaging in these activities. Working time is for work, so your employer may maintain and enforce non-discriminatory rules limiting solicitation and distribution, except that your employer cannot prohibit you from talking about or soliciting for a union during non- work time, such as before or after work or during break times; or from distributing union literature during non-work time, in non-work areas, such as parking lots or break rooms. Also, restrictions on your efforts to communicate with co-workers cannot be discriminatory. For example, your employer cannot prohibit you from talking about the union during working time if it permits you to talk about other non-work-related matters during working time

Chapter 11

School Days—Redo

During the election campaign, Sofie worked with two people attending New Mexico State in Las Cruces, about 20 miles from where she was staying with Yoli and Isidro. Conversations about their classes and professors made Sofie realize how much she misses school. She really wanted to return to school and get her degree. After a visit to the Admissions Office, a plan is in place to get her degree. It would take only three semesters if she enrolled at the start of the semester in January. Sofie now has a plan for the direction she wants her education to take.

She will re-enter her studies at NM State and then complete her degree at the University of New Mexico. She still has a keen interest in science and history and has studied about how historic science discoveries have triggered some volatile and civilization-altering eras. The recent discoveries of scientists such as Pasteur, Curie, Mendeleev, and Einstein have benefited the whole of humankind. Historically, the contributions of Galileo and Michelangelo altered people's perception of the universe, causing periods of chaos when their revelations conflicted with the norms of the day. The most significant science to date that has altered our civilization happened right here in New Mexico. What Oppenheimer and those scientists accomplished at Los Alamos has already changed the world forever. Whether it is for the better remains to be seen.

Sofie went to Grant County to visit her dad and Ernie during a break in classes. While there, her dad wanted to watch a Playhouse 90 production with her called "Judgment at Nuremberg", because it addressed the war criminals of Nazi Germany where they adopted Sofie. Ernie came over and the three made popcorn and sat down to watch. The production was riveting, and once the play was 15 minutes in, no popcorn was being eaten. Claude Raines was the Judge, with Melvyn Douglas as the prosecutor and Josh Lukas is the Nazi defense minister on trial.

When the telecast was over, the two men looked at Sofie and waited for her to react. It was her life that was forever altered by the actions of German citizens who contributed to the formation of the Nazi regime. Sofie was silent for a moment, but very aware that Dad and Ernie were waiting for her reaction.

Finally, Sofie says, "What comes to my mind is something I heard from a professor in my European history class. He said, *'The truth is, you are either fighting for justice or you are complicit in the injustice that follows.'* The theme in the play we have just watched has happened many times throughout history and is happening today. Take Stalin in Russia or Mao in China or The Red Scare here. The fact that injustice happens should surprise no one. It is replete throughout the world's history. It's the 'why' that continues to make educated people play the guessing game."

"Watson and Crick, two scientists at Cambridge, recently discovered the structure of the DNA molecule and a basic knowledge of how it works. Current research indicates that DNA not only carries the design for our morphology but, possibly for our psychology as well. This makes the question of nature vs. nurture in human behavior more relevant. Can some genetic sequences of DNA account for the differing actions of *'fight vs. flight,'* or phobias, or addictions, and on and on…?"

"Throughout the play, I couldn't help but wonder how someone as educated as Janning, the Nazi minister of justice, could betray the very people he had pledged to serve. His verdicts as a well respected judge in his community became increasingly harsh for defendants who were not of Aryan descent."

"It occurred to me that Naziism became a cult like the KKK and other groups who take refuge in the security of like-minded people. When lies were told, they turned a deaf ear, when lies were printed they refused to read the truth, when their voices were needed in the name of justice they refused to speak. Hear no evil, see no evil, speak no evil. ALL, possibly, determined because of some genetic code for fear of those who are different; Therefore, driving them to seek comfort by surrounding themselves with... *those who look like me.*' I'm not saying our genetic code dooms us, just maybe some predisposition, like how some people know their parents were alcoholic, therefore they drink only in moderation or not at all. Or perhaps how individuals can overcome phobias by confronting them. They know their weaknesses and must constantly work to overcome them. Anthropological studies have shown this fear of *'Others'* was justified in prehistoric times. Nomadic tribes would play havoc on neighboring communities by stealing resources and bringing disease. It was wise at that time to fear your neighbor.

"Wow," Ben says, "I didn't know New Mexico schools were that sophisticated."

Ernie jumps in with, "Hell, Ben, you don't need college for thinking like that. It has been a common occurrence in these parts for Gringos and Mexicans to segregate themselves for the past 200 years. Have you already forgotten what your little league baseball teams looked like, or neighborhoods for that matter? AND I surely can't forget what those miners and their wives out at Empire Zinc were fighting for. It was some of those same things Sophia just described and we saw in that play. There are a lot of honorable men out there who continue to work for just solutions, but there are still a lot who want to go backwards and keep their status at the top of the food chain secure at the expense of progress, I might add...WHY? What reason could they possibly have to care if their teammate has the name of Gonzalez? Maybe the nature side of the equation has some contribution to the issue just as the nurture side does."

Sophie continues with the discussion. "I would like to think a play like this will have a major impact on the issues of prejudice and injustice throughout the world, but we all know change comes way too slowly. In my case, I know my family has nurtured me to be honorable and treat others with the same respect I demand. But I also know some people who have had some very good nurturing and still turned out to be pretty shitty individuals. AND, the opposite is true as well; people with dire situations growing up become amazing success stories. I think you can tell how much this subject fascinates me. With the background our family has, this nature vs nurture thing has all but consumed me at times. And it has filled me with a desire to pursue answers through my education."

Sofie pauses then continues, "This may sound a little dramatic, but this past year has re-energized me to be more serious about what I'm doing and not be so self-centered and casual with my actions. I wake up every day now thankful for the three people who saved me and continue to inspire me."

"Speaking of inspiration" she quickly adds "hasn't mom been something this past year!! She has such a capacity to take on the impossible task, then completely own it. Just as you two did during the Empire Zinc strike, standing up with those women and oppressed miners. Hell, it cost you your job, Ernie. I told Mom, and I am telling you now, I will not let the occurrences of my recent past define my future. I still have some regrets about what I put my family through, but I will not dwell on the past. Like Ol' Pete Gorman says, *'Everybody has a past, but only YOU control your future.'* I have a demarcation line in my personal history with the acronym of AA (After Armando) just in case you guys are a little slow on the uptake."

"One other thing," Sofie says, "how in the world did you two pick this show to watch with me at this moment? I was trying to figure out a way to describe what I was trying to accomplish at college, and that show did it perfectly!!"

Chapter 12

Summer of 1961 - Sophia Gets a Job

Sophia is in one of her favorite places, the corner table just off the last row of the history section in the UNM library. She has a couple of hours before she needs to go to the junkyard for Chuy, take parts off a wrecked car, and deliver them to the shop. She likes this new job because of the flexible work times and she usually works by herself with her own tools. Last week, she and the yard mechanic even pulled the 352 engine from a Ford Fairlane 500 interceptor.

She has several volumes of recently published historical literature recommended by the advising professor for her graduate thesis. She hasn't chosen an actual title yet, but the thesis will focus on how authoritarian regimes can rise to power. Although this is a popular topic now, Sophia wants to incorporate some of the recently published scientific developments. Most interesting to her are the fields of psychology and genetics. She has just collected a variety of books and magazines and stacked them on the table. She is trying to sort them out by date of publication when she notices an odd-looking fellow moving through the library in her general direction. He is a dwarf. She realizes the guy can't be 4 1/2 feet tall. His physique is well proportioned, and as he moves closer, she can see he is around 50 years old. She tries not to stare, but he keeps coming toward her, eventually sitting at the far end of her table. He's carrying a small three-ring binder, which he sets on the table in front of him. Sophia's immediate thought is the poor chap needs a booster seat. He can barely put his elbows on the table.

Sophia tries to ignore the guy and goes back to sorting out her research material. She is looking forward to reading through a series of short stories by Isaac Asimov from his collected series, "Earth is Room Enough." Some of the stories speculate on what the U.S. might encounter when new technologies are used to influence human behavior. For instance, one story chronicles how a computer selects a single individual to elect the president.

She is curious how people could willingly give up their voting privileges, not to mention the motives behind those seeking to restrict the voting rights of others. There has been so much national controversy lately about denying voting privileges to certain segments of our society. It wasn't until just a few years ago that people of Asian descent were even allowed to vote. The poll tax is still used in some states today, primarily to restrict people of color from voting.

Author's Note

In 1951, a case was heard in federal court. The plaintiff was an African-American woman who "alleged that, apart from the payment of her poll taxes" she was "in every way qualified to register under the Virginia law as a voter." In the final ruling the courts again took the position that states were entitled to make their own laws, finding that "it is well settled that a law that is fair on its face and is also fairly administered is not rendered invalid by the evil motives of its draftsmen." The plaintiff's case was dismissed.

Despite courts confirming poll taxes, their popularity was on the decline. By 1962, just five southern states had poll taxes on the books: Alabama, Arkansas, Mississippi, Texas, and Virginia. That same year, the House passed the 24th Amendment, outlawing the poll tax as a voting requirement in federal elections by a vote of 295 to 86. The Amendment did not become part of the Constitution, however, until 1964, when South Dakota ratified it. Today, eight states have still not ratified the amendment.

The events leading up to WW II in Germany and Italy hold an obvious interest for Sofie. She has many questions nagging at her brain in which she would like to seek some answers. For example, why did parts of that populace willingly give up their freedoms? What or who convinced them things were so bad that taking backward steps was the solution? How did it happen?

'*The Power of Propaganda*' is a serious component of school curriculum currently being taught at all levels of education today. Taking the events leading to WWII as their model the education system today stresses the importance of *'think for yourself and double check your sources of information.'* She wonders if citizens were forced into authoritarian rule, or did they just get lazy? Believing they were unhappy just because someone told them so. Is there possibly some code locked in the DNA of our species that predisposes some individuals to think the worst, thus seeking an authoritarian figure to keep them safe from people different from themselves?

Well, Sophia thinks it will make a very good and innovative thesis topic.

Sophia is lost in her thoughts and has all but forgotten about *'short stuff'* at the end of the table.

The guy clears his throat and says, "interesting collection of reading materials you have there, Ms. Wallace."

Sophia immediately snaps her head up and says, "How the hell do you know my name? I have never seen you before in my life. And, believe me, I would remember."

He says, "Oh no, you are correct. We have never met. And I have only seen you a few times around campus. I knew this direct approach would startle you, but I believe the upcoming conversation will interest you. So please, if you will let me continue for a few more minutes."

"See," he continues, "I am going to offer you a job. And, it is a job only offered to a very few, as you will soon realize. To proceed with my direct approach, I work for a newly created branch of the federal government. My specific duty is to locate potential employees to help with our mission."

Sophia says, "And pray tell what is that mission, Mr. Whoever-You-Are."

"My name is Gordon Conner," he says. "It is a pleasure to finally meet you. Let me give you a little background that will help you understand our interest in selecting you as a candidate for this position."

Gordon continues. "First, we know all about your background of being adopted out of Nazi Germany at the end of the war by Ben Wallace and his two friends. We specifically target individuals like yourself for recruitment because they are highly motivated to help our mission once they understand just what it is we do. And second, all of you speak at least two languages fluently and most of the time three or more, like yourself. The direction of your education is also very appealing in that your dual interests of history and science will shorten the training period required. We have been monitoring and evaluating your growth over the past few years... As we must with all our prospective candidates. We have conclude you will become a valuable contributor to our mission if you so choose."

Sophia says, "Again I ask, Mr. Conner, what is that mission I am supposed to help you accomplish? You can't expect me to just jump at some job I do not understand, no matter how much you sweet-talk a gal."

He says to her, "No, of course not, Ms Wallace, so let me continue. In the interest of brevity, I will give you a synopsis of what will be expected of you. If you have no interest, I will be on my way, and you will never see me again. The primary objective for the job is to verify the viability of certain information. We are tracking projects and developments by the U.S. National Laboratories. We use the information we collect to identify the sources. For example, we need to determine what lab produced the data and what scientific team worked on the project. I am sure you have read in the local papers that there is a lot of communist and foreign activity in the State of New Mexico with White Sands, Sandia Labs, and Los Alamos. Our mission is basically to ensure that the science developed here is not compromised by any foreign entity. And if compromise occurs, quickly identify and deal with those individuals."

Gordon pauses and they remain silent for a while. Gordon finally says, "Well, Sophia, what's it to be? Interested enough for me to continue? I can stop now with no harm done. But if I continue much further, we may reach a point where a decline of the offer may cause some debriefing efforts on our part. I might add, any debriefing is uncomfortable for both sides."

After a minute or so, Sophia says, "So you want me to be a spy?"

Gordon laughs a little and says, "Well, kind-of, but not like in the movies with guns and all. But yes, there is some element of risk here. The foreign agents we deal with are quite serious. However, the people you will interface with are laboratory scientists working to develop technology for the US to use both domestically and internationally. The people are academic in nature, with some accountants and clerks thrown in the mix.

These are not dangerous folks. But you will be, as you say, spying on them."

Sophia is thinking about how her dad and mom delayed their careers when asked to serve their country. There were no guarantees for them; and they knew they would definitely be in harm's way. She surprises herself by saying, "OK, tell me more. I am interested in how this is going to work, and what my specific duties might be."

Gordon looks at her carefully and says, "Well then, I'll tell you how it will work for your specific assignments. Please understand it is different for other recruits who have their own unique talents."

Gordon begins, "With your specific set of skills, we believe you would be a great asset to us as an editor and proofreader for scientific material. Those people read through the data results and conclusions generated by the project scientists. For various reasons, the project results will eventually need to be published for dissemination, hence the need for editing. The reports coming from the project labs are all but unreadable by those outside the project team. Our job is to transform that document and make it readable to a broader audience without diminishing the impact of the work itself. The audience that will see the report is an important consideration. The format for internal use like peer review differs from those destined for the various scientific journals like Scientific American, Nature, and so forth. Other times, the staff will need to generate a report to document the results for continued funding by congress. This is altogether different, as you can imagine. If we had a person in such a position to preview firsthand knowledge, it would be very valuable."

Sophia says, "Stop right there! Whose side am I working for here? Didn't you just ask me to spy on my own team of scientists?"

Gordon says, "Yes, that is exactly what I am asking you to do, in part. Let me explain."

"The science community, at the New Mexico facilities in particular, is very hush-hush about what they are doing and the results produced. Rightly so, I might add. But in the past few years, they have become so secretive that even our own intelligence agencies cannot find out what they are working on. Therefore, when we encounter communication in the underground about these scientific events, we don't know what to believe, or even where it came from. Is it real or not? If we have some knowledge of the what and where, it makes our job much easier to identify the bad guys and from what sources they are getting their information from. Believe me, efforts like I've just described have brought several dangerous spy networks down."

Gordon pauses trying to asses Sofie's interest, and then he continues,"You are probably not aware, but there is a distrust between the two primary government agencies tasked with protecting the US from outside interference with our democratic mission. That distrust has prompted my group to establish this branch of our agency to basically spy on our own people, as you have so adeptly pronounced. It should not exist, but, in fact, it does. The FBI and our group have been sniping at each other for years and it has definitely been detrimental to our national security. Consequently, our national leaders and scientists no longer trust either agency. So, they no longer involve us regarding cutting edge developments produced in our own national labs. They don't realize this is most harmful to our national security. There is some hearsay that Dulles will step down soon. So maybe then the feuding with J. Edgar will ease up, and some cooperation will ensue. But until then, it is business as usual for us in the trenches. Our country cannot afford to get any further behind the Russians in the spy game."

Sofie then responds, "So if I agree to pursue this venture, what would be the next step? Surely, I have to know what to expect next in order to decide."

Gordon says, "Okay, this is what will happen in the immediate future, say one year. You will take classes at the University here to beef up your credentials to be accepted to the science editing division of a company we own. Then you will be available for assignment as the workload demands at one of the three major federal science facilities in the state. As part of the hiring process, we will provide you with the security clearance required to work on the documents destined for editing. The clearance level will increase with time, typically, three years to reach the highest level. Basically, you will be a temp-agency employee at first, moving from one facility to the next and from one assignment to the next. But here, let me emphasize the importance of every assignment regardless of the security level. Most breakthroughs in our business come at the lower levels. Remember, the Soviet agents are not sure what is most important to their superiors, so they try to get as much as they can. If we can pick up a communication coming into a Russian intelligence center about a specific project that you have recently identified, then we will know there are some operatives at work within that facility. This tells us where to target our mitigation efforts."

"I will be back here tomorrow at this same table and same time in twenty-four hours, Ms. Wallace. I'll need a decision then. I cannot provide you with any more information about this until you have signed a letter of intent to join our company. From my perspective, it is a challenging but rewarding career. It pays well. As you will see soon, I hope. And you will never get bored. One last thing, the company you will work for is an editing company. This company is incorporated in the State of Delaware and is completely legal. The company obtained a license to operate in five states that have federal research and testing facilities. This corporate structure will provide you with an excellent cover story for friends and family. Therefore, you can minimize the secrets you have to keep from them. Obviously, the owner of the company must always be a secret. Because of the reasons I have already explained, we cannot disclose the connection between the editing company and the CIA."

"If I can add my personal sales pitch here, it would be this: I cannot think of a better way to serve my country than by keeping our most important work out of enemy hands. If you accept this position, it will surely change your life, as it changed mine. But the change was for the better and I have never regretted my decision. I have told you more than I intended, but I have a good feeling about this. So, I think it has been worth the risk. Enjoy your evening, Ms. Wallace, and I look forward to a successful conclusion to this proposal tomorrow."

With that, Sofie watches him walk out of the exit and disappear and thinks, *'What the hell just happened here?'* Everyone told her life would get much more complicated after college. Something like this never entered her mind.

Sofie's head is spinning as she finally gets back to her house. Then it dawns on her she cannot share this decision-making process with anyone, even her family. Maybe after tomorrow she might tell them about the editing company job offer. Will this editing company pay for my college? When will I be placed on the payroll? Is there a contract to sign? Who will my supervisor be? Does this company have an office in Albuquerque?

Sofie decides she needs a list of agenda items for the meeting with Gordon tomorrow. But, she admits to herself, I am excited and very interested in the possibilities. WOW, she thinks, my life will really change if this opportunity materializes. It seems like just yesterday I was a pregnant college kid and felt so lost. I had no real idea what my future might look like. And now, someone wants me to become a spy? She opens the bag with the burger and fries she picked up on the way home but suddenly has no appetite and opts for a beer instead. She wonders what in the hell tomorrow will bring. Right now, though, finding a pencil and paper to make a list of questions is her priority.

After a fitful night filled with speculation and one of her bad dreams that she hasn't has in a while, Sofie enters the library and heads to her table. Gordon is already waiting. He seems very organized, with a briefcase open and a couple of file folders on the table. Sofie sits across from him with her list of questions ready to go.

Gordon says with a little chuckle, "Get any sleep last night?"

Sofie replies with a slight smile, "Like a baby."

Gordon looks at the notepad in front Sofie with her questions itemized, then says, "Let's get the Q&A session out of the way, then hopefully we can get to the important part of this meeting. Fire away, Ms. Wallace."

Sofie starts:

Question 1: "Is there a contract I will need to sign? And can my mom review it since she is a lawyer?"
Answer: "Yes, and yes. Since you will work for an editing company, these are normal procedures. The company also has an operating history complete with PNL statements. I can assure you, when your mom checks, she will find the contract will contain the standard language for an editing company, including a non-disclosure agreement."

Question 2: "Can I quit if I have to or want to?"
Answer: "Yes...but it's not easy, and there will be an extensive debriefing. When we initiate a debriefing process, we must alter our operating procedures. So we strive to prevent that event from

happening. Let's be real here, Ms. Wallace. This job is serious, and you really need to commit from the onset. I want to make that point perfectly clear."

Question 3: "What is the name of this company, and do they have an Albuquerque office?"
Answer: "Yes, we have an Albuquerque office, and you will be told the company name and meet your supervisors after you sign our letter of intent."

Question 4: "When will I enter the payroll and will they cover the cost of my classes?"
Answer: "Once we finalize your contract, you will begin receiving a monthly salary of $950, and we will cover the expenses of your schooling."

Gordon now with a little edge to his voice says, "Look, Ms. Wallace, are you interested in the job or not? We are very serious about you becoming part of our company. We'll do everything possible to make you happy enough that you never want to leave. You are just one of many we have hired in our brief existence and no one has quit yet. We have other candidates if this is not for you. But, in my opinion, you have all the qualities needed for this kind of work."

"So I ask you again…yes or no?"

Sofie looks Gordon in the eye and says, "Yes, Mr. Conner, the answer is a yes."

Gordon says, "I knew it. You are too smart to think an opportunity like this will come your way again. Here is this letter of intent. It is not a contract. That will be presented to you in the next few days after we have agreed on the details. This is nothing more than a summary of the conditions we just discussed, so I don't think Representative Beltran will need to read this document first. Just read and sign at the bottom. Tomorrow we will meet back here at 9:00 am, and I'll take you to our Albuquerque office to meet our regional manager. After a short meeting, we will give you the employment contract to sign. You will have three days to review and bring the signed document back to our office. Three days should be enough the time for Ms. Beltran to have her input."

Shortly after 9:00 am the next day, they are driving east on Route 66, past the Knob Hill area. They turn north for a short distance and pull up in front of a duplex office building. As they enter the front door of the office on the left, a voice from the back calls out, "Is that you, Gordon? I will be right with you, so make yourself comfortable."

Sofie and Mr. Conner sit in front of the desk. The guy who called out from the back walks in and Sofie jumps out of her seat and shouts, "*Hargraves, what the fuck are you doing here?*"

"Well Sofie," he says, "So good to see you, too. Even way back then, I had a hunch we would meet again."

Mr. Conner then quickly says, "Ms. Wallace, please keep calm and let me explain. Hargraves made a serious misstep in his first big assignment with us. I suspended him and gave him a demotion for his actions. He got off easy! I dare say if your dad had found out, he probably would have killed him. And If you would have stepped forward with a complaint, Calvin here would have disappeared completely. Over the past few years, he has proven to be very good at his job, and his good work has continued. Attracting good people, like yourself, and evaluating them is a vital component of our success. Plus, he gave you the highest evaluation possible as a future prospect, as I have already told you."

"So, Ms Wallace, if you feel you cannot work with Mr. Hargraves, that is understandable. You are free to walk away now, with only a minimal compromise to our operations. He told me you both parted at the end of the school year with some type of mutual respect for each other. Based on that assessment, we continued to keep you among our prospective employment ranks. I hope that is still the case and that you can look past the serious misstep Calvin made years ago.

Sofie says, "I am just shocked at even seeing Hargraves again, much less working with him in some capacity. Will he be my direct supervisor?"

Hargraves says, "No, that will be James Bradley. This is Bradley's office. My office is in Richland, Washington, and I rarely get down this way. Mr. Conner, in an effort for complete transparency, wanted to bring us together and gauge our reactions."

Before speaking, Sofie composes herself and says, "Look, you knew I would be shocked at this meeting, and I initially was. I'm still a little put-off. But, our experience was, as you say, years ago, and I cannot deny that I started the encounter and got some '*benefit*' from it as well. So, how can I realistically be so upset at this '*reunion*' to believe a working relationship is not a possibility? Plus, I have undergone a maturation process since then, if you know what I mean. '*Hell, you probably know exactly what I mean*'. We did part ways with a mutual understanding that what happened was a mistake. Well, there you have it, I guess, 'let bygones be bygones,' 'let sleeping dogs lie,' 'a miss is as good as a mile,' 'people in glass houses,' and so on. Welcome to adulthood. So where is my contract, and when do I get paid?"

Sofie takes her contract and heads home, where she plans to call Mom immediately at her D.C. office. She is determined to have her read this before she signs.

When Sofie calls her mom, Maggie tells her to go to her Albuquerque office right away. Her office manager there will have a copy of the contract ready for the courier service on the 8:00

pm flight to D.C.. Maggie says, "I will read it first thing in the morning and call you by 10:00 AM your time."

"Mom, they told me definitely not to make any copies of the contract."

"I don't care what they told you. They are just basically a temp-agency company from what you have said, and if they are recruiting YOU, my guess is that will not be a deal-breaker. No one will ever know but you and me, anyway. I promise I will tear my copy up immediately after review. Don't worry. I'm excited for you. This sounds like a perfect fit for your talents and the pay is terrific. Plus, they'll pay for continuing your schooling. Well done! You make me proud! I will do a cursory check on the company for you with some contacts I have, just to be sure."

As Sofie hangs up, she says to herself, "Ah, geez, lying to Mom is never a good thing. Keeping this secret maybe tougher than I thought."

Just down the street in a parked car, Hargraves says to Conner, "Putting that bug in her phone was a good idea. What do we do now?"

Gordon takes a minute and says, "Well, we agreed this might happen. Let's let it play out for a while. Her conversation with her mom was pretty benign. This may be an excellent test for our cover company. We'll see what Mrs. Beltran's cursory search turns up. If it reveals too much, it's still early enough that we have options. Is the other transmitter in the house behind the picture activated?"

Hargraves replies, "Yea, and the tracking device on her car as well."

"Good," Gordon says, "You know, new recruits are a pain in the ass. But we need to be sure we know what we're dealing with here. She is already breaking one of our directives by making a copy of the contract. We can't have her ignore any others, or we will have to take some actions nobody will like."

Sofie calls her dad to tell him the great news and finds herself truly excited now and proud of her initiative to get a good job so soon after graduation.

Ben says, "It sounds very exciting, and I like the pay for further schooling part."

Sofie promised she will write him a letter soon with more details and asks him to tell Ernest. "Tell Uncle Ernie I will write him a letter also so he can show Dave. This may sound a little corny, but feel like I am helping my country by working at these important government facilities. I feel like I am paying something back. Anyway, when I told Mom, she wanted to make sure you knew that there may be follow-on visits when security clearances are requested, so don't be surprised."

Sophia heads to her mom's office to have the contract sent to D.C.. While there, she has an extra copy made for herself. *'In for a penny, in for a pound,'* she thinks.

Author's Note

As an indication of the feuding between America's two lead intelligence agencies, I am including a letter from President Eisenhower to Allen Dulles, the director of the CIA. This shows the concern the president had for this situation. This letter makes it clear that the president and Congress had lost faith in both agencies. In this post-WW II period, intelligence gathering to monitor Russian activities was crucial to keep the USSR from taking over the eastern European countries weakened after the war. The intelligence we gather is also necessary to keep our sophisticated scientific research safe.

DWIGHT D. EISENHOWER
34th President of the United States: 1953 - 1961
Letter to Allen W. Dulles, Director of Central Intelligence, Regarding Board of Consultants on Foreign Intelligence Activities.
January 13, 1956
[Released January 13, 1956. Dated January 11, 1956]

Dear Mr. Dulles:

In the Hoover Commission Report submitted to Congress on June 29, 1955, relating to the intelligence activities of the Government, there is a recommendation that I appoint a "committee of experienced private citizens who shall have the responsibility to examine and report" on the work of the Government's foreign intelligence activities. I have noted your concurrence.

In accordance with this recommendation, I am constituting a Board of Consultants to review periodically the foreign intelligence activities of this Government, and to report their findings to me. While the review would concern itself with the sum total of these activities, it would be expected that major attention would be concentrated upon the work of the Central Intelligence Agency. A copy of the letter which I am sending to the prospective members of the Board is enclosed.

The work of this Board together with the regular reviews conducted by the appropriate Committees of the Congress will help to provide a method for assuring the Congress, the public, and the Executive Branch that this highly important and sensitive work is being efficiently conducted.

I know that you will afford the Board of Consultants the fullest cooperation in its work.

Sincerely,

DWIGHT D. EISENHOWER

Note: See Item 10 for letter to prospective members of the Board. See also Executive Order 10656 of February 6, 1956, "Establishing the President's Board of Consultants on Foreign Intelligence Activities" (21 F. R. 859; 3 CFR, 1956 Supp.).

Dwight D. Eisenhower, Letter to Allen W. Dulles, Director of Central Intelligence, Regarding Board of Consultants on Foreign Intelligence Activities. Online by Gerhard Peters and John T. Woolley, The American Presidency Project

Chapter 13

Hi-ho…Off to Work We Go

Learning Russian is harder than physics. She thought it would be the other way around. Her adviser let her double up, so she is taking two Russian language classes and two basic physics classes. These are tough classes, but she is finding that there is some redundancy, and it's not impossible to keep up. Her goal by the end of the year is to read some basic Russian and gain some proficiency in the atomic sciences. The physics classes are the basic beginning courses, and she hopes to gain a general understanding of terms and procedures. James Bradley has told her there are three sections in the physics courses she needs to concentrate on: atomic chemistry, fission, and fusion. These are the most important, according to Bradley, *'because that is what they do'* at the labs where you will work.

School goes well, and she meets two other employees in training during her weekly visit to James Bradley's office. Everyone refrains from chatting too much because they have been warned about the strict prohibition of discussing work assignments with fellow employees. However, she found out they both have similar stories to hers. Both were orphaned as young boys during the war. Gabe is from Italy, and Jason is from France. Sofie doesn't think their American families are nearly as supportive as her triparental structure. She doesn't feel like trying to explain the whole thing to strangers. So basically, the three new hires just discuss classes and speculate what the apprentice phase of their training will be like starting next year.

Sofie gets completely immersed in her classwork and before she knows it she has spent an entire year going from class, to library, to home with sleep on the weekends. She has missed family gatherings and has only seen her mom twice since school started and has not seen her dad at all. Infrequent phone calls is all the contact she has had. She misses her family more than she thought and hopes to be a better daughter next year.

When Mr. Bradley brings Sofie into the office, he tells her, "I'm impressed! Your mastery of the courses in such a short time justifies the reasons for your recruitment. Gordon said to tell you, '*CONGRATS on a successful year*' and your promotion. You're ready."

Sofie is thrilled when Bradley introduces her to the lead editor she will shadow for the next six months. She is excited to finally get to work in her new career. Sofie wonders if she will ever be able to tell her family about this '*spy business.*' After an extensive introduction, Mr. Bradley leaves to let them get to the 'nuts and bolts' of how business will be conducted during normal daily operations. Jeff Holmes has been working for TECH ED for only 20 months himself. "Pretty boring," he says. Jeff then begins to tell Sofie the basic procedures involved with the editing responsibilities.

One lab will call for an edit of a report destined for submission. They will tell us what the subject is and we will match it with the person on our staff best suited to develop the finished product. By best suited, we mean two things. First, we have to deliver a quality product, because we do operate a going business here. The primary component of a quality product is that you understand what the author is trying to convey to the people who will read the report. That audience will not always be scientists from the same discipline or even a scientist. The authors sometimes get really pissed at what they think is dumbing-down their product. The best way to deal with that is to put their unedited text in an appendix and reference that for all the technical people who need the complete details and math. Most of the authors know their limits of communication. And, you will get to know your limits on the technical science that needs to be communicated to a broader audience. Most will work with you willingly and get quite excited when you have put together a finished document for dissemination. They realize they do need your help after all.

Jeff then leans in a confiding manner and says, "I'm just betting you are the type that will get some inner reward at that moment."

Also, TECH ED provides invoices, employee resumes, tax information, and all the rest required of an enterprise of our stature. Various government entities routinely audit these records, so they must be professional and precise. Ms. Wallace, you need to ensure that the invoice information you give to Bradley every month is accurate, as it undergoes close scrutiny at several levels. There can be no discrepancies.

The second component has to do with our company's primary mission that these labs know nothing about. We must deliver a report to our head office in D.C. regarding every assignment we complete for our clients. This is regardless of how minor that assignment may seem to you. This report must be on Mr. Bradley's desk at the end of the next day after completion of the assignment. You must include a detailed summary of the project you worked on, the location, the project start and complete dates, plus the name of the project manager and/or lead scientist. If the assignment becomes lengthy, say, over a week, you may be required to submit an interim report as well.

To make this happen, you will most certainly need to ask numerous clarifying questions of the scientists and managers during the course of your edit. The scientists are quite proud of their work and always answer your questions enthusiastically if approached at the right time. They seem to always appreciate someone who is sincerely interested in their project. Since you are not allowed to remove any written material or job notes from the facility, an excellent memory is a must. Also, you must put in writing as much as you can remember from the edit and questioning as soon as possible. The notes you write must be attached to the report form delivered to Mr. Bradley.

Jeff asks, "Any questions so far?"

"I've got a couple," Sofie says. "Do they search you when coming and going from a lab?"

Jeff answers, "Always at first before you become a regular and then randomly thereafter. But don't ever be tempted to remove anything! Mr. Conner would skin you alive if he found out. You will get good at knowing what is important about each report quickly, and Bradley will help you implement the system he likes for each document."

"OK, what about the security clearances?", asks Sofie.

Jeff responds again, "The labs already have your basic clearance packet. You will begin editing work commiserate with your clearance, and then your level will progress as time goes by. After two years, I have just received clearance to edit some top secret documents and enter the laboratories and fabrication shops where the work is conducted."

Jeff emphasizes what Mr. Conner had said before about no edit being trivial, names, dates. and subject are all important and could very well contain a key to understanding what the Russians know and where they got their information from.

Jeff then says, "The first couple of reports you deliver to Bradley will be a rough go. He will put you through a ringer and it will make you feel incompetent. But just remember, they hired you for good reason and they want you to succeed. Just stay with it. You are very smart and will do just fine. Few people can do the job they are asking of you, and they know it. You have some serious value for them!!"

Sofie says, "So you think this is boring? I am so excited, and nervous, about my first site visit tomorrow, I am about to pee my pants."

Jeff was right about one thing: Bradley can put you through the ringer. He is very demanding about details and clarity, priorities one and two for an excellent report. After six months on job training with Jeff, she is getting to know exactly what Bradley wants. The form he asks her to follow is very helpful in organizing each report. She is also gaining confidence in entering these super-secure facility. It was quite intimidating at first. Now she knows where the department superintendents' offices are located for the work being assigned and who she must contact to begin the editing process.

She usually works alone in a secure office unless she needs to visit a specific location for instrument configuration, information clarification, or process procedures. She cannot leave her office without an escort. This is usually the lead scientist or one of his assistants who can answer questions quickly and accurately.

Sofie Wallace now has clearance to edit secret documents and enter facilities where the projects are developed. All the project managers and scientists impress her with their dedication to the serious work done at the project sites. They are inspiring in their efforts to make America the greatest nation on earth, and she is proud to be part of the greater effort. Plus, with her clearance level advancement, she has gotten a nice raise in pay.

She has been wanting to look for a place of her own to live. Now that can become a reality.

Uncle Ernest called to tell her he would be in town for a few days to attend a funeral service for his Tia Abuela Rosa who just passed away at 88 years in Corrales, a small community just north of Albuquerque. Ernie told her if she was still looking for a place to buy, his Tia owned two acres of land with a small house. No one in the family was interested in the property and they were going to sell it. Why not to you? Ernie says he will show her the property when he is in town next week.

As soon as Ernest showed Sofie the property, she says, "Yes-Yes-Yes. It is exactly what I had in mind. Kind of has the feel of your place in Grant County that I love." Ernie says, "Yeah, except for the river, the acequias, and the cottonwoods. My cousin wanted me to warn you that living here is impossible if you cannot get along with the ditch-boss. The Mayordomo, as he is called, is a cantankerous old Mexican named Carl Leyva. He and his wife Carla live on the property next to yours."

Sofie says, "Well, uncle Ernie, let's go right now and meet the notorious Carl and Carla. I bet they will just love a neighbor with such a lovable uncle."

When Sofie greets them in Spanish and her dozen questions about the river and canal operations are convincing, they welcome their new neighbor. After Sofie helped Carla fix a quick lunch out of leftovers in the icebox, they embraced her with open arms and asked when she would move in.

On the way back, Ernie says, "The car still looks beautiful and runs as smooth as ever. Is that vato Chuy still helping you out when you need it?"

Sofie says, "Yeah, I still go down there now and then when I need a tool and to change oil...He's OK, Ernie. You and Dave need to let that go. There was nothing Chuy could have done about Armando. He had no way of knowing something like that would happen."

"So, what's your opinion on this property, Ernie? If you think it will work with your family, I'm ready to buy as soon as we can arrange it."

Ernie says it may take a while because they'll need an attorney to clear the title. "It has been in our family so long and passed down through the generations that no one is sure who needs to sign on the dotted line, so to speak. But don't worry, everyone on my side of the family could use a little cash, and no one wants to do the work necessary to live in Rosa's old place. It's yours if you want it. Have Maggie help with finding the right lawyer to make this happen quickly and then move in."

Old Carl and his son helped Sofie make her new home more livable by putting in new flooring, doors, and windows. Surprisingly, the roof was in good shape and the septic system works, as does the water well. Sofie has cut her travel time to Los Alamos by 30 minutes and loves the peace and quiet of her new home.

Life is good on the home front, but her job is becoming more and more demanding since they elevated her clearance. The projects are more sophisticated and the project staff members are under noticeably more stress. The success the Russians have had with Sputnik and the declaration of a *'space race'* has set the entire research community on edge. Answers are now expected sooner rather than later. The establishment of the Lawrence Livermore National Laboratory (LLNL) in California as a competitor to Los Alamos also heightened the expectations for success. The downhill effect was accelerated research and subsequently, more communication and editing work for TECH ED.

Sophia often wondered if her mom ever read any of her edited documents as part of her committee work. Mother and daughter serving America together. What a nice thought that is.

The Los Alamos National Lab (LANL) is now heavily involved with many aspects of nuclear weapons testing and measurement of the detonations. In association with the detonation process to trigger a nuclear event, an intense combustion is required. LANL is experimenting continuously with gas mixtures to enhance the combustion process. Also, since the Sputnik launch, many of the top scientists and managers are leaving Los Alamos for private or academic sectors. James Bradley has told Sofie this has created a lot of concern in his chain of command regarding the secrecy of the research. There was also increased activity at Sandia Labs as it has assumed the responsibility of testing the nuclear weapons and physics packages designed by LANL and LLNL.

Sofie is doing more and more work at Sandia Labs, located just outside Albuquerque at Kirkland Air Force Base. Sandia has become the primary facility for producing workable weapons from the bench work prototypes developed at the National laboratories. Sandia's work now also includes the development of equipment for nuclear blast measurement and detection of nuclear blasts.

Fields of physics that Sophia had never heard of were now being developed and needed collaborative communication or proof of results to government offices in D.C. One of the recent developments that she and Bradley have become fascinated with is a project associated with the seismic detection lab. The rapid development of transistors to replace the tube in the electronic world has allowed the development of devises like the seismic intrusion detector. These detectors use a spike inserted into the ground attached to a small box that contains a battery transmitter and antenna. The device is very sensitive and can pick up nearby vibrations from even footsteps.

Author's Note:

Background on early work done at LANL and Sandia Labs.

Sandia Lab - Facility for Acceptance, Calibration, and Testing (FACT)

The Original Mission—NW (nuclear weapon) Ordnance

In 1945, "Sandia originated as a single-mission engineering organization for non-nuclear components of nuclear weapons." Its mission was to provide the ordnance, testing, and assembly of nuclear weapons. Sandia was the Z Division of Los Alamos Laboratory. In 1949, Sandia Corporation was established. The need to "redesign the bomb into a field weapon could not be done in a laboratory alone, but in a production center…with factory management." The University of California, manager of Los Alamos, became increasingly uncomfortable about being associated with the engineering aspects of NW work. Consequently, President Truman wrote a letter to AT&T's president informing him of the Atomic Energy Commission's (AEC) intent to ask AT&T to manage Sandia Laboratory. President Truman opined that AT&T/Westinghouse had "an opportunity to render an exceptional service in the national interest;" AT&T accepted the task and the opportunity. Although the statement applied to AT&T, we at Sandia have adopted the phrase as our vision statement—(We, Sandia, provide) Exceptional service in the national interest.

By the early 1960's, Sandia Lab had developed an array of nuclear blast measurement technology and technologies to detect nuclear detonations. One of its projects was the Unmanned Seismic Observatory which had stations scattered around the Globe. This work was done in support of the Limited Test Ban Treaty of 1963.

Chapter 14

The times they are a'changin

When Sophia enters her house, the phone rings and she immediately hears a familiar voice. "Well, for crying-out-loud, Tom Siefert. What the hell. It must be at least five years since we've talked. Oh my gosh, deputy. I hope this is a social call. Is everything OK?"

Tom says, "Sofie, stop talking, and I'll tell you. Yes, this is just a conversation between old friends. I moved to Albuquerque a few months back after I left the sheriff's department. Following my training back east, I've joined the FBI in their field office here. I saw your dad last week in Grant County, and he made me promise to call you when I got into town. So that's the short of it."

"Wow, Tom, what a leap!" Sofie continues, "I heard you got married to Janice Calhoun a couple of years back. I'll bet she is part of this newfound ambition of yours. I just never pictured you leaving Grant County with your ranch and all there. So tell me about it. I'm excited for you. I always knew you had too much talent to to stay in Grant County your whole life. I'm finding there is a lot of interesting things going on in this state and talented people like yourself are needed to keep us all safe."

Tom responds, "Well, that's what this call is about. It's an invitation to dinner at our new house so you can meet Jan and see our year-old twin daughters. And, we can catch-up on our career path adventures."

"Tom, Tom, Tom," Sofie says. "You could never do things the easy way. What's the matter with one at a time? Are you trying to do to poor Janice in?"

Tom says, "That's enough, Sofie. Geez, can't you just keep it friendly? Just show up for dinner this Friday. I want to hear about that fancy job you got. Your Dad can't quit bragging about you. Take this address down. It's in the Northeast, near the Winrock Shopping Center. Easy to find. See you 7:00 PM sharp. No...is not an acceptable answer."

"I'll be there with freshly made apricot empanadas. I can hardly wait!"

Dinner with the Sieferts was quite nice, and the three talked about what was new in Grant County. Not much, they concluded... same old ranching, mining, forest service, and college stuff. Although, the final implementation of a large (3 million acres) section of the Gila National Forest as a wilderness area has sparked a lot of community interest during the past year. Their conclusion is that rural New Mexico is slow to change and has yet to embrace some of the new movements sweeping the country. It sure hasn't been caught up in all the civil rights and anti-war demonstrations that are happening across the country. Although, Tom told her Ernesto Polanco's name keeps coming up when articles about 'La Raza' appear in the local papers.

Sofie replies, "Well, Tom, I suppose it's not surprising when we disregard the 'All Men Are Created Equal' part of our Declaration of Independence. After 200 hundred years, African- American, Mexican-American, and women, I might add, are still striving for the status you white males have enjoyed since the founding of our country. And my guess is the fight won't stop anytime soon."

Tom says, "As much as I agree with the principals they are standing up for, the methods the protesters are using is like job security for me."

Driving back to her house, Sofie thinks if only Tom knew that after all the years and their humble beginnings in Grant County, they would practically be teammates on the national security stage; '*It is a brave new world*'

The phone rings early the next morning and James Bradley is calling. He wants Sofie to come in to the office on Tuesday morning. It is a little unusual since most policy and work assignment changes are done when she delivers her routine reports. This space race thing and the competition mandates with the other national laboratories have everybody on edge. She is curious about how TECH ED might respond.

The sunset highlights the Sandia Mountains and transforms the majesty to all different shades of blue- red-orange-purple…What a show mother nature can put on! Sofie sits on a rickety old chair behind her house, just marveling at the beauty of New Mexico. It never ceases to speak to her spirit. Today, the colors on the mountain created by the setting sun are divine. These moments also produce a calmness that she seems to need more and more these days.

She and Carl have just walked the acequia ditch banks. They didn't say five words for the entire circuit, just a greeting when they began and a "good evening" when they returned home. They have been doing this for some time now and neither wants to break the spiritual feeling the river gives to its worshipers.

These are typical Acequias in the Coralles area. The first is the main channel bringing the river water, and the second is a typical feeder channel to the property owner. The Mayordomo will oversee an entire section of a local distribution. Duties of the Mayordomo include organizing the property owners for maintenance projects and setting water allocation volumes for each property, depending on water availability.

Sofie has overheard some work acquaintances say she has no friends. She always liked the aloneness and doing tasks by herself. School friends were not there at the beginning for a non-English speaker when she moved to Grant County more than twenty years ago. She played some team sports when young but never liked them much. She never joined clubs or attended crowded events like music concerts when growing up. Sitting alone behind her house, she wonders if the reading she did in college about how people can be brainwashed by authoritative leaders and lose their identities still makes her shy away from group activities.

The influence that some mass cult-like groups can exert on people makes her more and more comfortable with just her inner self. Discussions have come up before with her dad and Ernie, *'the self- appointed leaders of the Grant County Great Thinkers Society,'* about what in the world people lack that they are prompted to join the KKK, the Bloods, the Crips, the SLA, the Black Panthers, or other hate groups prominent today. As far as she is concerned, that goes for the evangelical brainwashers like Oral Roberts on his Abundant Life and Healing Waters televangelist broadcasts. Sofie thinks it is that same desire for acceptance that also gave rise to the Masons, Elks, Moose, and others. There is still nothing more rewarding to her than working on her car or exercise on the speedbag followed by a heavy bag routine. She now realizes the joy her grandma has when she gardens. She can't wait to get a garden started here. Maybe she will ask her grandparents to come help her. Yoli has dropped short notes about how well her son is doing in his adopted home. She finds these notes comforting, but so far, they have elicited no desire to seek a reunion with her son.

As darkness that only a river valley can bring encompasses Sofie, she realizes this philosophical thinking crap has been a refuge, so she won't have to think about what happened in the morning meeting with James Bradley. What he wants her to do now is in direct conflict with the TECH ED policies outlined by Gordon Conner when she was hired. For the past seven years, she has been operating with the responsibility of editing sensitive scientific research and making it readable to a broader audience. Her supervisors repeatedly warned her not to remove any materials or primary information from the labs.

Now that is about to change. Bradley told her in the meeting that CIA headquarters in D.C. has been picking up information from reliable sources that Los Alamos is developing their own nuclear reactor. They have identified the project as UHTREX. If this information is leaving the lab and ending up in Russian hands, then there is definitely an informant on the inside. Just a few weeks ago, our agency was unaware of this reactor, but now it has been referenced in several Soviet secret communications. With three mentions in the last week alone. Bradley says they are fairly certain UHTREX is the primary focus of the project Kurt Sanger is leading. Sofie had worked inside the Sanger lab on several occasions. Although the editing she did appeared to be unrelated to the UHTREX project, she was in the building where they suspect much of the reactor work was being done. At this point, they need to know two things to verify the validity of the correspondence they are intercepting: What makes this reactor prototype different from previous designs? And what is the intended use?

There were lots of other questions surrounding this project, but these two pieces of information will allow them to pinpoint the source of the information breech and confirm the existence of this project. This development is so recent that they were not convinced it was real. It could be misinformation disseminated by the LANL to throw the Soviets off. However, if D.C. gets the information they need, the misinformation question will be answered. Plus, they would have a missing link in a spy network they had been working on for years now. To say this was their agency's highest priority at this time would be an understatement.

Bradley had said, "Sofie, I know this goes completely against the company's established directive. When D.C. told me what they wanted, I objected strongly. But since then, I have become convinced that we must take the risks here because the rewards would be so great. We cannot fall behind the Soviets in the nuclear power arena. That is not an option. *'Period'.* D.C. knows how productive and successful you, personally, have been at deflecting critical data from entering enemy hands, plus your accurate project reporting has led to the identification and arrest of enemy agents, both here and abroad. They have specifically directed me to place you on this critical assignment. I told them I would have this discussion with you, but that the decision must be yours and yours alone. Their counter to that was that if you declined the assignment, you must take a transfer overseas for the duration of this investigation at a minimum. Their thinking was you were such a logical choice for this assignment that Los Alamos might question why another person other than you was working in the Sanger building…so your transfer would provide the answer."

This upcoming editing assignment would allow Sofie access to the Sanger complex. It was scheduled to start on Monday of next week. It would be one of those chronology documents headed to the various legislative committees that monitor the lab's progress and provide their funding. She had worked on those before and had access to highly classified files. With her tenure, she would have unaccompanied access to most parts of the complex in order to produce the comprehensive report they need. After all these years, Bradley had told her, she was well known and respected throughout the complex. It was the perfect vehicle to gather the information they were after. She remembered Bradley saying, "Make no mistake about this, though, you will need to snoop through files outside of the designated assignment and take some pictures with a mini-cam to provide the details we need. The camera is small enough to be concealed, so detection is highly unlikely except with an extremely detailed personal search. As you know, labs where radiation research is conducted avoid the use of x-ray for searches."

When Bradley finished talking, Sofie had remained silent. This was a lot to comprehend. As she had listened to Bradley talk, she got the distinct impression that things would never be the same after this assignment. Definitely NOT business as usual. It's not that she hadn't thought about the possibility of TECH ED's mission drawing her into a more serious and perilous arena. But she really did not anticipate that it would involve LANL or Sandia, where she knew and appreciated the dedicated people working on America's top-secret technology. She expected 'The Company' would move her to another arena of operation if she had ethical concerns about an assignment. How in the hell could she turn down this assignment and still have a future with the CIA? If she declined, what would quitting look like? A scary thought to her just now.

Sofie had asked Bradley, "What happens if I get caught with sensitive information on a camera?"

Bradley had told her, "Of course we would stand with you and take responsibility for creating this assignment. But honestly, no one is sure how a situation like that would play out. It could take on a life of its own for all the players involved, including you and me. There are no guarantees here and obviously there is a significant danger in this project. But Sofie, D.C. has mandated this project will be done, and they have identified you as the best chance for success."

Sofie had made it plain that she didn't like it and didn't appreciate being put in this position. *'It wasn't what she signed up for!'* She had no training or preparation for that kind of subversive activity, and it didn't seem well thought out to her.

Bradley's response had sent shivers down her spine. "Sofie, this is the CIA. *'It's what we do'*. Job specialization is not always possible. We hire people like you who can think quickly and make sound decisions in stressful situations. You are the best one in our organization for this assignment. Period. So, you need to decide... in or out. We need an answer by Thursday at the latest. Times, they are a changing."

As soon as Sofie left his office, Bradley picked up the phone. When the voice on the other end answers, Bradley says, "Sam, do we still have that phonemic in place at the Wallace house?"

"Yeah, Sam says, "but we haven't listened in for a while. I got to tell you that girl is as boring as they get. Nobody outside of her family calls her and she very rarely talks to anyone over the phone or in her house."

"Well, we need to start again and see if we can get some recording device for long-term playback within range of the microphone planted in her phone." Sam told Bradley this job will be tougher than in her old place. The place she lives in now is more remote and people here are more suspicious of strangers moving about their neighborhood.

Bradley cuts him off, saying, "Sam, you and Jay just get it done…and soon. Today would be best, but no later than by the end of the day tomorrow. Got it?"

Chapter 14 1/2

HELP!...I need somebody!

Sofie gets up from the chair and makes her way through the dark to her house and picks up the phone and places a call. When Tom answers, Sofie says, "Tom, I need to talk with you confidentially. Can you meet me tonight or early tomorrow at the latest? This is not a social call."

Tom says, "I will be at your house in less than an hour," and hangs up. Sofie smiles to herself and thinks, to hell with that aloneness shit! It sure is nice to have friends.

When Tom walks up to the door, Sofie meets him with a beer in hand and leads him through the house to the backyard where two chairs await. The beautiful New Mexico silence is all around them and neither breaks the spell for quite a while. Finally, Sophie says, "Tom, I am going to tell you a story. It's long and complicated, so bear with me, but please feel free to ask questions or get more beer."

She starts at the beginning with Gordon Conner, James Bradley, and Calvin Hargraves. Tom says, "Stop right there, not Hargraves the math teacher?" Sofie answers, "The very one, but just be patient. All will come out." So she tells the story. Tom becomes completely captivated. She tells him, "While I am getting me something stronger than beer and peeing, why don't you mull that tale over in your pretty little head?" Sofie returns shortly with a bottle of tequila and two glasses.

Then Tom says, "The CIA and something called TECH ED, what the fuck have you got yourself involved in?"

"That is exactly why you're here, Tom. I'm not sure anymore. To put the last piece in place for you, I was just asked this afternoon by Bradley to smuggle secret documents out of LANL. I can assure you, you would not be sitting in that chair right now if I wasn't scared shitless. I think I may have been unwittingly spying on my own country these past seven years. After saying that…excuse me a sec while I go throw up in that ditch over there."

When she returns, Tom says, "Sofie, I am new to this FBI stuff, and I really don't know what to do here. This is serious business and people well above our paygrade need to be involved. And I mean right now."

Sofie answers abruptly, "Well, Tom, we need to figure this out because I need to give them an answer by the day after tomorrow. And, Tom, I am not really sure myself what's going on here. TECH ED seems to be legit, with quite a few employees depending on their paychecks, so please, be as careful as you can. I am so dreading going to work on Thursday. You have always had hero written across your chest. Now is the time to deliver. I have no one else to turn to. Can you just imagine what my mom, the human wrecking ball, would be like if I told her the story I just told you? Talk about your atomic explosions!"

Tom says, "OK, my supervisor gets to the office before 5:00 AM every day so he can talk to the chief in the Justice Building in D.C. if necessary. I will ambush him and really give him something to talk about. Maybe we can play this squabble between the FBI and CIA to our advantage here. If nothing else, we should be able to get some concrete info on TECH ED fairly quickly."

"Oh, my god…Sofie, my mind is racing to think of what this might mean, no matter which direction it takes. So, just in that ditch right over there, huh?"

When Tom returned from the short walk to the ditch, he seemed better. "Look, I'm leaving now. It is already 1:30 AM, so I am going straight to the office to work on some kind of flow chart with dates and names to present to Stan Bolling first thing. Shit–it is already Wednesday!"

Sofie says, "If you're going to the office, I am going with you. You would call me every 10 minutes for names and dates, anyway. This way, it will be much more efficient, and it's the only way you'll have something completed in time. I just can't stay here by myself!"

They quickly gather a few items they might need and Sofie retrieves the contract she signed when joining TECH ED. They fail to see the sedan with two passengers parked up the road from the house.

Sam turns to Jay and says, "What the hell do you make of that?" Jay says, "Looks like she finally got a boyfriend. A good lookin' gal like that should be gettin laid every now and then. Should we follow them?"

"Nah," says Sam, "we got our orders. Just make sure *'the thing'* on her phone is still transmitting and find a place to situate the recorder. This is the perfect chance to do it, so let's get going."

Tom and Sofie go straight to the conference room when they get to the FBI office. Tom puts on a pot of coffee and lays some pencils and notebooks on the table, then says, "You work on the chronology of this starting with the dwarf Gordon appearing and ending with Bradley giving you the assignment yesterday. I know the time period has spanned several years, but try your best to get all the important assignments you have worked on and the locations. If it's incomplete, it won't matter that much now. Just get as much down as you can remember. I'll work on the narrative you just told me, hopefully, getting all the names in the right places. If we split the tasks, we may have this in shape to present to my supervisor in a couple of hours."

Stan Bolling walks into the conference room at 5:00 am sharp. Tom meets him at the door and says, "Stan, this is Sophia Wallace, and she has an incredible story to tell you. We have been working on this for the last three hours and it needs your immediate attention, especially before you call headquarters. Sit down and I will get you a cup of coffee." Stan looks at them both, then settles his gaze on Sofie and asks, "Ms. Wallace, is this going to change my schedule for today?"

Sofie returns his gaze and says, "It will."

Tom tells Stan he and Sofie were going to the little bakery on the corner for a bite to eat while he reads the two documents in front of him.

When they return with a dozen pastries, Stan has his feet up on the table, staring off into space. He puts his feet down, looks at Sofie, and says, "Ms. Wallace, in my twenty-plus years with the bureau 'THAT' is the most incredible story I have ever heard. *'I don't know what to make of this'*. Tom, where do you think we should start? You have obviously been thinking about this longer than me."

Tom responds, "Sofie and I think this all hinges on TECH ED being part of the CIA, as these guys claim. If it is, there is no real harm done to our national security. Just a lot of red faces at the CIA which would get a belly laugh from J. Edgar. However, if we determine there is no connection, as Sofie now suspects, *'then…Katey bar the door'*. As you read, TECH ED is operating in our National Lab system at Oak Ridge, LLNL. LANL and Sandia plus Hanford and White Sands."

"OK, let's make the call to headquarters," Stan says as he reaches for the phone. "Ms. Wallace, is there anything else I should know before I call back east?"

Sofie says, "Just one thing…my mom is Margaret Beltran."

Bolling cradles the phone and says, "You mean like Representative Beltran, Chairman of the House Armed Services Committee!"

"The one and only," Sofie replies.

Bolling's face is pale as Tom intervenes and says, "Yes sir, if we don't do this right, there will be a lot of shit headed down our hill."

As Bolling dials the phone, he says, "Boy, the chief is going to get a charge out of this one. Don't you two move from this room. This is going to get intense, and I mean soon."

After about an hour of back and forth with headquarters, several more people have joined the conversation on the D.C. end. Finally, someone takes immediate action and orders a stenographer into the room so that the chronology and the narrative can be duplicated for the FBI personnel in D.C. to study. Sofie goes to Tom's office to dictate the documents to the D.C. stenographer. When she returns to the conference room, Sofie overhears the serious discussion on the speakerphone. As best she can tell, they are all giving this the attention it deserves. Several questions are posed in Sofie's direction, and she answers them all as concisely as possible.

Finally, she says. "Gentlemen, if I may; I need some urgency here! Come next Monday morning, what I know to be a high-level CIA manager has asked me to carry a camera into a top-secret section of Los Alamos. My objective will be to take pictures of files about a small atomic reactor that very few people know about. I am not comfortable with that mission. I need your help!"

When the phone call finally ends, Bolling turns to Sofie and Tom and says, "Pardon the expression, but you two look like shit. Why don't you go home, clean up, and get a couple hours of shut-eye. Let's meet back here at 4:00 pm. That should give those hot-shots back east time to get us some answers. Over the past few years, I have developed a good working relationship with someone at the CIA who is in a position to help us. The name Beltran will strike fear in the CIA more than the FBI. The CIA is newer, and they are not sheltered by the likes J. Edgar. I promise you, Ms. Wallace, I will exert all the leverage necessity to expedite the answers we need by your Monday deadline."

"Now that we have some semblance of a plan of action," Sofie says, "I plan to call Margaret when I get back home. She needs to hear what is going on from me first. She will want to jump right in the middle of this, I'm sure. But I think I can convince her otherwise. She will like it that Tom is involved and that the FBI has initiated some immediate action. I'll tell her she will receive the documents I just read to headquarters by the end of the day. Let your D.C. FBI guys know Representative Beltran will be calling for those documents. So go ahead, scare the shit out of your CIA friend. Inform him that The Armed Services Committee is aware of what is expected from the CIA. However, if we don't have some suitable answers by next Monday morning, I can assure you, all hell will break loose. My Mom will not let me carry out that mission at LANL…..out of fear for my safety and for national security. Time is ticking. This has been the longest day of my life. It can't still be Wednesday!!"

Sofie pauses for a moment and finally says, "I have to tell them by tomorrow. Whether I am in or out for this assignment with Sanger. What am I supposed to say when James Bradley calls Thursday morning?"

"You have to tell them you are in," Bradley says. "If you do anything else, it might raise suspicion on their part. Questions will be directed at you that will be hard to answer and may trap you in some inconsistencies. We cannot let them think that it is anything other than business as usual at this stage."

"OK, then," says Sofie, "Keep them at bay until the trap is sprung. The sooner the better, I hope."

Bolling says as they are leaving, "I pray that some part of the fractured mess that is the CIA, knows about TECH ED. Who knows, maybe some good will come of this, and pave the way for more cooperation. This is no way to run the U.S. security forces."

Tom tells Sofie to follow him to his house, where they can clean up and eat something. Janice will take the twins somewhere so we can get a little sleep. Sofie thinks she ought to object, but it makes little sense to waste time driving to Corrales and back. Besides, she is dead tired and needs to lie down soon.

At 4:30 pm Wednesday afternoon, they are back at the FBI office, and Sofie is on the speaker phone again. This time it is Bolling's CIA contact, a man named Alan Dover. He informs them that the results of his quick investigation into TECH ED are mixed, but he tells them this story has definitely captured the attention of the director when it was explained to him that TECH ED had access to the sensitive science and technology being developed at the national labs. All branches of the CIA are now in an all-out effort to determine the reporting chain of command that monitors TECH ED'S activities. So far, they have not found the reporting entity, and that is becoming quite worrisome to all involved. TECH ED, however, appears to be a legit company. In 1959, TECH ED incorporated in Delaware as a privately held company with stock issuances to five individuals and a small electronics company named Light Year GL, which provided the capital for the start-up. They have a well-known accounting and legal firm on retainer; and their employees all pay taxes, have social security numbers, etc., just like every legit company should have. They did discover TECH ED is listed as a branch of the Operations Division in the CIA reporting structure. However, that group was supposedly disbanded more than a decade ago and apparently does not submit operations reports to anyone within the CIA. And amazingly, according to what his supervisor uncovered, they still get appropriations money for staffing and operations. In his words, '*What a cluster-fuck.*'

Sofie and Tom continue to listen as Dover reveals the history of TECH ED. "Ms. Wallace, uncovering this plot with Agent Siefert may make you both national heroes, but the powers that be will do their best to sweep it under the rug as fast as possible. This company has apparently eluded scrutiny by all the various agencies responsible for national security for what looks to be 10 years. The whole thing is so ingenious, brilliantly thought out. Using our own loyal citizens, like Ms. Wallace and the laboratory staff, to produce reports on our advanced technologies is quite diabolical. They also played our 'Spy Agencies' for fools by taking advantage of our discord, jealousy, and lack of cooperation. It couldn't have been anyone else but the Russians behind this. We have been playing catch-up to their spy machine since World War II."

The phone goes silent for a moment before Dover starts up again. "One last thing for today, if I may. When each department learned about this crisis, they all eventually asked who was responsible for exposing this devious operation. Without fail, everyone said HE must have some serious balls to face this down and certainly deserves some sort of recognition. Ms. Wallace, so far there is only a tight circle of people who know of your heroics, so the size of your ovaries is safe for now. You have all our highest respect. Thank you, Sofie Wallace."

After the phone conference ends, Stan shares with them how the operation to deal with TECH ED will be structured. Bolling puts both hands on the table and squares his posture. He says, "So for now, we fear the worst…..that TECH ED is a front for pilfering information from our most secret sites. This is rapidly becoming a very scary situation."

It has been decided that the FBI will take the lead role in the effort to shut down TECH ED and detain all the employees for questioning. Starting as soon as Friday. The CIA then will develop some plan to mitigate the significant damage to our national security. As the CIA director reportedly said when he gave the status of the situation to the President, "It is our fuck-up... We deserve a chance to fix it," to which the President was rumored to have said, "It will be impossible to repair the damage this negligence has done to us. I envision a new director in our future soon, along with some restructuring."

After the meeting ended, Sofie says, "Well, I feel more like a fool than a hero. I don't care what that windbag says. Oops, sorry Stan, I hope he is not a good friend. That ovary crack was demeaning. If I… oh, what the hell, we don't have time for this petty crap now. Why does everything boil down to heroes or villains? We've got too much work to do; I cannot dwell on that asshole."

Sofie rises to her feet puts both hands on the table and says, "So, Stan, you FBI guys are in charge here, I assume you have the authority to hire me on the spot because I really need to work on this. Plus, you guys need me. I know more about their organization than all of you put together. I need to make these guys pay. And I am going after them starting now…either with or without you! I sure hope you spy guys can keep a secret. This situation obviously requires some quick, precise action. The net must be cast accurately and broadly enough to capture the biggest fish. If they get off the hook here, I and a lot of others are going to be really pissed. Look, I know you will have to coordinate a plan nationally to act simultaneously at all the sites, and I know it will have to happen soon. I just think I can contribute to the New Mexico part…I'm talking way too fast, aren't I?"

Sofie takes a deep breath, then continues, "I'll tell you what. Let me go home and call Margaret before she finds out some other way and then I will be back here tomorrow around noon to see what you geniuses have cooked up."

Tom says, "I have a minor adjustment to that plan with your permission. Why don't you call her now while we are here to give you some support and ease her mind as well? She will see that we are on top of this."

"OK, if you guys are game, I am. It's about 8:00 pm there. So let me try her office first." Sofie dials and the office manager answers immediately informing them that Ms. Beltran is out of the country until Friday on unexpected NATO business. She told me to stay in the office until 9:00 and keep the phone line clear, so I have to go now, but I will tell her you called. Does she need to call you immediately or can it wait until she returns? She is involved in quite serious developments with our European allies."

Sofie says. "No, no. Friday will be fine," then hangs up.

"That's it for me today, then," Sofie tells them. "I'm heading home for tonight. I assume you spy agency guys can keep your activities a secret until Friday. If Mom gets wind of this before I've talked with her, well, I just don't want to think what might happen."

Sofie picks up a Blake's Lotaburger and is thinking about what she can tell her dad. It will have to be convincing without revealing the true details yet. When she gets home, it's her favorite time of day. The sun is low in the sky, changing the color of the mountains. She heads to the chairs behind her house to enjoy her burger as the light fades.

Dad answers on the second ring. It is so nice to hear the voice of someone who loves her. Tears well up in her eyes and it's only then she realizes how much stress she has been under the past couple of days. The importance of the moment suddenly overwhelms her. The next few days will reveal everything. After some small talk, Sofie just blurts out, "Dad, I'm quitting my job as of this coming Monday."

Ben says after a brief pause, "Wow, what brought this on? Just a week ago, you told me how much you were still enjoying the work you were doing and viewed it as important."

"Well, things have changed, and the company wants to go in a different direction. I just don't want to be caught up in something I don't completely understand. I wish I could tell you more right now, but I have some confidentiality clauses in my contract that I need to honor. Would you do me a favor and tell Ernie for me? He'll want to talk too much, and I just can't do that right now."

"Sure thing," Ben says. "I told him I would go out to his place Friday after work for a beer and some of Lupe's cooking. It will give us something to talk about other than baseball and cars. Hey, have you told Maggie yet? I bet she was surprised. I'm sure she didn't expect it."

"No, you are the first to know," she says. "I understand Representative Beltran is presently in Europe on NATO business. Isn't that something cool to say about your mom?"

"Yes, indeed. Margaret is something else. She always has been."

"Look, Dad, I hate to cut this short, but I have had a couple of long days, and I am worn out. OH! One thing before I go: I had dinner with Tom and his family the other day. Thank you for insisting he call me. He's so adorable in the family setting created by Janice and the twins. Plus, now that I will be unemployed I can plan a trip home for a long visit. I'll call again in the next couple of days. Say hello to Dave for me. Adios for now." As she hangs up the phone, she is already thinking of bed.

Chapter 15

Breaking Up is Hard to Do

As soon as Sofie hung up the phone, Sam and Jay were hunting a pay phone to call Bradley. When Bradley answers, Sam says, "Boss, I think we got some trouble brewing here. We were monitoring the gals place just like you asked when she called her dad. Boss, she's going to quit the company, and I mean like soon. She told dad Monday was her last day. What the hell do we do now? She can't just pack-up and leave that quick, can she?"

Bradley says, "This is exactly why we started our surveillance again. She didn't like her new assignment. I thought she was overthinking it. She asked too many questions about the implications and adverse reactions. Learn anything else?"

Nah, she only mentioned she just had dinner with an old friend named Tom who just moved here with his family. Must be the guy we saw her with on Monday, like we said in our report. We just thought he was some sort of one-night fling. It was the first time we'd seen him. Oh yeah, she mentioned she tried to call her mom, but she was out of the country now.

Bradley says, "I can't remember anything about a Tom in her background report. I'll check with Hargraves to see what he knows. Anyway, we have to act quick on this situation. We better have something in place before Beltran returns. Get back to the office ASAP."

Bradley thought about the situation for a while. It was well past the time to act on Ms. Wallace. This had been brewing for a while…. If Ms. Wallace wasn't so good at her job, we would have removed her before Beltran started moving up the house leadership ranks. Gordon thought something might slip during a phone conversation between Sofie and Beltran that would benefit our cause, so he was reluctant to let her go. Gordon needs to know the current situation. The time had come to deal with Sofie Wallace.

As soon as Sam and Jay hit the office, they were in Bradley's office, developing a strategy to deal with Sofie. He tells Sam and Jay, "You guys plan to act on Thursday. We can't afford to have Beltran and Sofie enter into some detailed discussion. There is too much at risk here."

Bradley immediately calls Gordon Conner. He has to use several phone numbers dedicated to emergency use for situations just like this to track Gordon down.

Gordon is in Belgrade, and Bradley doesn't even know what time it is there. He just knows this is too important to care about time. He's fearful about what might happen in the next 24 hours. He needs help with this now!

After hearing Bradley's report, Gordon says, "Well, it had to happen someday. She has been one of our best assets, but all good things come to an end. Have your guys pick her up and find out what she knows. We have done this before. However, this is a little more high-profile so make your plan a good one. Anything else I should know about?"

Bradley told him about this guy named Tom who had just moved to Albuquerque from their hometown. Gordon says, "Lots of guys named Tom, but check with Hargraves. It might mean something to him."

Bradley continues his narrative, "We are acting fast here, so any info Hargraves could provide will not alter our immediate plans anyway. Sam and Jay will pick up Sofie Thursday night, so we should have a good idea of what she is planning by Friday morning. That sodium pentothal drug works pretty fast and we should get some ideas of what she knows or if she has involved anybody else."

Before Gordon hangs up, he says, "Make sure you get this right. Get the information she has, but try not to make it too messy...if you get my meaning."

Things are in motion and moving fast at TECH ED. Sam calls Bradley to tell him everything is in place for Thursday night to act on the girl. Bradley told them they could use the safe house near the intersection of Rio Grande Boulevard and Alameda. "It's close by, vacant now, and somewhat secluded. It'll be perfect for what needs to be done. There is a phone line in that house as well, so call me when you get there with Wallace."

When Sofie wakes up Thursday it is already late but she is still tired, the phone is ringing. She knows it will be Bradley looking for her answer. As she walks to the phone, she composes herself and goes over the answer she has rehearsed in her head. After their greetings, Sofie starts in, "Look Jim, I'm sorry about my reaction the other day. I have become so used to this routine that I forgot who I work for and more importantly, why. I'm sure I can do this mission and you are right. There is no one more qualified to pull this off than me. So I'm in. Set everything up for Monday as you planned."

Bradley tells her he's very relieved to hear that. Furthermore, he was so confident that would be her decision he has not even thought of a back-up plan.

Well, that went just great. Sofie thinks maybe too great? Oh, what the hell...I'm just getting paranoid here. All of this will be over before Monday rolls around, anyway.

After talking with Bradley Sofie walks the canal route by herself trying to clear her head. When she returns she places a call to Tom and relates her phone conversation with her boss. She assures Tom that nothing will happen at the TECH ED office before the FBI action on Friday. She declines Toms invitation for dinner, saying she is still exhausted and just wants a good nights sleep before the events on Friday.

Sam and Jay got a real good chuckle out of that!

Sofie wakes in the middle of the night around 2:00 am, she believes. Lying there, she tries to enjoy the silence, but her mind can't stop thinking about what the upcoming few days will bring and how many lives will be changed in the wake of events to come. Her attention is peaked when she hears a strange noise in the house but can't quite tell where it's coming from. The mice have been long gone, so the noise is perplexing. There it goes again. She is on full alert now. Kitchen or maybe the living room, she thinks. *Someone might be in her house.* The little 38 is on the top shelf in the closet... What a shitty place to keep a gun. Now she will have to slip out of bed quietly and move across the open floor. Rolling out of bed to keep low, she moves over the floor quietly and only straightens up to enter the closet. Suddenly, as she is about to enter the closet someone appears from the dense darkness. Instinctively, she uses a straight left to his face followed by a right cross to the jaw, and just like Dave said would happen, the guy crumples to the floor. The punches were delivered with a lot of force and the guy is not moving. While Sofie moves closer to provide some finality to the situation, someone grabs her from behind and holds a rag over her mouth and nose.

Slowly, Sofie regains consciousness. She is bound and gagged in some confined space and can hardly move. Maybe the trunk of a car, maybe even her own car, because she now detects the familiar sounds and motion of movement. How long have I been out, she wonders? She wonders who could be doing this to her…

but she knows... Reality hits. She has been kidnapped by some Soviet TECH ED thugs. Surprisingly, with this reality comes some calmness. If they had wanted her dead, she surely would be by now. It must be information they want.

How the hell did they find out so quickly about her intentions? This situation could turn very nasty for me when they discover I won't be talking about anything I know. Maybe I can make-up something up to throw them off until rescue or escape is possible. Chances of that seem pretty slim, she thinks.

As she becomes more aware, Sofie concludes she is in the trunk of her own car. But she can't figure out if that is good or bad. The travel motion and sounds stop, and she hears both doors open and close. Two men are talking, but she can't follow the conversation. No one comes to get her out of the trunk. After what feels like an eternity, the trunk lid is flung open and someone blinds her with a strong flashlight beam. Her legs have been cramping so badly she cannot even stand as she is dragged into the house and thrown on a bed with no mattress, just the springs. Her hands are unbound, but immediately re-tied to the frame.

When her eyes regain some focus, she sees a guy standing over her with a big bandage over his nose. Before she could laugh, he delivers a blow to her face, and she gags on the blood running into her mouth. The guy is still looking down at her when another guy comes in and says, "Knock it off, Jay. There will be time enough for that later. Ms. Wallace here needs to answer some questions."

They take her from the bed and re-tie her to a chair. She is still in her sleep clothes and feels very vulnerable, which is their intent. Sofie says, "Hey, I know you. I saw you come out of Jim Bradley's office when I was there a while back. Name's Sam, right?"

Sam tells her, "Well, Ms Wallace, that's an excellent memory you got there. For your sake, I hope it continues. We need answers to some questions, and we don't have a lot of time to waste. So this will get mighty unpleasant for you in a hurry...if you follow my meaning. I got a short list here if you are ready to start."

"For starters, who have you told about your intentions to leave TECH ED? And why are you leaving on such short notice? While you're at it, tell us who this guy you've been palling around with the past few days is?"

Sofie asks them how they know she is thinking of resigning. The words are no sooner out of her mouth when a burning electric jolt hits the bottom of her left foot.

"Now, Ms Wallace, like I said, we have no time for such evasions. Hopefully, you are beginning to understand the seriousness of the situation. We need truthful answers and we need them now or there will be more pain in your future."

When Sofie doesn't respond, another jolt hits her right foot with more amplitude than the first one. "This can continue, Ms. Wallace, with the prompting applied to even more sensitive parts of your anatomy."

They ask questions but receive no answers. The electrical probe is moved to other parts of her anatomy. Sofie becomes so delirious with pain, she could not respond if she wanted. When she regains consciousness, she is back on the bed and alone. She doesn't think she told them anything, but she feels drugged and is not sure.

Tom arrived at Sofie's house early Friday to discover no one was home, and her car was gone. She knew the importance of the meeting this morning, and Tom was immediately concerned. Inside he finds the bed unmade, blood on the carpet by the closet door, and no coffee in the pot. He immediately calls Bolling and tells him his suspicions. Tom says he'll call Ben in Grant County to see if he has heard from Sofie.

Ben recounts his phone call with Sofie yesterday to tell him about leaving TECH ED, but has not heard from her since. Tom tells him, "Ben, I can't lie. This could be serious. Sofie came to me with the concerns she had about quitting her job on such short notice. After hearing her story, we both concluded that she had every right to be worried. We were supposed to meet again this morning, but she's not at her house as we had planned. That is all I can tell you for now, other than no one knows where she is. If you hear anything, please call my office immediately. The number is on the card I gave you."

As soon as Ben hangs up, he calls Ernie. "Ernie, have you heard from Sofie?" Ernie said he hadn't talked to Sofie for about a week. After relating his conversation with Tom, he tells Ernie, "I am headed to Albuquerque as soon as I hang up. I didn't like the tone in Siefert's voice."

Ernie says, "not without me, you're not." So now there are three men racing to Albuquerque. Yes, Dave is with them. The posse is back together. Driving has given Ben time to think and what he can't figure out is why Tom knew about Sofie quitting her job and why the FBI is involved. He thinks, 'Just wait till I get that Siefert in front of me.'

Five hours later, the three arrive at Sofie's place to find several cars parked out front. Tom recognizes them and heads over to find out what's up. Ben is all keyed up and heads straight for Tom. He can see the look on Ben's face, but he has rehearsed what he needs to say. Hopefully, this will appease Ben for the time being, and they can continue with the effort to find Sofie.

Without going into too much detail, Tom tells the three men that Sofie's job was not quite as it appeared on the surface but had some Federal Government ties. He said Sofie contacted him yesterday, trying to get some information about the federal agencies involved in her work. As of now, she and her car are missing and kidnapping has not been ruled out.

Dave says, "Tom, who the hell would kidnap Sofie?"

Tom ignores that question and tries to bring Ben up to speed on what has happened. But Ernie interrupts, telling Tom they are here to find Sofie, and he knows how they can do it faster than a bunch of FBI prima-donnas.

Tom cuts him off immediately, saying, "The FBI is in charge of this, and you guys just need to stand down. There is nothing you three can do right now."

Dave gets in the middle of the conversation and tells Tom, "We have ways that law enforcement can't understand or use. For instance, once you said Sofie's car was missing, I knew that Ernie and I could locate the car much quicker than a bunch of Anglo lawmen. That car is very recognizable. Sofie has worked on it in more than a few shops in the valley over the years. She's even shown it in local car shows. That custom dark green paint job is primo. I can assure you every chicano in this area knows that vehicle. Right now, Ernie and I are on our way to every shop in this vicinity. If that car is still in this valley, we will find it; and I mean today. Just please stay out of our way, and we will let you know the moment we find it."

Ernie and Dave were right. Every garage they stop in knows the car and the good looking *'guera'* driver. Finally, they find someone who has seen the car today. Well, his cousin saw it parked beside a house just off Rio Grande close to the Alameda bridge. The guy tries to find his cousin, but everyone he calls has no idea where he might be. It is now Friday night and he might be anywhere.

Dave and Ernie go to the guy's apartment. Nobody is there, and neither is his car. Ernie says, "No good to drive around these dark streets without at least a general location. Let's go back to Sofie's and stay with Ben by the phone. Maybe something will break. If not, we will be back here at sunup and hope this little *'vato'* is here then. We gave enough guys that phone number for Sofie's house…maybe it will ring."

When Ernie and Dave get back, they find Tom is still there with Ben. Dave tells them they might have a lead on the car but won't know its whereabouts until morning. Ernie takes Tom through their efforts to find the car, and Tom concurs, "It is the best lead we have, and even if the guy is a no-show tomorrow, a mass search to locate the car can be started as soon as there is enough light."

Tom had updated Ben on exactly what Sofie was doing for TECH ED and why she was leaving so abruptly. Tom also told him that the FBI was closing down and arresting suspected Russian agents at various locations across the country as they speak. But he could not or would not speculate on whether that boded well for Sofie's safe return.

Tom shared with them what the FBI found in Sofie's house and held up a tiny transmitter in his fingers. "We took this out of the phone right after you left today. We don't know how long it's been there, but it is definitely a Russian design. The U.S. still has nothing this sophisticated. We also found the recording devise tucked away in a camouflage box under the front porch. There's nothing on the tape, which leads us to believe they just started listening live to get some info. They may have heard Sofie's call to Ben where she talked about leaving. The brevity with which Sofie was leaving TECH ED and that phone call probably precipitated her quick disappearance. Our guess is they need some answers from her about who she has contacted and about what."

So Ben says, "That may mean we still have time to reach her!"

Before it's even light, Dave and Ernie park outside the guy's apartment, but there is still no car and no one answers the knocks loud enough to wake the neighbors. They head back to the cousin's house to see if he knows anything. The guy that answers the door proves to be the guy they were looking for.

When Dave and Ernie tell him who they are, he says, "I heard my cousin was looking for me. I just got here a few minutes ago. I remember the car and the street where I saw it parked. It was strange because I have never seen it in this neighborhood before. I thought that house was still vacant."

Dave and Ernie find Sofie's car parked to the side of the house, just like Ronny said. They walked around the house but couldn't see or hear anything coming from the inside.

Ernie says, "I'm not waiting any longer," and picks up a bench from the back porch and busts open the door. They pause, listening for evidence that someone might be there but hear nothing. They move quietly through the house, searching for Sofie.

They find her unconscious, tied to the bed frame, and still in her sleep clothes…but she's alive. Dave finds the phone in the living room and calls Tom immediately, telling him to get the ambulance there quickly.

When Dave returns to the bedroom, Ernie says, "She's been tortured and appears to be drugged. Dave, I almost passed out when I saw her. Who could do this to someone like her? What could she possibly know?"

"Tom says the ambulance is on the way," Dave informs him, "and they will take her directly to the VA hospital. They're expecting her."

The two men look at each other in disbelief. "Tom better have some good answers," Ernie says. *"Just look what they've done to my girl!!* Let's at least get her off this bed frame and cover her with a blanket. For God's sake, Dave, she has burn marks all over and a front tooth is missing."

When they move her to the front room and place her on the couch, Sofie regains some consciousness and starts yelling profanities. She is delirious and in obvious pain. Ernie holds her and tries to comfort her, but she has no recognition of her surroundings or who is there.

Tom, Ben, and the ambulance all arrive at the same time. The medics waste no time in getting Sofie on board and en route to the VA. Ernie wanted to confront Tom for some answers but decided he would rather be with Sofie during transportation to the hospital. One of the FBI guys took Ben to the hospital, with Dave following close behind.

When Ben arrives at the hospital, Ernie is waiting just outside the emergency room. "She is in bad shape. They had to sedate her so they could evaluate her condition. The ER Doc said to give them an hour and they would have some answers for us. But for now, she is stable and in no immediate danger. They'll know more after the initial exam. He said they also need to find out what they drugged her with, and that may take some time."

Ben says, "While we have a little time, let me fill you in on the basics of what is going on." Ernie and Dave can't believe what Ben is telling them. How could something like this happen, especially to someone like their Sofie?

"Geez, Ernie, this is right out of some spy novel, and our girl Sofie was right in the middle of it. Tom and his boss are calling her a genuine hero. He says arrests are being made all over the country, thanks to Sofie's quick and decisive actions. This is some kind of big deal our girl initiated. Tom says Margaret is being debriefed and will provide more details when she arrives, which could be some time later today."

When Ben finishes, Ernie says, "Arrests. Uh! Is there any chance you and I can get to whoever did this to Sofie? For God's sake, Ben, you should have seen the way I found her. Fuck the arrests. Jail is not what these fuckers deserve. You, me, and Dave need to deliver this punishment personally."

When Margaret walks in the hospital, it is like the Red Sea parting. Hospital staff, security, and government agents, most of whom don't even recognize her, but they all step aside. She wears that commanding presence. She walks straight to Ernie and Ben and delivers a long, loving embrace.

"Boys, our daughter has started a national security firestorm that was unimaginable last week. Soviet spies are fleeing for their lives all over the country. And as rumor has it, some of our top brass are looking for alternative employment. But what price did it cost our girl?"

Maggie continued, "Tom has tried to fill me in, but he's still pretty shook-up about what happened to Sofie. I think he was looking for me to let him off the hook. But I looked him in the eye and told him he and his office definitely share some responsibility for Sofie's condition. She is a civilian, after all, and came to you. You should have anticipated the danger she was in. *'You get no cover from me.'*"

Maggie then tells them, "I am famished, so let's go get something to eat so we can be back when the doctors have something to tell us. I will fill you in on everything I know. But this is an unfolding story, and a lot is still happening."

Chapter 16

All the King Horses

Three days later, when Sofie finally regains full consciousness, her dad is the first person she sees. He is sitting in a chair, reading a book. He doesn't know she's awake. Sofie just watches him and thinks about the time she first saw him. A giant with huge hands and a tender touch gently lifting her up and keeping her safe.

She tries to talk but can only squeak, to which her dad jumps up and is immediately by her side. "Water," she says. He fills a cup and holds her head upright with that special tenderness he has. As she drinks he remembeers the first time he gave her water from his canteen.

She lays her head back down and asks, "Where am I...and how long have I been here?" Ben tells her, "Three days in the VA hospital in Albuquerque. They did a number on you, kiddo."

Sofie asks after a pause, "So what is the verdict? Am I going to make it?"

"So far, the outlook is good, but there are some concerns. I'll let the doctor explain. But for now, don't worry. Hopefully, you will improve significantly in the next few days. Let me go get your mom and Ernie. They just went to the cafeteria. I'll go find them." Before he leaves, he goes to her bedside and kisses her cheek gently.

Sofie asks with tears in her eyes, "How many times have you done that in the last three days? About a million, I'm guessing. I'm sure I felt everyone. I love you, Dad. OK, now, go get the other members of this patchwork family we have."

When her dad has left, Sofie realizes she can't move one of her legs and she feels extremely tired and queasy. She feels the darkness closing in around her. When she awakes, all three parents are in the room. They all share the same worried expression. Her dad says, "We are all so eager for you to be better. But the nurse said you may drift in and out for another day or so. We will all be back tomorrow when the Doctor makes his morning visit. Until then, just know we love you and one of us will always be near."

It has been four days of drifting in and out of awareness. Thank God they finally removed the catheter to her bladder and reduced the dosage of that awful tasting medicine to just once a day. Dad said the doctor would be here soon to explain what had happened to her and what her recovery would look like. Today marks the first day she has regained some extended cognitive thought since she was abducted.

Dad and the doctor walk in together, and the doctor asks her if it is okay for her dad to be with her while he goes over the diagnosis and prognosis with her. "Of course," says Sofie.

The doctor says, "Well, then let's begin. You are a very lucky girl just to be alive. The quick actions taken to get you here made all the difference. Ms. Wallace, there are lots of concerns here but the fact you've been poisoned tops the list. The physical abuse and the symptoms related to the injection of sodium pentothal into your body have already begun to ameliorate, but you received a lethal dose of thallium. We at the VA have seen it before as a favored poison used by the Russians, and fortunately, we quickly made the diagnosis. Your delivery into our system rather than a private hospital is making all the difference in your recovery."

Sofie says, "Doc, I don't feel so recovered or even particularly lucky at the moment. What is my immediate future going to look like?"

"The gastric lavage, forced diuresis, and the treatment with Prussian blue has stabilized your system and has lowered the levels of thallium to below the toxic level. All good news there… however, there are some physical and mental effects that will linger. The term we use is toxic neuropathy. Recovery, in both extent and time, is unpredictable, but I can assure you in just a few weeks, you will be much better. You will probably have some hair loss, so don't be too alarmed. You will also have some coordination problems for a while, but those will also get better with time. Mentally, you will probably have some periods of anxiety, possibly accompanied by bouts of paranoia. These also will abate and disappear over time. We are talking over a period of a year or two, though."

Sofie can hardly believe what the doctor is saying. Things could have gone so differently.

"They meant to kill you and damn near succeeded. You made some serious enemies for them to take such a brutal measure. Thallium poisoning causes painful and progressively debilitating effects; and if treatment is not initiated quickly, an agonizing death is unavoidable. Thank God they located you in time and got you to this hospital. That is a lot for you and your dad to take in, but let me assure you once again, you will recover to lead a normal life. However, it is possible that you may never regain the total vigor you previously experienced…Time will tell."

Ben says, "Thanks doc, and thanks to your team for everything. Let my daughter and I digest what you just told us. I assume if we have some questions, either you or your staff will be available. Oh, hey I just thought of one. When can I take her home?"

The doctor says, "About three more days here and she should be ready to leave as long as she has someone to stay with her for a while to monitor her progress."

When the doctor leaves, Sofie turns to her dad and says, "Twenty-five years after you rescued me, those fucking Russians almost killed me again. It looks like Team Wallace foiled them... again! I hate those bastards! Pardon my language."

Later that day, Sofie wakes to find her mom in the hospital bed with her, sound asleep. Mom's eyes flutter open.

"Nice nap," Sofie says.

"You scared me to death," Maggie says.

"Oh, Mom, I have too much to do to leave this world yet."

"Well," Maggie replies, "I can not tell you how many brave young soldiers said those very words and never lived to see the next sunrise. I loved those boys! *'Such optimism lost to the world forever...It broke my heart'.*"

Maggie then give Sofie a progress resport on the federal actions currently unfiolding. "Just so you know, there are now nine Russian spies in detention centers from coast to coast. Some had infiltrated our research facilities years ago. The quick action taken by you and Tom gave them no time to execute their escape plans. We are still trying to figure out how the CIA could have overlooked TECH ED all these years. They suspect there may be someone in their ranks providing cover."

"What happened to Gordon and Calvin?" Sofie asks.

Maggie says, "They are still MIA. They were obviously the first to know of your plans to *'out them.'* I know what you are thinking...but let me assure you, nobody could have resisted the torture you endured plus the truth serum injection, so don't blame yourself for giving up some information. I don't want to hear another word about it. Is that understood?!"

Over the next three days, Mom, Ernie, and Dave parade through her hospital room, all trying to be cheery and optimistic. But she can sense the uncertainty in their speech and body language. She knows they are just reflecting the uncertainty she feels about her own future. She can't wait to get home and walk the acequia with Carl.

Home at last!!! Even if she just sleeps all the time except for meals and some rehab…. walking with her *fucking cane,'* it feels good to be in her own house–in her own bed–with her little 38 in the nightstand. The doctor was right about the paranoia.

Just like the doctor promised, though, she can feel herself getting a little stronger each day now. Her dad is so good. Sleeping on the couch, the big lug, and helping her with all of her daily necessities. And, she does mean ALL.

When they were talking after dinner last night, he told her he quit his job. "I'm going to help Maggie with 'research and investigation' for upcoming legislation. Maggie explained to me she really needed someone on her staff to sort through all the lobby bullshit and why it is so important to get legislation right the first time. It didn't take me long to say yes. I've been stuck in a rut doing basically the same thing for over 25 years. Hell, I'm 50 years old, and I think a change would be invigorating. However, the thought of working for Maggie scares the shit out of me!!"

Her dad continues to update her and says, "Maggie said I could use the house in town when you can fly solo again. This way, I won't be too far away if a need arises. So it won't be hovering!!"

When her dad has finished Sofi says to him, "Don't worry Dad any reasonably sane person I know would be a little scared to work for Maggie."

A knock at the door pauses their conversation. It's Tom and his boss, Stan Bolling. They have come by to give Sofie a progress report on the demise of the Soviet spy ring she helped demolish.

Bolling tells them, "We've made twelve arrests in the U.S. with another seven fugitives identified and on the run. Eleven more are under arrest outside the U.S. Most of them were in Europe, where they were attempting the same scheme that brought them success here, until Ms. Wallace caught on to their game. However, Hargraves and Conner are still MIA. People have reported that Conner is in Israel and there have been definite sightings of Hargraves in Vietnam. It's only a matter of time until we catch them. One thing before I forget to mention it. There will be some FBI investigators contacting you as soon as you feel up to it, wanting some additional info."

Sofie asks, "Will this investigation be into my motives and actions? I have really nothing else to add to the detailed report we worked on in your office. And, obviously, you guys are having success arresting spies and covering up *'your blunders,'* so what else could I possibly contribute?"

"No, no," says Tom. "This is just standard bureau procedure to see if you recall anything since then."

Sofie replies, "I'll tell you what. If I remember anything, I will call you personally, Tom. So please, I think you have enough to keep you FBI guys busy for a while. Maybe later, OK. Now, can I get back to my afternoon nap? I've grown quite fond of them."

Tom tries to mollify the situation as the two men leave, but the air has gone out of the room and the whole situation ends rather poorly. Ben tells her that maybe she could have handled that better but just gets the cold stare from Sofie.

"I don't trust that Bolling guy. He talks way too much. Let's just let Tom deal with that bureau shit for now."

Before Sofie can get to the kitchen to make some tea, there's another knock on the door. Sofie yells out, "Tom, just go away–not now–come back later."

A voice on the other side of the door responds, "It's not Tom, it's Marvin."

Ben, who has been marveling at how his daughter handles herself in the difficult situation with the FBI, gets up to answer the door. There is a tall, wiry looking guy in the doorway. He is obviously of Native American heritage but speaks with no accent as he introduces himself.

"I am Marvin Barton, the nephew of Carl and Carla. I will be staying with them for a while, and they told me to come over here and introduce myself. And, since I love them dearly and respect their wishes, here I am on your doorstep. If the timing is bad, perhaps I can return at a more appropriate time."

Ben says, "Not to be rude, but my daughter has had a tough day already. Maybe you could return later. Why don't you come back tomorrow, if you don't mind?"

Sofie adds, "Marvin, please come back later. My Dad is right…Now is not a good time. Any relation of Carl and Carla is welcome here, so please do come back."

She faces her Dad and says, "Did you hear the way that guy spoke? His English was impeccable. I bet he is an interesting individual. I sure hope you didn't scare him off permanently, 'Mr. Protective Father Figure.'" Sofie smiles and gives her dad a kiss on the cheek as she heads to bed for a siesta.

Chapter 16 1/2

Que Sera, Sera

After another month of rehab, Sofie loses the cane and is walking the acequia with Marvin and Carl almost every day. Marvin gave her a Peterson Field Guide to Western Birds as a 'get well' gift. Her dad, not to be outdone, bought her a nice pair of Nikon Binoculars.

Aren't men something? She laughs to herself and thinks… Maybe I haven't lost all my powers after all.

More and more, it is just Sofie and Marvin walking. It has become apparent why Marvin is here. His uncle is getting weaker and weaker as the cancer progresses.

Carla has said. "There is nothing to be done. It is just a waiting game now until the end comes…as it comes for us all."

Marvin took her to the petroglyph site on the western mesa overlooking the Rio Grande Valley. Of all the pictures drawn by those ancient people, the spiral is Sofie's favorite. Marvin told her most interpretations present the spiral as a labyrinth of an individual's journey in the quest for truth.

As they stood together, admiring the view and the ancient artwork, Marvin asked her to show him where she thought she was on her own personal journey. She knew at that moment she would love him forever. They could talk and laugh about anything.

He told her about growing up on the rez near Farmington and graduating from the University of Denver, where his interests lay mainly in the sciences concerning ecology.

Growing up in the Four Corners area where coal mining, oil, and natural gas facilities abound, it wasn't particularly an overreach to speculate on whether those activities were damaging our environment permanently.

Marvin gave her some back issues of Scientific American magazine that provided evidence that burning fossil fuels for energy is indeed changing the chemistry of the atmosphere, soil, and oceans. The buffering effect can't last forever before things will get serious. Rising atmospheric temperature and the acidification of the oceans, if left unchecked, will cause irreparable damage to our ecosystems in the years to come.

Marvin tells her, "Mark my words; in fifty years, by 2020, our planet will have reached a tipping point, from a chemistry standpoint. It will be a state from which we cannot recover… unless we change our energy production to more sustainable methods. The trouble seems to be that the people who can make the most change either deny the science or they just don't care."

Author's note

Carbon pollution is changing the ocean's chemistry, slowing its ability to uptake CO2, making it more acidic and harming the marine life we depend on. The ocean has absorbed about 29 percent of global CO2 emissions since the end of the preindustrial era (usually defined as 1850 to 1900). In the past decade (from 2008-2017), we've dumped into the atmosphere about 40 gigatons of emissions of heat-trapping gases each year from the burning of fossil fuels and land-use change—or the equivalent to 252 million blue whales.

If you are wondering:

1) a gigaton is a billion metric tons (2,200 pounds each)

2) the weight of a Blue Whale is about 300,000 lbs

Data is from The Union of Concerned Scientists with a membership of over 200,000.

Sofie then tells him of her sustainable social theory she has been developing. The assassination of Martin Luther King has made her believe that if we don't live by our American Proclamation, 'All men are created equal,' we are doomed. Lasting peace is not sustainable when one group of people sees themselves as superior to their neighbors. Mass destruction weapons have proliferated in recent years. Since mankind has now developed the how…it seems only a matter of time when some race or creed of people will act out of hopelessness or fear and our world will change forever.

Sofie looks up at Marvin and says, "Gee, did we just spout a scenario of hopelessness for the whole planet and the human race to boot?"

"Oh, no!" says Marvin. "Humans are good at finding flaws, but we are also good at finding solutions. I believe when more and more people can see all the benefits that social and environmental sustainability brings, the goodness in humans will prevail... I am not sure we will live to see it through."

Marvin pauses for a moment, then says, "Hey, I just had a great idea. Why don't you come with me to Farmington next week when I'm scheduled to give an informal presentation to members of the Navajo Tribal Administration? They want me to help them understand some of the issues that might arise as a result of the coal-fired generating station that is operating nearby and scheduled for expansion."

Sofie is immediately excited. "Oh boy…road trip! A few must-do items come instantly to my mind. Can I meet your family? Can you give me a personal tour of Chaco Canyon? And can I drive you in my car?"

Sofie shares her inner thoughts for a road trip with Marvin. She tells him, I really need to do something like this. Getting out from under my Dad and Mom's constant vigil is something I am almost desperate for. I feel my sanity almost depends on it. Without you, Marvin, I know I would have sunk to some diminished mental capacity the doctor at the VA warned me about. I don't mean to be so needy….but …"Marvin, I am developing some serious feelings for you, and the thought of spending a week with just you excites me to my core. How's that for being one of those pushy modern broads you read about in the popular magazines?"

Marvin looks at her with what could be called a pregnant pause and then says, "To use one of your favorite words…WOW!"

Sofie edges into Marvin's space, looks him in the eye and almost pleads, "Please Marvin, don't make me ask!!"

Marvin then pulls her into an affectionate embrace while saying, "Sophia that is what I want too. I think we are so good together. I have never had such a longing for anyone before. The thought of just leaving on this trip without you almost paralyzed me. It's time we started experiencing *'all that life has to throw at us.'* As for your three requests, the answers are yes, yes, and yes!"

Marvin tells her, "The first 'yes' about meeting my family may be a little different than you might think. It is Navajo tradition that I must introduce you to both my maternal and paternal clans. *'That's a lot of Dine'* for an outsider to take in. AND when they find out I am presenting them a Biligaana as my partner there will be a curiosity factor making for a big turnout. Oops, did I just say 'my partner'? Is that a step forward in this relationship? Is it the right step? Please, Sofie talk to me."

She says, "It's the perfect step. Don't you dare tell my Mom and Dad until we tell your family first. I'm much too excited about meeting your family to deal with mine right now. OK, Marvin, it's time for you to tell me that everything will be fine, and your family will love me!!"

Marvin laughs, "Navajos just don't let their feelings show on the first meeting. You will not be able to tell one way or the other how they feel about you after just one meeting. However, I'm sure with your diverse background and multilingual skills, they will be very impressed. Several family members on my mother's side speak Spanish like my aunt Carla. Plus, the fact that Carla loves you like her own…you are home free, as they say."

Marvin then holds up two fingers and says, "Two things you should know though. Navajo is a clan-based society, and all members of a clan, both maternal and paternal sides, are expected to participate in the child raising duties. When my dad did not return from his deployment to the Philippines in WWII, my mom's clan, mainly Carl and Carla plus my mom and Carla's brother Sam, took over most of my parenting duties. Thank goodness. They were amazing."

The second thing is that the Navajo have a matriarchal society. So you need to impress the girls.

We will talk more about this as we travel and you get to interact with more Dine. We will probably stop by my uncle Sam's place outside of Bloomfield. He's a real character with a great sense of humor. He'll like you immediately and the word will spread quickly. He is a notorious gossip.

Sofie thoughtfully says, "My, oh my, Marvin, you have really given this whole trip some thought. Makes me feel welcomed already. I want to be a part of this. How fun! Both our families are 'non-traditional' as defined by the good old USA standards. I'm still trying to process that we both lost parents in the war. We know that loss but here we are thanks to a lot of people that care."

Sofie and Marvin have the Ford packed and ready to go first thing in the morning. Sofie decides she better call Ben and Maggie to let them in on the 'road trip' venture so they won't worry. She calls the number for Ben at her former residence but Maggie answers and there is a little awkward pause. Sofie can't help herself and jumps right in saying, "Gee, Mom, this is the third time in a row I have called Dad and you answer…What's up with you two…anything you want to let me in on??"

Maggie says in a flat tone, "Maybe a conversation for the near future. Do you need to talk with Ben?"

Sofie is sure she has now ticked her mom off somehow, but she says, "No, I just wanted to let you both know that I am taking a little trip with Marvin to Farmington where he is giving a presentation to a local group about the expansion of the Four Corners Power Plant. I feel I need some change to my recovery program plus I have been feeling so good lately that I am getting cabin fever and want some adventure to boot."

Maggie says, "Well, it sounds like you have made up your mind on this so you and Dr. Barton have a nice trip. Just call us a couple of times so we won't worry."

Now it's time for Sofie to pause and her mom jumps right back in, "You didn't know about Dr. Barton's recent doctoral degree from The University of Denver? Pretty impressive friend you have made there! I bet this will give you something to talk about on your travels. Be careful my dear, in every way, if you get my drift. You and I will sit down for a nice chat when you get back. I have things to share with you as well. Enjoy yourself, and I agree this adventure will be good for you in lots of ways. I love you and take care."

Sofie doesn't even have time to respond before the line goes dead. "What the hell!" Sofie says louder than she wanted. Something is going on with Mom lately. Maybe it is just the pressure of her job…but… something is not right. 'Nice chat?' Again… what the hell! Marvin has a PhD! Now that's big deal. How come he didn't tell me? Lots of things I don't know about are whirling around, and come to think of it, Dad has been acting different lately too.

Maybe it's just me and some delayed effect of the poison. One thing for sure is that Marvin has some explaining to do mañana. I really thought our relationship was farther along.

Chapter 17

Six Days on the Road

A golden New Mexico spring day greets Sofie as she comes out of the bedroom to put some coffee on. She opens the front door to let the day in and finds Marvin sitting on the front porch sipping coffee. She doesn't even bat an eye and says, "Why Dr. Barton, how nice to see you this morning. Let me get my coffee and I will come out to join you." Marvin's head sags a little as Sofie turns to head inside. Sofie sits on the bench next to him and without looking his direction says, "If you're ready, let's get an early start and we can find something to eat down the road."

Marvin looks at the side of her pretty face and says, "I've been meaning to tell you but…"

As his voice trails off, Sofie says, "Not like you haven't had the chance in the last couple of weeks."

There then ensues a long silence before Marvin begins. "This education thing is new to me, my family, and my friends back home. Let's just say it has changed some of my relationships and not always for the best. I have hence become a little apprehensive about calling notice to my accomplishments."

"Hold it right there, mister," says Sofie "You can't use the words 'hence and apprehensive' in the same sentence without advertising your education. There is no reason you should not have told me, and proudly, I might add. Getting a doctorate degree from a prestigious school like UD is amazing. Look, this serious relationship business is new to me too but we will never go far if we conceal our past from each other."

Silence.

"OK," Sofie says, "let's just hit the road and use the next week to get to know each other better and see where we stand when we get back. I have a lot to tell you too, that quite frankly may make you run away…I don't think so…but it might. I really want this relationship to work so let's get it off to a good start. Deal?!!"

Sofie declares herself the driver since it is her car which makes Marvin the navigator since it is his trip to his hometown. They head north on the same route Sofie had traveled to Los Alamos but, when they come to Bernalillo, they turn west on U.S. 550. Marvin has just told her the first stop will be at Nageezi to meet his uncle Charlie Atcity, from his paternal side. He and his wife Tillie run the trading post and post office there. It is a good place to get info on the road to Chaco, which can be a very bad trip at times. When they get to Nageezi, Marvin tells her they will enter Navajo time where things slow down and interactions are more drawn out. It is considered impolite to rush through a conversation or a visit. So, you can almost count on being asked to share dinner and spend the night.

When they arrive at Nageezi, Sofie is surprised to learn that they were not expected. Charlie is a tall man and very handsome, just like his nephew, while Tillie is quite diminutive. At first, they appear to be an odd couple. But after a little observation, the couple seems to almost be dancing around each other as they move about the kitchen and living area of their noticeably, small house. Tillie lets Sofie help with dinner while the two men move outside to do whatever men do out there.

Charlie tells Marvin the road into Chaco is all but impassable now and their car would never make it but they are welcome to stay in their guest house out behind the trading post. The visit is very cordial and the conversation definitely picks up as the evening progresses. Sofie continues to learn more and more about Marvin.

She can see that his aunt and uncle are very proud of him. Tillie enjoys recounting some of Marvin's impressive accomplishments.

Marvin had attended the Navajo Prep school run by the Methodists in Shiprock where he was an outstanding basketball player. Using his excellent grades and athletic skills he got a scholarship to the University of Denver. Sofie is surprised to learn that he has a professorship and teaches class at UD. Although Tillie couldn't explain why he is not on the University of Denver campus this current semester. Maybe he took some time off for Carl and Carla she thinks.

After dinner, Sofie and Marvin go to their guest quarters and sit outside under the beautiful star-lit sky that is beginning to fill with light as the waning three- quarter moon breaks over the horizon. Marvin is lost in his own thoughts and seems to be content to just sit beside Sofie. Sofie has noticed that Marvin is definitely different in Nageezi on the Navajo Reservation than in Corrales. His energy seems directed inward as if he is careful what words escape through his mouth.

Finally Marvin breaks the silence and says, "Sorry about the road to Chaco. I was really looking forward to the visit there. I have only been there twice and have not seen the canyon in about ten years." Sofie does her best Navajo impersonation and just nods her head but says nothing.

Sofie jabs Marvin in the ribs and says, "Your aunt and uncle are very nice and they are very proud of you, as am I. I knew there was something special about you since that first time you knocked on my door and my dad tried to shoo you away. I am so curious about your past exploits and family history. I would like to ask you a million questions right now but I think more than that I would like to let your personal history just play out over the next few days. Revealing bits of your home life and past experiences *'little by little'* for me to see. I have been so caught-up in my own circumstances these last few months I haven't given you even the courtesy or opportunity to delve into your biography. Now I just want to be a companion as you so graciously introduce me to your world."

Marvin smiles and says, "You have become more than a companion to me these past weeks and I think you feel the same. That is why we are here. I have gotten to know your family and friends and have been quite impressed. Now I want you to meet my family and friends. Through all of this I hope we can build a lasting bond and trust. A foundation we can build on for a life together."

"Marvin, that is the best proposal possible. No girl has ever felt so loved or wanted as I do now. I have never told a man I loved him until this moment. Now I know why…I never have!…I love you, Marvin. WOW! I can't wait to see what tomorrow brings."

Marvin and Sophie are awake early and take a short hike around the Nageezi Trading Post. The relaxing pace allows them all the time needed to take in the beautiful landscape just now catching the first rays of sun. They enjoy a leisurely breakfast with Charlie and Tillie before packing up the car and heading north to Bloomfield to meet Sam and Talulah Joe, an aunt and uncle from his maternal side of the family. Sam worked on the construction crew building the large natural gas plant at Blanco and has worked for El Paso Natural Gas ever since.

They arrive at Sam and Talulah Joe's home on the San Juan River at noon on a Sunday. There are already quite a few people there and the beautiful outdoor dining area has been set up in honor of their arrival.

Sofie finds that Sam and Tully are far less traditional than were Charlie and Tillie. They have been living off the reservation for quite some time and Sam works as an electrician at the EPNG plant.

Everyone makes a big fuss when they arrive and Sofie can hear three languages being spoke from the people at the gathering, and just like Marvin had told her, they are impressed with her Spanish fluency.

It is a joy-filled afternoon in a beautiful setting and ends quite predictably with the men sitting together, talking sports, rodeo, and farming. The children present are involved in some games and are completely self-entertained while Sofie is fielding a variety of questions about the status of her relationship with Marvin. Some questions seem very nosey and little indulgent. She tries to deflect from answering with some humor, but they persist to the point where she finally smiles and says, "That is none of your business," at which everyone has a big laugh and moves on to other topics. She learns more and more about Marvin and how highly he is regarded among his family and community.

When Sofie and Marvin finally retire to their bungalow for the evening and are sitting outside, Sofie asks him, "Just what the hell are you meeting with this group of people about on Tuesday? I gather from snippets of conversation I overheard that it seems somewhat important."

"Well, let's go inside, and I will show you the focal point of my talk. It centers on four overhead transparencies I have created. Let me go to the car to get my briefcase, and I'll meet you back in the house."

Marvin sits down at the small dining table next to Sofie and retrieves the transparencies from his briefcase. "I'm assuming you have had enough science and chemistry basics to follow along. In fact, this may be a good opportunity to evaluate the academic level of the material and whether it matches the level of my audience. They will be men of education, such as yourself, with varying degrees of scientific knowledge. It will be good for me to see your reaction and hear your critique."

While Marvin sets up his presentation, he gives Sofie the basics. Several large industries had been developed in and around Navajo land in the past several years and all seem intent on expansion. Some of the chapter leaders were hearing concerns from their community about the waste products and long-term affects these industries might impose. They knew I had some education in this field and asked me to help them with understanding what the long-term ramifications might entail.

"My God, Marvin, you sure can string the words together, can't you? My guess is the presentation might be more productive if you just took it down an intellectual notch. Even though I am sure these are very smart men, it is not a university setting."

"OK," Marvin responds. "I am sure that's good advice. The audience for this presentation includes some industrial personnel, Tribal administrators and a few chapter house leaders. All are quite intelligent, but some of them I know will need this review of basic science and how it relates to fossil resource management. It is precisely why they asked me to speak. The industrial revolution has been evolving for over 200 years now. But only since WWII has the entire globe gone on a modernization binge, and the search for energy sources is driving civilization to burn more and more fossil fuels. Research in this area started before the 1950's. However, the current research of the 1960's is revealing that serious damage is being done to our planet and may create dangerous conditions as soon as the end of this millennium. Those conditions, if not addressed now, will alter human behavior and possibly render some geographic zones uninhabitable."

Marvin shows Sofie his first overhead transparency for his presentation.

First Transparency

The Carbon Cycle

Carbon is one of the most common elements found in living organisms. Chains of carbon molecules form the backbone of many organic molecules, mainly:

Carbohydrates ——— Sugars

Amino Acids ———— Proteins

Lypids ——— Fats

Carbon is constantly cycling between living organisms and the atmosphere. The movement of carbon through the environment is called **The Carbon Cycle.**

Living organisms cannot make their own carbon, so they need some metabolic processes to get carbon into their systems.

PHOTOSYNTHESIS

In the atmosphere, carbon is in the form of carbon dioxide gas (CO_2). Recall that plants and other producers capture the carbon dioxide and convert it into the carbohydrate glucose ($C_6H_{12}O_6$) through the process of **photosynthesis.** Thus the energy from the sun is stored in the form of glucose. The chemical equation is

$$6CO_2 + 6H_2O \rightarrow C_6H_{12}O_6 + 6O_2$$

(carbon dioxide + water -> glucose + oxygen)

RESPIRATION

As animals eat plants or other animals, they gain the carbon from those organisms. Through their metabolic process of **respiration,** the carbon is then returned to the atmosphere as CO_2. Respiration is the reverse of photosynthesis and provides animals with the energy they require. The cycle is then complete.

$$C_6H_{12}O_6 + 6O_2 \rightarrow 6CO_2 + 6H_2O$$

(glucose + oxygen -> carbon dioxide + water)

Carbon is also released to the biosphere as an organism dies and decomposes. In addition, the carbon bound up in living organisms can also be returned to the atmosphere though destructive events like fire. <u>Cellular respiration and photosynthesis</u> can be described as a cycle. Photosynthesis uses carbon dioxide and water with energy from the sun to make glucose and oxygen. Then respiration takes the glucose and oxygen to make carbon dioxide and water completing the cycle.

"I want the second transparency to emphasize the cycling of carbon that is happening at this very moment has been happening for millions of years and has created a stable environment. Plants and animals have evolved to use all the available resources including carbon. The key components in our atmosphere today in relation to the carbon cycle are oxygen at a concentration of 20.95% and CO2 at .032% of the gases in the atmosphere."

Second Transparency

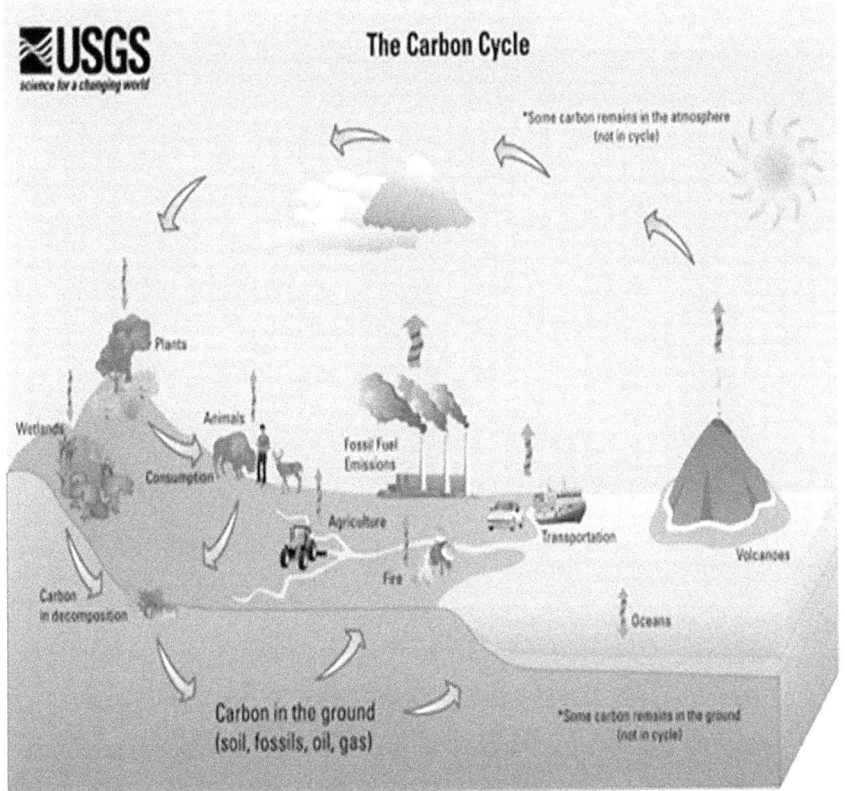

Plant photosynthesis and animal respiration keep the balance of the two components close to these levels at all times and has done so for millions of years. This historical balance has insured stability and predictability to the flora and fauna of our planet.

"Before I present the third transparency, I want to make it clear to all that there is a huge bank of carbon in the geosphere that has been '*isolated*' from the evolutionary processes in play today."

"I have a suggestion here," Sofie says. "As an example of the isolated carbon in the geosphere I'm thinking that the coal and oil reserves found below the earth's surface right here under Navajo Land… '*is that isolated bank of carbon*'. That should really get their attention."

Third Transparency

Millions of years ago in the Carboniferous period (362- 286 million years ago) there were so many dead plants and animals (primarily invertebrates) that they could not completely decompose before they were buried. They were covered over by soil or sand, tar or ice even before the age of dinosaurs (250 million years ago). These dead plants and animals are organic matter made out of cells full of carbon-containing compounds (carbohydrates, lipids, proteins, and nucleic acids).

What happened to all this carbon?

When organic matter is under pressure for millions of years, it forms '**fossil fuels.**' Fossil fuels present themselves today as coal, oil, and natural gas.

As seen on the previous transparency, when humans dig up and use fossil fuels, we have an impact on the carbon cycle.

This carbon would never be introduced to the atmosphere and therefore never influence the carbon cycle without intervention by humans. The burning of fossil fuels releases more carbon dioxide into the atmosphere than is used by photosynthesis.

So, there is more carbon dioxide entering the atmosphere than is coming out of it.

This carbon dioxide is referred to as a **greenhouse gas.** The carbon dioxide gas lets in light energy but does not let heat escape, much like the panes of a greenhouse.

To end my presentation I'll emphasize these points on a fourth transparency.

Fourth Transparency

* All energy for life comes from the sun.

* Plants use the photosynthetic metabolic process to store this energy in their structures. Complex carbon compounds are formed in the plants with that energy stored in their molecular structure.

* This energy can be regained using the respiratory process of animals that break the complex molecules back to their simpler forms for reuse in the photosynthetic process again. Hence the cycle continues.

*This cycling of carbon has been consistent enough over the past millions of years to produce a stable environment for evolution to continue in a predictable manner. It is only recently that humans have developed the technology to disrupt this pattern by bringing into play literally a gigaton of carbon that was unreachable to the photosynthetic process in the past.

*The cycling process has now been overwhelmed with all the CO2 discharged into the atmosphere when fossil fuels are burned. Therefore, it is now lingering in our biosphere.... in the atmosphere, in the oceans and in the soil.

This excess carbon will alter our planet in ways that are unpredictable today. But we know the changes will be profound without some concerted effort to limit their emissions.

Sofie looks at him and says "My-oh-my, Dr. Barton, that ought to raise some questions in this meeting of yours. I really like the summary on a final transparency to give your audience some time to absorb the totality of your talk."

Marvin acknowledges that a fourth transparency really does solidified the presentation and says he glad he decided to include it in written form rather than just verbally summarizing such a complicated subject.

"Well, I hope you don't want me to make too many more changes in the presentation because it is way too late for much more. I was hoping to just WOW you with my brains and charm and you would say, 'That's just great the way it is'."

"Well, mission accomplished!" says Sofie. "I do have one suggestion if you haven't already thought of it though. Give all those in attendance a hand out of the transparencies you are using. In the technical presentations that I have attended, they tend to be very helpful and provide a perfect place for note taking. Other than that, I did think it was quite organized and very concise, although it is a shame to waste all your charm and looks on a bunch of middle-aged men. Maybe I ought to tag along just to bolster your male ego if nothing else."

Marvin can't tell whether she is serious or not so he just silently sits there waiting for whatever comes next. No other words were spoken even when they relaxed in bed next to each other enjoying the silence of the San Juan Valley.

Sofie did tag along for the drive but went to see the generating plant which is the focal point of this big meeting, while Marvin gave his presentation.

When Sofie returned, Marvin was waiting for her just inside the Shiprock High School library with three other Dine. They were some relatives of Marvin and couldn't resist meeting Marvin's biligaana partner. They all exchanged polite greetings, and it was quite obvious they were all very proud of Marvin and his accomplishments.

As they headed back to Sam and Talulah's place in Bloomfield, Marvin tells her there has been a slight change of plans and one of the Tribal Administrators could not attend the meeting. He sent word that he would like to visit with me tomorrow at his office in Window Rock and be briefed on how the meeting went. So we will need to leave a little early tomorrow to make it to Window Rock in time to meet my Uncle Ray before he leaves the office at three.

Sofie asks, "So you have an uncle high-up enough in the Tribal administration that he could request a briefing on a meeting he missed?"

"Yeah," Marvin says, "Uncle Ray is kinda high- up, but I haven't seen him in a while, and besides, I would really like him to meet you. So off we go mañana. What did you do while I was in the meeting?"

Sofie tells him of her self-tour of the area around the power generating station and adjacent Navajo coal mine and railroad operation. "That is some operation they have with the coal being mined that close to the generating plant. Kind of messy and dirty up there, and I'm guessing some concerns related to that surfaced in your meeting." (See Appendix E)

Marvin nodded in the affirmative but made no further comment.

Chapter 18

It's a New Dawn and a New Day and I'm Feeling Good

The next morning, Marvin and Sofie are in the car after Tally fixed them a parting meal to tide them over for their trip across the reservation. Window Rock is the capital of the Navajo Nation and was located right on the Arizona-New Mexico border, halfway between Gallup and Ganado, about a three hour drive from Bloomfield.

Marvin tells her there is no other capital in all the world more beautiful than Window Rock with magnificent red bluffs and rock formations. "Nothing even comes close," he says. "I think they just built a new motel there, and they even have a restaurant that people say is very good. My uncle can sometimes get pretty busy and may not have time to entertain us at his house in the Navajo way. So if this motel looks good, we can stay there or move on to Gallup and stay at the El Rancho. We will get to Window Rock in plenty of time to eat and do a little sightseeing. I can't wait to show you around. I don't get to Window Rock often, so I like to take it all in when I do."

After being tourists for a couple of hours, with Marvin driving Sofie's car for the first time, they pull up in front of the Tribal Administrative offices. Sofie looks across the parking lot and spots a cherry 57 Chevy painted yellow. She tells Marvin, "My uncle Ernest has one just like that down in Grant County." When they enter the offices, the receptionist and Marvin greet each other like old friends and they chat partly in Navajo and partly in English. Finally, she tells Marvin, "The Chairman is off the phone, so you can head back to the conference room. I think everyone is already there by now."

Sofie grabs Marvin quickly and firmly yanks him around to face her. Her voice gets louder than she intended.

'Just stop right there, mister.' I'm not walking through that door and finding out that your uncle Ray is none other than Raymond Nakai, am I?

Marvin, you've got to stop with this modest, unassuming way you have been with me…AND I mean it!!! It may be fine with others, Dr. Barton, but not with your supposed partner… companion… bride…whatever we are at the moment.

Marvin hangs his head for a moment then replies, "OK… OK! Sophia this is all new to me…being involved with someone I am seriously in love with. I guess my thinking is a little off, but I am beginning see that you love me too and I need to open up more. Can we just get through this meeting and talk about this later tonight? Ray is dying to meet you after all the favorable reports from the other family members we have been staying with along our journey."

As they open the door, the first person Sofie sees is Dad and then Maggie. The room is completely filled with all her family. Even Dave is there. She literally almost faints as she leans on Marvin for support.

Maggie says, "You two having a little lovers spat in the hallway out there?…Nothin' serious, I hope."

The only thing Sofie can say at the moment is, *"What the hell!"*

Her grandpa and Dave are sitting next to each other and have these big, huge grins. Marvin locks eyes with Raymond who just shrugs like he has no control over the situation. Ben grins and gets up to guide them to the two chairs nearest the door as if everything is falling into place as planned.

Ben gives Marvin a firm handshake and Sofie a fatherly hug. He whispers to them and quietly says, "Don't worry, this is not all about you."

Raymond quickly adds, "But the timing of all of this is quite fascinating, and it has been exciting and fun to help coordinate. I think now, though, I will let Margaret take charge of this gathering since she is the one that initiated the original plan. You two youngsters don't need to worry. This is not a hostile Indian ambush but a joyous occasion. The fact that you are totally surprised is a testament to how Navajos can keep a secret. No one along your journey through Navajo Land must have given you even a clue as to why you two are here. Take it away, Margaret."

All eyes turn to Margaret who is sitting next to Ben, and Sofie notices for the first time they are sitting very close together and are holding hands.

Maggie wastes no time looking Sofie square in the eye and then she and Ben say together like it was rehearsed, "We are getting married."

For the second time in just minutes, Sofie thinks she might faint. Luckily she is sitting down and holding on to Marvin. Everyone in the room cheers and says, "It's about time!"

Maggie holds her hands up to calm everyone down. "Let me do a little explaining here to remove any speculation. Ben and I have loved each other for a long time now, but I came to depend on him more and more for advice and moral support since I became a state representative. And our love seemed to intensify after what happened to Sofie and the whole spy ordeal."

Ben puts his arm around Maggie and says, "Sofie seems to be in such a good place for the first time since the poisoning attack, and her relationship with Marvin is going to become permanent if I am to believe my observations and the accounts from Marvin's family. All this taken into account, Maggie and I just don't want to wait any longer."

Sofie slowly regains some focus and says, "OK. That explains why you are holding hands and all; but what the hell are you doing here in Window Rock?"

Maggie jumps back in, "That one is easy to explain. Ray and I have been friends since I first campaigned for office back years ago, and we have continually been in touch over the years regarding the amount and nature of all the new industry happening across the Reservation. So, when we needed someone to perform a quiet family wedding away from the maddening crowds, I asked Ray if he would do this for us. And he has so graciously said yes."

Ray turns to Marvin and Sofie, "Let me intervene here, if I might. Margaret called a few months back as a concerned mother about her daughter who was developing quite a close friendship with a Navajo man and wanted to know if I knew anything about a Marvin Barton. *'Now, is that some coincidence for you or what?!'* We had the biggest laugh over the phone and neither one of us could get a word in for all of the questions being asked back and forth. The timing is another piece of fate. Margaret and Ben were just going to tell you about their wedding plans when they found out about the reservation tour you two were planning. So the timing was just impossible to ignore and now the wedding plans are set. The coordination to make this event happen with your arrival here was no small feat, I can guarantee you that. Ella is not here today because she is cooking and finishing the final details for the wedding tomorrow at a friend's house just outside of town. It is a beautiful site and has been used for occasions like this many times. It will be perfect."

Margaret and Ray look at each other for a moment and the Ray nods to Maggie in the Navajo way by lifting his chin in her direction. She stands to command the attention of all in the room and states, "The wedding is not the primary reason for this gathering. So, with Chairman Nakai's permission, I will take the lead in revealing some of the plans we have been formulating. After much discussion with my future husband and Chairman Nakai, I will not seek re-election in the upcoming year. Instead, with my lead, my law firm will be retained on a permanent basis by the Navajo tribe, and I will represent them in dealing with the many exciting and innovative changes happening on the reservation. And you all will come to see, as I have, Chairman Nakai is a true visionary leader. Our country is in dire need of good leadership at this point in our nation's democratic growth. I can still recall the moment I recognized Raymond was a man I wanted as a friend and ally. He was delivering one of his famous speeches. It was at the Governor's Interstate Indian Council in 1964. In it, he said, '*Getting together is a beginning, keeping together is progress, working together is success.*' So that little sidelight about my future is just a small part of the Chairman's plans, and now I will let him detail some of the vision he has. So, Chairman, the audience is all yours."

Raymond comes to his feet and chuckles to himself and says to all in the room, "I am sure the parties in this room who thought this was just going to be a wedding event are saying to themselves, '*What the heck did I get myself in the middle of?*' But everyone in this room loves Margaret and Ben, so we just decided to use you all as a test audience and gauge your reactions to all of this restructuring– whether it be personal or political."

The Chairman pauses for effect before he continues, "A little background might be in order here for those not familiar with the recent developments happening all over our beautiful Navajo Nation. There has been a big effort to bring industry to the reservation and this has split our people into basically two factions."

He continues, "As you can imagine …One side says *'the white man is doing it all again!'* They give us Natives what appears to be worthless land then discover some value they did not know existed at the time, like the Dakotas with gold or Oklahoma with oil. The exploitation that followed has had a devastating affect on the resident Natives. The other side says *'what the heck,* I finally got a good paying job with El Paso Gas, and I ain't going back."… *.I am tired of living in poverty.*

"So basically you have the traditionalists who believe in the old way of life and don't want that to change… The land and respect for our home should be preserved at all cost has become their mantra. And on the other side is the younger members of our community who want to move into the 20th century with indoor toilets, running water, electricity and a paycheck. In addressing this dilemma, some titanic battles have been fought both in and out of Tribal Council Chambers. However, with my re-election, a progressive agenda is now the course of action throughout the Navajo Nation. That course then prompted my call to Representative Beltran seeking some advice from an old friend, as I like to do. During those talks, I voiced my concern about all the industries that are basically 'invading' the reservation. The list included some big names such as:

Peabody Coal
Public utility companies
Various oil company interests
Kerr-McGee uranium
Natural Gas exploration/transportation companies
United Nuclear Corporation
Black Mesa Pipeline

These companies have employed many Dine' workers to help them generate enormous profits while the Navajo Nation still remains well below the poverty level. Things must change. We need to negotiate better contracts with the companies which will benefit the Navajo Nation and yet protect our sacred relationship to the land and people."

I will make an obviouss understatement here by saying, "This is an immense undertaking. These companies are already entrenched on our land with existing agreements to do business with what is just minimal compensation to the Navajo people, only a few hourly wage jobs without much future."

At this point, Ernie cannot contain himself any longer and says loudly with a distinct edge to his voice, "I have lived that existence, and I know the damage it can do to your spirit. Those young men holding those hourly wage jobs love the newness of the paycheck but will soon become frustrated and angry when they realize how expendable they are at the whims of management."

"Mr. Polanco, I thought that might rouse your Mexican ire," says Raymond with a note of camaraderie in his voice.

"Margaret, Ben, and I have discussed the events that happened in Grant County many times, and it is one of the primary points in my case to convince Ms. Beltran to help us gain some higher ground in our contractual relations with these big corporations. I would also like to take a moment to thank Ben for agreeing to help us with our effort to understand the agendas of large corporations and how they might react to contract changes and labor force demands. His long-term service in management has already helped us strategize how we will initially proceed. Plus, he did give up his recent employment to join forces with Margaret's law firm."

"That brings us to the final agenda item of this meeting before we get to the wedding plans. The Tribal council would never agree to let a bilagaana have the authority to solely represent our interests in these issues, so I did not even propose that approach. Instead, the council and I have agreed to create a new position that will report directly to the chairman and must attend all regular council meetings. The title of that position will be Director of Natural Resources, and the person we have nominated to head up that new division is Marvin."

Sofie's head snaps around to face Marvin, and she says, "*For God's sake. I just give up!!*' It's a good thing I love you, Marvin, because a girl can only take so many twists and turns in her life without someone to lean on."

Marvin has a stunned look on his face as he looks at his uncle. Raymond has the soft Navajo grin of someone who has just sprung a well-laid trap and the prey has no escape route. Uncle Ray broadens his grin and tells Sofie, "This is the first Marvin has been informed of what his Nation expects of him and his beautiful education, so go easy on him. This one is on me and your parents."

Isidro is watching his granddaughter's anxiety build over the course of this gathering and is worried about the long lasting affects of poisoning. Before anyone can utter another word he says, "Pardon me Chairman, but there is one more agenda item that needs some attention here. The people in this room are the ones needing to hear the plans Sofie and I have been working on. You guys aren't the only ones who can keep secrets. We have kept it to ourselves until we gathered all the research data necessary to make the final decision to proceed with our venture".

This announcement has had the perfect reaction Isidro wanted. Sofie is now beaming and looking directly at him with '*I love you*' written all over her face. Isidro asks Sofie if she wants to introduce their plans. She shakes her head and says, "*It's all yours, Grandpa*".

Isidro reaches for his wife's hand as he begins to talk, "The idea came to me while I was attending one of those local grange meetings and I just could not get it out of my head."

Sofie is loving the way he is drawing this out.

"So, Yoli and I drove up to see Sofie during her recovery to discuss the idea and see if she was interested. Well, the initial phase of the plan came back from the university lab with a very favorable report."

Bless my Grandpa, thinks Sofie.

Margaret just blurts out, "For heavens sake, Dad, just come out with it already. We are all dying here!!"

Yoli just says, "Patience, mija."

Everyone is just staring back and forth between Sofie and her grandparents. Isidro leans into the table and says to them, "May I continue with my story now?"

"Well, as I was saying before I was so abruptly interrupted, I just picked up the results for phase two of our project on the way up here and there is nothing to prevent us from proceeding. Sofie and I have just purchased ten acres of good farm land not 1/4 mile from her house in Corrales, and I plan to put the sign up on my way home announcing the future location– Vino Encanto."

"New Mexico State ordered both merlot and pinot noir varietal cuttings when the soil samples results were favorable. Sofie knows enough chemistry and I know enough about farming that we both are confident this venture will be successful."

At that, Isidro leans back in his chair with a smug look on his face that all but shouts out '*How's that for some family news!*'

Marvin says, "*My-oh-my…how's that for some non-disclosure.*"

Chapter 19

Old Man River

It is a particularly beautiful spring morning as Sofie and Marvin walk beside the river that has drawn generations of inhabitants to her banks. It has defined New Mexico history since the earliest people came from the north in prehistoric times. Neither she nor Marvin has said a word since they began their walk, and Sofie is thinking about her new duties as mayordomo. Taking over from Carl and Carla has had some challenges. No woman has done this before and no one so youthful and new to the area as well. Although she hated to do it, she finally got Isidro to walk with her a couple of times on his last visit and that seems to have swayed the old-timers that had been voting against her. The landowners' meeting went well last night. Sophie had properly identified the repairs that were needed along with developing a maintenance schedule through the irrigation season. Her pay is not much but every penny counts since work on 'Vino Encanto' has started. Renovating those old buildings on the new property to house the winemaking equipment has turned into a money pit. Isidro has found a young couple to come live and work on the property while they work through the complicated H-2A visa procedures that just recently took the place of the Bracero program that had guided immigrant labor actions along the Mexican Border for two decades. Isidro has told her the young couple has had some experience with growing grapes, plus they remind him of when he and Yoli came to the U.S. all those 50 years ago.

How they are going to pay for all of this is a little up in the air at the moment. But as Sofie has seen, her family is quite resourceful and she is confident a path forward will materialize, somehow. On a brighter note, Isidro is bringing up the cuttings for planting along with some labor to help as well. The cuttings have done well in the hydroponic phase and are now ready to plant as soon as the soil is prepared properly and the irrigation is in place. Isidro is amazing. Getting this venture off the ground has taken a lot of time, energy, and resources. At 70+ years, he has been there every step of the way. They have split the responsibilities. He will handle the farming and she will be in charge of winemaking.

Marvin breaks the silence and she pushes her thoughts aside. He asks her, "What you thinking so intently about anyway?"

Sofie leans into him and tells him her thoughts had just drifted back to the wedding. "The setting, in the natural beauty of that canyon with the timeless red walls, emitted an aura that made me realize my mom and dad have been together for a really long time in spirit, although, not always physically side by side. I am so happy that now they are truly bonded in love that will last for eternity. Your uncle conducted the perfect ceremony. You told me about how important the number four is to the Navajo and how it would be included in the ceremony. Everyone in attendance had dressed using their own creation of the four colors; black, white, blue or yellow. Raymond also referenced the four seasons and the four directions accentuating the everlasting earth we inhabit. Wasn't Mom just stunning in that yellow dress beside my handsome father in a black suit with a the turquoise bolo?! I didn't start crying until your cousin Carlos started playing the flute and the sound echoed off the cliffs. By the time they brought out the gourd filled with water to wash each others hands for the purification, I could hardly stand up...as you know."

"I became so caught up in the emotion of that moment I could not focus on the ending of the ceremony when your uncle talked about the most important word in the Navajo language, 'Hozho.'"

When you said it refers to the balance one must have with life and can be translated as.. peace, balance, beauty, and harmony, it seemed like the perfect sentiment for a wedding. His final blessing to my parents about following the 'Beauty Trail' was so eloquent. I'm glad it was written on the program. It has become my guiding philosophy since that day."

"May it be beautiful before me. May it be beautiful behind me. May it be beautiful above me. May it be beautiful below me. May I walk in beauty."

"Marvin, I want our wedding to feel like we are bound for eternity…like theirs. We can never duplicate that ceremony and I don't want to even try. Maybe something in Grant County, there is plenty of beauty there to go around for sure. Anyway, you asked."

The Nine Commandments

Authors Final Note

This fictional story basically throws people into events in New Mexico that happened from the time surrounding statehood in 1912 until about 1970. So basically a 60- year period. I grew up in Grant County and even worked at the Empire Zinc Mine in Hanover when I was just out of high school in 1966. I also travelled the Navajo Reservation when I worked for El Paso Natural Gas Company in the late 70's through the 80's. I got to know a few of the Dine' that worked at the EPNG facilities. I was always struck by their sense of humor and the thought that they always knew more than I did. Over the years I have come to realize New Mexico is a wonderful compilation of many cultures with deep roots in this wonderful place.

My grandmother moved to Grant County just after statehood all by herself to treat 'consumption' in one of the sanitoriums. She was soon followed by her two older sisters (My Great Aunts). My grandmother began teaching grade school and soon married into the Watkins Clan. My mom was born soon after and lived her whole life in Grant County. She was elected as county treasurer and served in that capacity until her untimely death.

Also, my dad was a soldier in WWII stationed in the Philippines. He was taken as a prisoner of war and spent the next 3 years in various Japanese prison camps until the Atomic bombs were dropped.

My wife is also a native New Mexican. Her uncle served alongside my Dad and was a prisoner as well. However, we didn't know that until we met years later in high school.

Finally, one thing I wanted to note in writing this book was that I discovered what a remarkable man Raymond Nakai was. When he took office in the early 60's, the Navajo Nation was in serious turmoil as a result of all the new industry moving to Navajo land. The conflict of the modern vs. the tradition was not unlike what we *continually see through out our country and even world wide. His approach to that dilemma is documented in an appendix at the end of this manuscript where he delivers a State of the Union address to the tribal council. Here is a quote that embodies his leadership and should be a mantra for all leaders.*

'Only he who makes his people strong is strong, and only he who rules free men is great.'

The appendix A that follows is a speech he gave to the tribal council in 1966. A kind of a 'state of the union address,' if you will. It is a document that should serve all free men who attempt self-government.

Acknowledgement

Many people helped me with this effort including best friends Mary Lou Morrow and John Arsola. First readers with valuable incite were Judy Ringnell and Jenny Petty. Robbin Freeman took a mess of sentences and tenses and edited that into a readable manuscript. And, what about that jacket cover my friend Fred Barraza designed! His wife Jenny, and longtime friend of mine, is the gal standing beside the car. Finally my wife, the incredible Joanne provided her talents, patience, and love to get this over the finish line.

Jason Collins and the team at Citi of Books put the finishing touches and introduced me to a whole new world.

This is a fictitious book surrounding historical events that took place in New Mexico. Any foul balls in these pages are off my bat. I am a scientist by nature and education. Not much of a literary bent to me. I loved doing the research and fitting it into the story.

Hope you enjoyed it!!!

Appendix A

SPEECH OF RAYMOND NAKAI CHAIRMAN OF THE NAVAJO TRIBAL COUNCIL

It was Emerson who wrote these words:

"The world is a proud places
Peopled with men of positive quality,
With heroes and demi-gods standing around us,
Who will not let us sleep."

Yes, here in our Navajo Reservation we find that we have men of negative as well as of positive quality. I suppose we have our cowards and demi- demons as well as our heroes and Demi-gods. For those of you who have been with us here on the Navajo Reservation for a short period of time, our Navajo world might seem an unfamiliar one, in some ways a frightening place, and as Emerson stated you will soon find, as we have found that we cannot, indeed we dare not SLEEP.

Now, some of the things that I will say might seem to be strange words coming from the leader of the Navajo people, but my remarks have a purpose, and that is, unless we speak frankly to those whose friendship and assistance we seek, we will never get to the heart of the problems facing our Navajo people. For instance, there are some so-called Navajo leaders and their non-Indian advisors who have been engaged over a number of years in much unseemly name-calling, accusation, and blind striking-out at any visible target. I ask the question: Could it be that they are trying to relieve their disappointment and salve their wonder pride? Whatever the reason, it must be plain to them, as it is plain to most of us that the only ones who are the ultimate losers in this waste of time and energies, are our Navajo people who are in so great need of the good will and assistance from all of us. For the truth of the mater is that there is so much to be done, so much that has been left undone, so much that you as our missionaries, as the messengers of God among us, can do and do well, for you are fortunate to be dealing with our Navajos in the grass-roots level. The reason I know that you can do a good job is that we here in Navajoland already have witnessed and profited from the efforts of your colleagues of the past. But let me throw out one thought of caution. The Navajo world and its people are changing and the approach you will have to use in assisting us, must also change to meet the present needs of the Navajo citizen in the mid-60's.

We all know that a peculiar combination of circumstances thrusted many of our Navajo citizens into a position in the white man's world before many of us were ready to fully understand and assume this new way of life.

These experiences can be overwhelming in many ways. For instance, certain age groups of Navajos who under present circumstances must work and compete with their non-Indian brothers, are finding themselves ill- prepared with respect to the position which they would like to assume in our so-called modern world. With some of our older age groups, many of the ways of life and values which they hold dear will not die and we have to understand this and find ways to reconcile their values and those of the outside world if we are going to be able to help this most important group of our Navajo citizens. I do not have any sympathy with those who believe that we should write-off this group of our Navajo population, and concentrate only on the so-called anglonized-youth-groups of Navajos. When this present chapter of our Navajo history is finally completed, it might well be that our older Navajos held the key to a proper transition of our citizens into the white man's world. For this transition aspect of our life is admittedly enormously complicated by emotion, culture and also with the unsolved social problem of prejudice.

My administration has continued to make tremendous strides towards providing a better life for our citizens, but the task remains unfinished. For those of you who may choose to assist us in this matter you will soon find that it is very complicated and that many imperfections to our approach must still be eliminated. One, which I have found very trying as Chairman of the Navajo Tribe, but which I am glad to meet as a necessary challenge, is that the activities of Window Rock, our Navajo Capital, have suddenly been placed by everyone in the spotlight; including those trying to make personal gains at the sacrifices of our Navajo people. They are ready to point the most b brilliant spotlight on activities of my administration which have of necessity remained unfinished , and we have gotten little help from those who now come in sheep clothing, ready to exploit. During this election year, our efforts will be relative to many of our long range programs.

This is not to suggest that you and I are incapable of meeting the challenge confronting us, and that we should throw up our hands in resignation because of these handicaps under which we labor. It is to suggest that in preparing to face our responsibilities, we in our Navajo government, should not overlook the assistance that can be put in good use. From the Federal and State agencies, and of course, that to be performed by you, our missionaries here in our Reservation.

All these groups have done a great deal in many important areas of Navajo life. But suddenly, as witnessed by these gatherings, we are painfully aware that we have not done enough. We have not been asleep, but perhaps we have been drowsing. Our approach still reflects a great deal of unimaginative acton, which starts with great promise but always seemed to stop short of the hogan door. Our programs must of necessity be concentrated and geared to the most urgent needs of our Navajo people in this day and age - this need is not to be found in Washington, Gallup or Window Rock, but rather out in the field, in the hogans, where the Navajo lives, where you my dear friends have and must continue to do your great work among the people.

Since this gathering will devote much time to a discussion of what should be done in this critical situation, it would be unbecoming to attempt to offer the answers now, even if I were qualified to offer them. But perhaps you will consider a few general suggestions, which are offered as such:

It should first of all be noted that many of these suggestions will require the cooperative help from the Tribe and the Federal government but in my opinion the missions on our Reservation, can and should play the leading part in initiating and carrying many of these programs through.

I start by suggesting that we greatly expand our programs in adults education in hope of kindling and increasing awareness of the importance of our Navajo responsibility in the overall American society. All concerned would then learn the necessity of greater willingness to make necessary sacrifices to meet the challenge of the times. This will not be an easy undertaking, but crucial questions are being posed to our Navajo citizens every day and we cannot wait for decisions until years from now when today's students will have risen to the present positions of their non- Indian brothers. By then, it will be too late.

The second suggestion is tendered with full recognition of the delicate relationship involved. It is that we improve our working understandings among the Federal, State, Tribal and missionary activities. Our Navajos are more and more looking to us with a critical eye and are as anxious as we are to correct the deficiency that there is much talk and planning, but little true action that permits and talked about benefits to reach the hogan door. We can make all our tasks far easier if we consider the problems and sincere efforts of those of other groups.

There may be disagreements among us as to some of our methods but about our objectives there should be no disagreement.

Whether it be the State, Federal Government, Tribal or missionary activities, or any other large or small group each should be given the opportunity to take its place and each permitted to contribute to the strength of our efforts and it shall be repaid by giving strength to our Nation. I believe flexibility, adaptability and a wide range of programs to be far superior to reigning uniformity. The task before us I to prove the validity of our belief.

The part that our missionary friends can play is many fold. For not only can you help our people in the local level where much help is needed in their social and economic needs, but we know that this will be done in a Godly way that will preserve truth, impart truth, discover truth. On the latter point, we must not barter away our birth-right for the temporary advantage of just becoming like our non-Indian brothers. Let us devote our major efforts to good spiritual teaching and to the discovery of new knowledge upon which all material progress depends.

Some of you might be with us for the first time may say that if the Navajos, through their own tribal government and with the assistance of the Federal Bureaus have come so far in so short a time under such handicaps, what could we do? With your great advantages, if you chose to dedicate your energies, your resources and your intelligence to the task of regaining confidence in the area that should by all measures be your own the Spiritual side of all our lives, the possibilities are unlimited. The more optimistic among us feel with certainty that if we have enough moral courage and conviction, we cannot only catch up with our non- Indian neighbor boss: we can pass them and take a commanding lead in many fields which our Indian forefathers left as our heritage.

Motivating the Navajos, specially our Navajo youth to develop that necessary moral and spiritual courage, that necessary conviction, should be part of our task. For it will develop into a bright gleam of hope that should we succeed, we could bring to all the Navajos, and for that matter to all American Indians throughout our great Country, the well- being, the shining future that have through the ages been the persisting dream of mankind. This must certainly be the destiny intended by our Creator for those he made in His own image. Should we fail that gleam of hope may flicker and go out for another thousand years.

My own conviction, based partly on fact, partly on faith, is that we will succeed. I am encouraged in this belief by this Convocation and the feeling of great expectation that seems to be with all of us here present.

Let me leave you with this thought:

"The distinctive features of great religious groups is not their ability to behave well or righteously at all times, but their capacity to produce greatness at a vital moment."

This is such a moment in our Navajo history. Can you help us produce that evidence that other Americans are presently enjoying? If our Navajos are to experience this evasive gift, then you must help us produce much of the leadership, much of the moral strength, most of the trained intelligence so necessary to the task. At this critical period in our Navajo development, we cannot sleep.

(Raymond Nakai, Chairman of the Navajo Tribe al Council, addresses the Navajo Tribal Council on June 1, 1966)

Appendices B, C, and D that follow contain information I found during my research, most from Wikipedia, that I thought a reader might find interesting.

Appendix B

Carbon Cycle

Formation of Fossil Fuels

Millions of years ago in the Carboniferous period there were so many dead plants and animals (primarily invertebrates) that they could not completely decompose before they were buried. They were covered over by soil or sand, tar or ice. These dead plants and animals are organic matter made out of cells full of carbon-containing compounds (carbohydrates, lipids, proteins and nucleic acids).

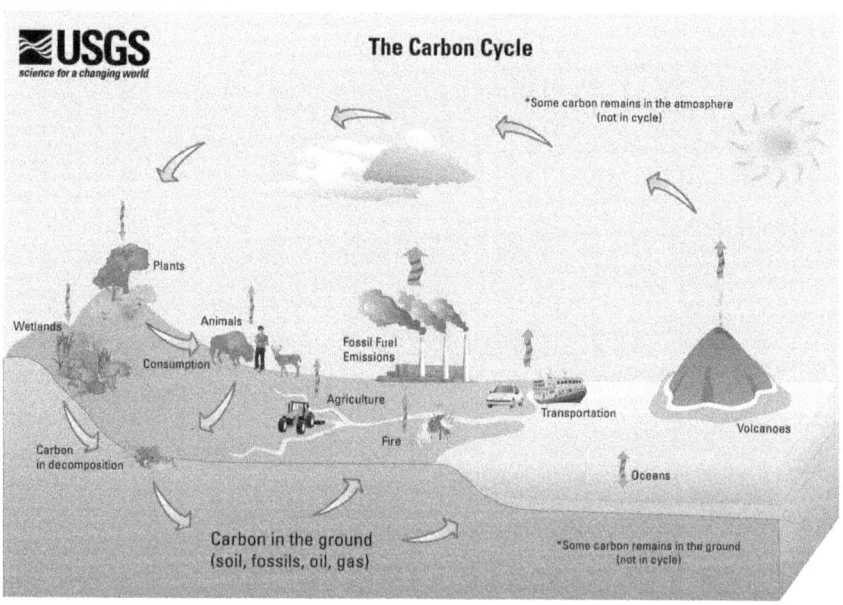

When organic matter is under pressure for millions of years, it forms '**fossil fuels**'. Fossil fuels are coal, oil, and natural gas.

When humans dig up and use fossil fuels, we have an impact on the carbon cycle (Figure below).

This carbon would never be introduced to the atmosphere and therefore never influence the carbon cycle without intervention by humans. The burning of fossil fuels releases more carbon dioxide into the atmosphere than is used by photosynthesis. So, there is more carbon dioxide entering the atmosphere than is coming out of it.

This Carbon dioxide is referred to as a **greenhouse gas**, since it lets in light energy but does not let heat escape, much like the panes of a greenhouse.

Appendix C

Author's Note related to Chapter 17 about Chaco Canyon:

It is truly a spectacular place with a special ambiance revered by Native Americans and historians alike. When you visit the site you see The Chuska Mountains on the horizon some 50 miles to the west and it takes a while to realize the monumental effort it took to bring the construction beams to the canyon without the benefit of the wheel.

Ruins at Chaco Canyon

Chetro Ketl, built during the 10th and 11th centuries, is one of the largest great houses in Chaco Canyon, New Mexico. Despite the harsh, high desert environment, thousands of people once lived in and around what is now a World Heritage Site at Chaco Culture National Historical Park. Credit: National Park Service

This photo from the 1930s shows the back wall of Pueblo Bonito, the largest structure found in Chaco Canyon, New Mexico. Archaeologists estimate the intact structure was 5 stories high and had about 500 rooms. University of Arizona tree-ring studies of building's wooden beams revealed the structure was built in phases from 850 to 1120. Credit: George A. Grant/ National Park Service

Appendix D

Los Alamos National Lab

In the years since the 1940s, Los Alamos was responsible for the development of the hydrogen bomb and many other variants of nuclear weapons. Additional work included basic scientific research, particle accelerator development, health physics, and fusion power research as the initial steps in Project Z (Z pinch).

A concept of Z-pinch fusion propulsion system for rockets was developed through collaboration between NASA and private companies.

By the early 1960's, Sandia Lab had developed an array of nuclear blast measurement technology and technologies to detect nuclear detonations. One of its projects was the Unmanned Seismic Observatory which had stations scattered around the Globe. This work was done in support of the Limited Test Ban Treaty of 1963.

[1] The energy released by the Z-pinch effect would accelerate lithium propellant to a high speed, resulting in specific impulse and thrust values previously unattainable. A magnetic nozzle would be required to convert the released energy into a useful impulse. Researchers thought that this propulsion method had the potential to reduce interplanetary travel times. For example, a mission to Mars would take about 35 days one-way with a total burn time of 20 days and a burned propellant mass of 350 tonnes.

Tokamak

Although it remained relatively unknown for years, Soviet scientists used the pinch concept to develop the tokamak device. Unlike the stabilized pinch devices in the US and UK, the tokamak used *considerably more energy in the stabilizing magnets, and much less in the plasma current. This reduced the instabilities due to the large currents in the plasma, and led to great improvements in stability. The results were so dramatic that other researchers were skeptical when they were first announced in 1968. Members of the still-operational ZETA team were called in to verify the results. The tokamak became the most studied approach to controlled fusion.*

Appendix E

Four corners power plant circa 1970

Appendix F

The information in this Appendix came from Wikipedia. I have left the [.] marks so the references can be easily accessed in the Wikipedia Page.

The Bracero Program (from the Spanish term bracero [bɾaˈse.ɾo], meaning "manual laborer" or "one who works using his arms") was a U.S. Government-sponsored program that imported Mexican farm and railroad workers into the United States between the years 1942 and 1964.
The program, which was designed to fill agriculture shortages during World War II, offered employment contracts to 5 million braceros in 24 U.S. states. It was the largest guest worker program in U.S. history.[¹]
The program was the result of a series of laws and diplomatic agreements, initiated on August 4, 1942, when the United States signed the Mexican Farm Labor Agreement with Mexico.[²] For these farmworkers, the agreement guaranteed decent living conditions (sanitation, adequate shelter, and food) and a minimum wage of 30 cents an hour, as well as protections from forced military service, and guaranteed that a part of wages was to be put into a private savings account in Mexico. The program also allowed the importation of contract laborers from Guam as a temporary measure during the early phases of World War II. [³]
The agreement was extended with the Migrant Labor Agreement of 1951 (Pub. L. Tooltip Public Law (United States) 82–78), enacted as an amendment to the Agricultural Act of 1949 by the United

States Congress,[4] which set the official parameters for the Bracero Program until its termination in 1964.[1]

In studies published in 2018 and 2023, it was found that the Bracero Program did not have an adverse effect on the wages or employment for American-born farm workers, [5] and that termination of the program had adverse impact on American-born farmers and resulted in increased farm mechanization.[6]

Since abolition of the Bracero Program, temporary agricultural workers have been admitted with H-2 and H-2A visas.

Appendix G

The information in this appendix came from an EPA Publication "Quivira Mines" updated May 8, 2025.

Uranium mining in New Mexico on Navajo Land

The U.S. Environmental Protection Agency (EPA), in consultation with the Navajo Nation, has finalized a plan to address the release of radionuclides and metals at the Quivira Mines site in the Navajo Nation near Gallup, New Mexico. EPA's plan includes removing uranium mine waste rock from the three areas of the site and transporting it to a newly created off-site repository at the Red Rocks Landfill property east of Thoreau, New Mexico. This removal action process will begin in early 2025 and continue for 6-8 years, including permitting, construction, operation and closure of the new disposal repository. This action for the Quivira Mines site is one of many actions the EPA is working on with the Navajo Nation and the states of Arizona and New Mexico to address risks from uranium mine waste. These solutions include off-Navajo disposal options in addition to consolidation of waste on the Navajo Nation.

The Quivira Mines are an inactive uranium mine operation located northeast of Gallup, New Mexico. Commercial exploration, development, and mining of uranium at Quivira Mines began in the late 1960s by the Kerr-McGee Corporation (Kerr-McGee) and then its subsidiary, Kerr-McGee Nuclear. Kerr-McGee Nuclear later changed its name to the Quivira Mining Corporation which was later sold to the predecessor company of Rio Algom Mining LLC. Mining continued until 1986 resulting in recovery of an estimated

1.3 million tons of uranium ore from CR-1 and CR-1E. The uranium ore body is located approximately 1,500 to 1,800 feet below ground and accessed via vertical mine shafts at the CR-1 and CR-1E locations. The mine workings were within an aquifer containing groundwater, and were therefore referred to as "wet mines", which required ongoing dewatering during operations. Water was pumped from the underground mine workings and discharged to a series of as many as 7 treatment and settling ponds before being discharged to Unnamed Arroyo #2 and the Pipeline Canyon Arroyo. Ore was transported approximately 50 miles from the site to the Quivira Mining Corporation's Ambrosia Lake uranium mill located to the east and north of Grants, New Mexico.

About the Author

Michael Chintis was born and raised in Grant County, NM. His mom was also a Grant County native. His dad came to New Mexico from Indiana in the late 1930's to play football and basketball at New Mexico State Teachers College in Silver City.

His wife, Joanne, is also a New Mexico native. Both received degrees from the local university and have traveled extensively for both work and enlightenment. They spend most of their time at their Mule Creek, New Mexico home on 20 acres in beautiful Grant County.